GHOST IN TROUBLE

Also by Carolyn Hart

GHOST IN TROUBLE

Carolyn Hart

wm

WILLIAM MORROW
An Imprint of HarperCollins*Publishers*

This book is a work of fiction. The characters, incidents, and dialogue are drawn
from the author's imagination and are not to be construed as real. Any resemblance
to actual events or persons, living or dead, is entirely coincidental.

HarperCollins books may be purchased for educational, business, or sales promo-
tional use. For information please write: Special Markets Department, Harper-
Collins Publishers, 10 East 53rd Street, New York, NY 10022.

FIRST EDITION

Library of Congress Cataloging-in-Publication Data has been applied for.

ISBN 978-0-06-191501-7

10 11 12 13 14   OV/RRD   10 9 8 7 6 5 4 3 2 1

To Rona Edwards and Tiffany Ward
in great appreciation

CHAPTER ONE

I lounged on a deck chair, comfortable in an orange polka-dot bikini. A breeze fluttered the brim of my wide-brimmed straw hat. Unlike the sun, Heaven's golden light never burns, but a lovely white straw is always flattering to a redhead. Oh, you're wondering about Heaven. Heaven, Montana? Heaven, Florida? Not even close.

I said Heaven. I meant Heaven. Quite possibly that calm statement either amuses or offends you. The worldly dismiss Heaven as a fable. With kindly, condescending smiles or cold sneers, they refuse to face up to the Hereafter. Their choice is to whistle while Rome burns. That's fine. They can tap-dance until the curtain falls, but they mustn't expect to take any bows. However, I would be lacking in candor—never one of my failings—if I didn't frankly state that Heaven is my customary residence.

I am Bailey Ruth Raeburn, late of Adelaide, Oklahoma, population 16,234. My husband, Bobby Mac, and I were lost in a Gulf storm on *Serendipity,* our beloved cabin cruiser. Bobby Mac was—and is—a fishing fool. It was his determination to track a tarpon that led to our precipitous arrival here in the latter part of the last century, but we've never lost our love for sea, sand, and serenity.

Today the *Serendipity,* as bright and fresh as on her launch day, rocked in a swell in turquoise waters. I enjoyed happy memories and admired Bobby Mac's muscular back as he struggled against the strength of a determined tarpon.

Bobby Mac and I fell in love in high school. I was a skinny, redheaded sophomore and he was a black-haired, laughing senior. We are still in love and having fun a lifetime and beyond. He's definitely the handsomest man in Heaven, but most of all I treasure his boisterous eagerness. Bobby Mac never met a steak he couldn't eat, an oil well he wouldn't drill, or a beautiful woman he didn't notice. Of course, he always assured me I was the loveliest of all. What a guy, then and now.

I was content, drowsing in the golden light, enjoying the gentle rock of the boat, occasionally waving to friends in other boats, feeling quite sublime.

A telegram sprouted from my hand.

I knew at once the telegram must be from Wiggins. Who else still tapped a Teletype to make contact? Wiggins had sent me a telegram! Nicely enough in Heaven, there's never a need to wait. A message arrives at once. A friend remembered suddenly appears. Wherever you want to go, there you are. Solitude is yours if you wish. Companionship is available instantly. In need of spiritual rousing? Saint Teresa of Avila strides along a mountain path, smiling, talking, welcoming everyone. Ready to laugh? Lucille Ball and Desi Arnaz's new skit is as funny as their long-ago movie about the vacation trailer. Want to perfect your culinary skills? Julia Child's kitchen is simply Heavenly and her reminiscences of World War II derring-do riveting. You suddenly recall your childhood friend who helped you staff a lemonade stand on hot August days? Why, here she is, smiling, arms wide. Perhaps you always wanted to play the piano? Fingers flying, ragtime pounds.

I jumped to my feet. "Bobby Mac, a telegram!" I tore open the yellow envelope, read aloud, my voice rising in eagerness, "'Urgent Delivery to Bailey Ruth Raeburn. Skulduggery afoot in Adelaide. Come at once if interested. Wiggins.'"

At the bottom of the telegram was Wiggins's special stamp of a shiny silver locomotive bearing the legend: *Department of Good Intentions.*

Bobby Mac held tight to his bending rod as he looked over his shoulder. "Are you sure, sweetheart? You had quite a challenge when you helped Susan Flynn."

I flapped the telegram, dismissing the past. "Everything will go better this time." Wiggins, who can be a bit stiff, had actually unbent with an approving smile after my last adven—mission to earth.

Bobby Mac grinned. "What are the odds? You have a talent for trouble."

I blew him a kiss and zoomed away. Bobby Mac understood. He couldn't resist the lure of fishing. As for me? I was already excited.

Skulduggery.

How Heavenly.

Dashes of pink and gold highlighted the arched clouds at the entrance to the Department of Good Intentions. There was a welcoming glow, warm as a friendly smile.

As I'm sure I've explained before, the department is under the supervision of Wiggins. In the early days of the twentieth century, he was station agent at a train depot. When he came to Heaven and was given the opportunity to continue assisting travelers (and all earthly creatures, whether they know it or not, are surely travelers in the best sense of the word), he joyfully re-created a small, redbrick country train station with a wooden platform and tracks running away into the sky.

When the signal arm dropped and the Rescue Express thundered on the rails, sparks flying, dark smoke curling to infinity, my heart raced. I wanted to leap aboard immediately, a blithe spirit.

The first time I'd approached the department, I'd felt anxious. I had no idea whether I would be welcome. Happily, Wiggins had immediately made me feel at home. In fact, he'd commented that he'd been expecting me.

Wiggins obviously had been well aware that I wanted to offer my services to his department. He knew how grateful I was to the brave and generous sailor who'd saved my life when I was a girl and I fell off an excursion boat en route to Catalina. I still remembered the shocking coldness of the sea. A deckhand jumped into the water and saved me. Thanks to him, I enjoyed a full and happy life. Ever since I arrived in Heaven, I'd been eager to offer help to someone in trouble.

Wiggins and the Department of Good Intentions gave me that chance, sending me to my beloved hometown in hilly, south-central Oklahoma. I knew the terrain, understood the mores.

Admittedly, there had been a few mishaps. Perhaps I'd become visible—not a desired status for a Heavenly emissary—a bit more often than the department wished. You will note that I avoid using the term *ghost*. Wiggins insisted that we consider ourselves emissaries. Ghosts, you see, have an unfortunate reputation on earth and evoke quite pitiful reactions of fear and shock. In any event, I had appeared a good deal more than Wiggins considered desirable. Moreover, he remained doubtful about the pleasure I took in the new styles. I'd pointed out that a naked emissary or, Heaven forfend, an emissary droopily draped in an ill-fitting sheet, would surely be more shocking. I'd simply taken advantage of the ease afforded me as a traveling spirit. All I had to do was envision clothing and I was clothed. I saw no reason to eschew fashion. What was the moral worth of appearing as a frumpy emissary?

He'd had no answer to that.

Now, as I hurried through the station waiting room to his office, I could scarcely contain my excitement. I passed under the lintel with the sign marked STATION AGENT. There was no door. Heaven has no need for doors. No one is shut in. Or out.

The office was just as I remembered. From his golden oak desk positioned in the big bay window, Wiggins could look out and see the platform and shining silver tracks. He sat in his desk chair, head bent, green eyeshade hiding the upper portion of his face, finger rapidly tapping the telegraph key.

I didn't want to interrupt. I edged inside, waited behind him. Was I ready? I'd dressed more formally than usual in a pale blue springlike tweed suit. Not a heavy tweed. Indeed, a rather ethereal tweed as befitted a vivacious though equally ethereal redhead. A rose floral pin added a softening note and rose leather sandals afforded a jaunty air. I felt a moment of unease. Too jaunty? Quickly the artificial flower and sandals changed into a matching blue. My nose wrinkled. Boring, but perhaps it would be best if Wiggins thought me a trifle boring.

I patted one of the jacket's patch pockets. Wiggins's telegram crinkled. In my other hand, I held a roll of parchment which contained the Precepts. Unlike my first visit to the department, I now knew the Precepts well, but I hoped bringing the parchment roll might impress Wiggins. While he was engaged, I unrolled the parchment and admired the ornate gold gothic letters:

PRECEPTS FOR EARTHLY VISITATION

1. Avoid public notice.
2. No consorting with other departed spirits.
3. Work behind the scenes without making your presence known.
4. Become visible only when absolutely essential.
5. Do not succumb to the temptation to confound those who appear to oppose you.
6. Make every effort not to alarm earthly creatures.
7. Information about Heaven is not yours to impart. Simply smile and say, "Time will tell."
8. Remember always that you are *on* the earth, not *of* the earth.

This time I would remember each and every Precept. This time . . .

"Wiggins, I'm here." I intended to sound cool and casual, but my voice, eager, bubbly, and excited, gave me away.

Wiggins's wooden chair swung about. He came to his feet, large face breaking into a warm smile. Shining chestnut curls poked from beneath the green eyeshade. His walrus mustache gleamed in Heaven's golden glow. He was unmistakably of his time, high-collared white shirt stiff with starch. Arm garters between his elbows and shoulders puffed the upper sleeves. Substantial suspenders and a wide black belt held up heavy gray wool trousers. Black leather high-top shoes glistened with polish. His golden brown eyes glowed. "Bailey Ruth. Good of you to respond. I knew you would. Your intentions are always of the best."

There was an unmistakable emphasis on *intentions*.

I dismissed a suspicion that he sounded like a man trying to convince himself.

"In any event"—he looked harried—"matters may soon be out of control. We are very concerned. I feel that a woman's delicate touch is needed. And there isn't anyone else available who knows Adelaide."

I decided to overlook the implication that he'd scraped the bottom of the volunteer barrel.

He waved me to a seat beside his desk and settled in his chair. His face furrowed. "Before we get into the particulars, let's discuss the Precepts. The last two times you were dispatched in such a rush, you hadn't had time to study them. I'm sure that accounted for"—he cleared his throat—"a rather wholesale departure from the directives."

He opened a drawer and pulled out a thick folder. When he opened it, I recognized the untidy mass of paper that had comprised my initial report. He skimmed through it, murmuring aloud about the flying crowbar in the mausoleum, impersonation of a police officer, liberation of the tan-and-black hound . . . His face drew down in a frown as he reminded himself about my Christmas visit at a historic Adelaide home. " . . . serious breach of Precept Two . . . and Precepts Three and Four . . ." He looked discouraged. "Your efforts are well meant but"—he shook his head—"so often you don't stop and think."

Actually, I often did stop and think, but possibly I should not share that truth with Wiggins. I scooted to the edge of the hard wooden bench. "Wiggins, this time I will have everything under control." I placed one hand on my heart, looked deep into his golden brown eyes, and quoted the Precepts verbatim. From memory. In the sixth grade I'd won a prize for reciting "Thanatopsis." The Precepts were a snap in comparison. If I do say so myself, I spoke with resolution and beautifully clear diction and concluded, "Now that I am aware of my obligations, you can count on me. I shall be the most tactful, behind-the-scenes, unobtrusive emissary ever!"

A flicker of a smile touched his face. His eyes softened. "A willing heart counts for much. That's what Heaven is all about."

I maintained a look of selflessness or as near as I could manage, selflessness not being a customary attitude for an energetic, exuberant redhead who loves to tango, reel in a fish, or cherish a romantic moment in the moonlight.

Slowly, he nodded. "Very well." He slapped my folder shut, reached for a slim file on his desktop. "Kay Clark intends to stir things up. That can be dangerous." His tone was grave. "Foolhardy. She has returned to Adelaide after an absence of many years. She is still as willful and headstrong and reckless—"

I watched a flush mount in his cheeks. I'd never seen Wiggins so exercised.

"—as ever. Of course, free will complicates everything." He looked at me doubtfully.

"Free will." I gave him a bright smile.

He looked pained.

Possibly that wasn't the response he'd hoped for. Quickly, I achieved an expression of thoughtful inquiry and folded my hands prayerfully. "Free will." My tone was musing, almost rueful. I tried to imply that I spent much of my time engrossed in this fascinating topic. Actually, I'd never given free will a thought.

"Ah, well." His tone was long-suffering. "We can only work with the materials we have at hand. But there is that complicating factor . . ." He flipped through sheets, muttering to himself. "Oh, my." He shut the folder. "I'm in a quandary. Perhaps another volunteer would be a better choice."

"Wiggins, please pick me. You know how much I love Adelaide. I can handle anything. I promise."

Wiggins leaned back in his chair, stared at me. "Very well. Let me give you a brief history. The family circumstance is exceedingly complicated and the situation is exceedingly volatile. You'll be spending most of your time at The Castle."

"The Castle!" I felt a quiver of delight. The Castle was Adelaide's showplace, built by J. J. Hume, an oil baron. Bobby Mac found oil, too, but he was a wildcatter, not a multimillionaire. The Castle, a Mission-style mansion with a series of descending terraces, sat high on Spotted Owl Ridge. The spectacular centerpiece was an active pump jack in the middle of the garden. As J. J. had told his wife, "Roses are fine, but nothing smells as sweet as fresh crude."

I'd attended charity balls and civic functions there. Every small town has its aristocracy. In Adelaide, the Pritchards and the Humes fulfilled those roles in strikingly different fashion. The Pritchards were aloof, elegant, and the great patrons of St. Mildred's Episcopal Church. The Humes . . . Suffice it to say that J. J. was a hard-drinking, rabble-rousing iconoclast, though his long-suffering wife, Millie, was a stalwart Baptist who loved her Sunday school class and spent much of her life murmuring, "J. J. didn't mean . . ."

I beamed at Wiggins. "The Castle is amazing. It has a ballroom and a balcony and terraces. A terrazzo-paved avenue framed by Italian cypress leads from the lower terrace to the site where the Millie number one was drilled." At Wiggins's puzzled look, I smiled. "The oil well in the garden. I think J. J. had a sense of humor. Honestly, to frame a pump jack and tank battery between rows of Italian cypress!"

Wiggins continued to look bewildered. I gave him a crash course in oil terminology, explaining how when a well was completed—and the Millie No. 1 was a fabulous well, pumping three hundred barrels a day—the rig was replaced with a pump jack. The big silver tank held the recovered oil. "J. J. said a pump jack and tank battery were better than sculpture any day. Of course, every big windstorm knocked over the cypress, but J. J. had new ones planted the next day. Does The Castle still belong to the Humes?"

I had a vivid memory of J. J.'s darkly handsome grandson Everett. My daddy referred to Everett as a good-for-nothing lout. But oh, how he could dance. I had once been tempted . . . But that was long ago. Bobby Mac had simply picked me up from the dance floor (actually high school gym) and carried me out the door. What a guy. My attraction to the brooding Everett dissolved in the mists of memory, overwhelmed by images of Bobby Mac. Especially that wonderful summer we'd tramped through Europe . . . As I recalled, Everett came to no good end.

" . . . and so the current family included J. J. IV, known as Jack." Suddenly I realized I'd missed a goodly portion of Wiggins's reply.

" . . . and Diane, his brother's widow, is no match for Kay Clark. Diane seems to believe everything she's told. Not a sensible course in life. Diane lacks sophistication. She has a sweet nature." Wiggins sighed. "It is sad that those with kindly hearts often are vulnerable to manipulation. Although I will admit that Kay's scheme is clever. However, duplicity is reprehensible even if in a good cause." A reproving sniff. "As for the Humes . . . oh well, free will."

"Free will," I repeated with an air of complete understanding.

"But, given all of those facts, are you willing to do your best?" His gaze was searching.

"Of course." I didn't want Wiggins to know I had no idea of the facts or my duties. Once I arrived, I'd quickly discern what I needed to know. Look, listen, act—that was my motto. I shot a quick glance at Wiggins. Had he picked up on my thought? It might suggest impulsiveness. "I will proceed with caution."

Wiggins looked pleased, as well he might, since my lack of caution had always been one of his concerns.

I felt ennobled. This time I would be a model emissary. "Behind the scenes."

Wiggins's obvious relief was almost pitiable. "Bailey Ruth, I should have known I could count on you." His voice was admiring. "Such a refined spirit."

How lovely to think of myself as a refined spirit. And soon to be a traveling spirit. I was ready to go, but I didn't want to hurry Wiggins. Perhaps he would think of me as not only boring but far above earthly temptations.

"Although an emissary such as you, endowed with both beauty and charm"—he gave me a gallant nod though his eyes were worried—"is perhaps in more danger of reverting to worldly ways. Not," he added hastily, "that I would expect you of all people to forget Heavenly attitudes." It would have been nice had his voice contained more assurance.

"Reversion." I dismissed the possibility with a casual wave of pink-tipped fingers. Wiggins worried a good deal that one of his emissaries, when on the earth, would revert to earthly attitudes, that is, succumb to anger, jealousy, suspicion, or any of the other undesirable passions. That possibility was the least of my worries. Why would I revert?

"All right." He was businesslike. "We fear for Kay Clark's safety—"

A staccato *dot dot dot* sounded from the telegraph sender on his desk.

Wiggins's eyes widened. He bent near, tapped a rapid response.

The sender's *clack clack* was frenzied.

Frowning darkly, Wiggins pulled down his eyeshade, wrote with a dark-leaded pencil on a pad. The instant he finished, he pushed back his chair, gestured to me.

"You must leave immediately. An emergency. I hope you arrive in time." He dashed to the ticket window, grabbed a white slip of cardboard, stamped it.

I took it, saw the bright red marking—ADELAIDE—and ran for the platform. The Rescue Express was thundering on the rails. I grabbed a handrail and swung aboard, eager for my journey. Over the mournful yet exuberant peal of the train whistle, I heard Wiggins shout, "Save Kay Clark if you can!"

I clung to a handrail as the express shot across the sky. I was on my way and the refrain sounded in time with the wheels.

. . . on my way . . . on my way . . . on my way . . .

CHAPTER TWO

Frogs wheezed, barked, and trumpeted in a dimly seen pond. I took a breath of pure happiness. Not that I don't appreciate the scents of Heaven, but the rich smell of a hot summer night in Oklahoma brought glorious memories: hayrides, marshmallow roasts, and Bobby Mac's embrace. The ever-present breeze wafted a hint of fresh-cut grass, water, and magnolia blossoms. Over everything, I delighted in the sweet fragrance of gardenias blooming in cloisonné vases that sat next to a marble bench in a small cul-de-sac facing the pond. Aromatic evergreens on either side and at the back formed the cul-de-sac. Cream-colored lighting in clear glass torches rimmed the pond. The cul-de-sac was shadowy, but not in deep gloom. The spot was well screened from the terrace though overlooked by a balcony.

In a rush of happiness, I forgot my mission for an instant. Truly, I was inattentive for a very short span of time, though we all know how life can change in a twinkling. I had no thought whatsoever about Kay Clark. I was too absorbed in the perfume of my favorite flower. The Castle's hothouse gardenias were famous in Adelaide. In warm weather, gardenias also grew in tall vases along the terraces and on the parapets of the third-floor balcony.

I had a vague sense of surprise that I had been dispatched suddenly. Certainly everything appeared quiet and peaceful at The Castle. Lights high in rustling trees and at the top of the terrace steps shed some radiance, but the huge house lay dark and silent except for occasional dim lights on the balcony. I knew it must be late, that hour of the night when foxes prowl, coyotes howl, and cats slip through darkness unseen.

Quick steps sounded.

I watched with interest as a woman hurried toward broad steps that led down to the terrace. She neared a lamppost and was briefly illuminated. I was captivated by her haircut. Her dark locks were so perfectly messy with artfully tousled midlength bangs and layered strands razored at the ends.

I brushed back a curl and wondered if I might try that style. I admired her outfit as well, a lime green Irish linen jacket with deep square pockets and linen slacks. Her green sandals were a perfect match. She didn't slow as she left the pool of light behind her. She crossed the dim terrace, evidently seeing well in the moonlight. The slap of her steps silenced the frogs.

I replaced my tweed suit with a white blouse and turquoise paisley cropped pants. White woven straw flats seemed a good choice for summer. Certainly I wasn't motivated by an earthly pang of envy. Even though I wasn't visible, I liked to be properly dressed.

She came directly to the cul-de-sac, but she didn't sit on the bench. She frowned and turned to look toward the dark house. Hands on her hips, she was a model of impatience. The frogs resumed their boisterous chorus.

In a moment, she glanced at her wrist. I assumed she wore a watch with a luminous dial. She tossed her head impatiently. A very nice effect with that tousled look. She glanced out into the garden on the other side of the pond, then up at the house, as if looking for someone. Evidently she had expected to be met.

I looked, too, but there was no movement in the garden or on the terrace below the steps from the house. I was curious that she remained near the bench. I assumed the cul-de-sac was the place designated for an assignation. Was I about to witness a romantic interlude? I shook my head. There was nothing of sensual anticipation in her rapid pacing. Instead, she exuded brisk determination.

Suddenly I heard an odd crackling.

The sound was ominous, out of the ordinary, frightening.

I looked up and for an instant froze in horror. An enormous vase directly above the cul-de-sac teetered on its pedestal on the third-floor balcony. The vase tilted, then hurtled down toward the impatient woman, so near to me, so near to death.

With no time for thought and little room to maneuver, I zipped into the cul-de-sac, whirled, and shoved her, shouting, "Jump!" I pushed with all my strength. We tumbled together out of the cul-de-sac.

The vase struck with enormous force where she had stood. The sound of her cry was lost almost immediately in the thunderous crash. Shards of porcelain and clumps of earth flew in every direction. A huge chunk of vase struck the marble bench. Clumps of dirt pelted us. The sweet scent of gardenias cloyed the air.

She landed on the flagstones well in front of the main portion of the fractured vase. I felt certain she'd escaped injury except for scratches to her hands and knees from her tumble forward. She struggled to her feet and turned to stare at the wreckage.

I regret to say she was swearing in a clipped, angry tone. I zoomed to her side. "Oh, my goodness. Thank Heaven you're all right." I was too excited to remember silence was my goal.

Her head jerked around as she sought the speaker.

I clapped cautionary fingers to my lips. From this point forward, I must remember to be unheard as well as unseen. However, despite my vocal lapse, I was confident Wiggins was pleased. I had arrived in time to save a life. Wiggins had warned of skulduggery, so I was sure the vase hadn't tumbled of its own accord.

The vase! Who engineered its fall? I zoomed upward and hovered above the empty pedestal. There were the occasional lights along the parapet, but none offered much illumination. I saw no one, heard nothing.

I didn't know which direction to take. I listened hard and heard the unmistakable click of a closing door. Quickly, I moved from one French window to another, trying the handles. All were locked. But a fleeing person would obviously click the lock once inside.

All was not lost. The woman on the terrace clearly had expected to be joined by someone. Perhaps I had now fulfilled my mission. Perhaps I had been sent simply to save her life and now Kay Clark would be forewarned and could take appropriate action. I confess I felt a quick sense of disappointment. It wasn't that I was reluctant to return to Heaven, but Heaven knew I just arrived.

However, I didn't hear the whistle of the Rescue Express.

I zoomed back to the ground. I stopped beside a weeping willow not far from where she stood.

The near victim looked at the empty parapet, the remnants of the vase, the mounds of dirt, the cracked marble seat. She exuded determination, which seemed an odd response to near annihilation. Moreover, nothing in the way she stood indicated distress. Indeed, there was a cocky lift to her shoulders. She kicked a dirt clod. "I'll be double damned." Her husky voice was brusque and, oddly, not so much shocked as satisfied.

"I sincerely hope not." Once again, I clapped fingers to my lips. Surely Wiggins would forgive my exclamation. Damnation is no joking matter in Heaven.

She swung toward the sound of my voice. "Who's there?" She took a step nearer the weeping willow. She was partially in the shadow of the evergreens and partially in a swath of moonlight. She reached into a deep pocket and yanked out a small but deadly looking revolver, holding it steady in an unwavering hand. Moonlight glinted on the gun. Her left hand dipped into the opposite pocket and retrieved a flashlight. She switched it on.

The stark beam was shocking after the dimness.

Me and my big, open mouth. That was how I got off to a bad start in my first visit to Adelaide. I'd spoken aloud and then had felt it necessary to appear to calm the situation. The effect had been unfortunate. Earthbound creatures are sadly unimaginative. If you come and go, that is, appear and disappear, the conclusion is immediate that you are a ghost. It is to no avail to speak of a Heavenly visitor as an emissary. The earthbound cling to stereotypes, believing that ghosts are horrid specters rattling chains and exuding a chill that turns hearts to ice.

Nothing could be further from the truth. Take me. I'm a redhead who likes to have fun. I am, if I say so myself, cheerful, energetic, and friendly. However, Precept Four was clear. I glanced Heavenward and gave a thumbs-up. I was determined to remain unseen. Precept Four was clear as could be. Moreover, this woman obviously was in no need of reassurance.

She took two steps toward the willow. The fronds drifted in the breeze. The flashlight beam whipped back and forth. She held the small pistol with apparent competence. "I have a good ear. Come out with your hands up or I'll shoot."

She aimed directly at me. That wasn't a problem, but I felt she was much too ready to wield a weapon. Public safety was paramount. I felt a pang of dismay. Had that pompous thought actually entered my mind? Maybe there was a basis to Wiggins's continuing worries about reversion.

She raised her hand, straightened her arm.

"Don't shoot." I spoke crisply. "I pushed you out of the way. Why attack your rescuer?"

"Who are you? Why are you hiding?" Her tone was equally crisp. "Did you know the vase was going to fall? Or do you claim to have ESP? Whatever, you are a little too handy on the spot to be innocent." Her disdain was obvious. "Come out or I'll shoot. One, two, three—"

I became visible. I spared an instant's thought to be glad I'd changed out of the tweed suit. Certainly I didn't want to appear unfashionable in front of a woman who obviously had style even if at the moment she lacked charm.

She took a stumbling step back, deeper into the shadow of the evergreens.

I reminded myself that I was not, repeat not, taking pleasure in her discomfiture. Her reaction was understandable, since becoming visible is a striking phenomenon. Colors swirl and slowly take form. It's quite arresting. I regretted I hadn't chosen more dramatic tones. Turquoise flatters a redhead, but the gentle shade lacks emphasis. I changed colors in midswirl, and, voilà! I was clothed in a scarlet tunic and gold trousers. I added matching gold sandals and a multitude of gold chains. I was sure I was clearly visible in the light of the flash.

The hand with the gun sank to her side.

She had only herself to thank if my sudden appearance scared her.

Immediate upon the uncharitable thought came contrition.

I hoped Wiggins wasn't keeping count of these small errors on my part. As the colors swirled and resolved into me, I forced a conciliatory smile and moved toward her. Wiggins might not be pleased at my appearance, but surely he wanted me to prevent a shooting spree. What was it Wiggins had said about Kay Clark? . . . *willful and headstrong and reckless* . . .

Without hesitation, she walked toward me.

I was impressed. She had to be shaken by my unorthodox arrival, yet she moved with determination to meet me. She stepped fully into the light from one of the torches as we came face-to-face.

I struggled to breathe. Despite the passage of years, I recognized her at once. Her oval face was elegant in its perfection and her beauty perhaps more striking in the mature woman than in the less polished late teen. Of all people . . .

Was this the circumstance which had concerned Wiggins, made him doubt my suitability to serve as an emissary?

She swore, her husky voice shocked and uncertain.

"You!" I sounded hoarse.

Kay took a step back. "I don't believe this." Thankfully, the hand holding the gun remained at her side.

Now I understood Wiggins's reservations about sending *me*. He had spoken of Kay Clark. How could I have had any idea of her identity? If only I'd attended to Wiggins's words more carefully, but my thoughts had been distracted by memories of Bobby Mac and Montmartre. Still, I was indignant. "You're Kay Kendall." I would never forget that face.

Kay Kendall—I suppose I'd have to remember that she was now Kay Clark—had been beautiful as a very young woman. She was beautiful as an older woman. What was she now? Nearing fifty, at least, but time had touched her lightly. Now there was the faintest of shadows beneath her eyes, an attenuation of her high cheekbones, giving her a poignant aura of vulnerability. Her face was elegant and memorable, high forehead, straight nose, pointed chin with a tantalizing cleft, raven dark hair lightly flecked with silver, compelling dark brown eyes. Kay Kendall Clark was arresting, fascinating, unforgettable. Few could resist her magnetism; though, like moths drawn to a flame, those entranced by her might forever rue their encounter.

"Bailey Ruth Raeburn?" Kay's rich contralto voice rose in disbelief. "Oh, wait a minute. You're dead." She blinked uncertainly. "I must have a concussion."

"No such luck." This time my fingers flew to my mouth in dismay. I must not quarrel with my charge. "You're fine. Besides, I didn't push you that hard."

"You're dead!" Kay repeated accusingly.

"Yes." And she was impossible. What was Wiggins thinking? Of course, it wasn't in my purview to judge whether Kay Clark, aka Kay Kendall, deserved to be rescued, apparently from a foolhardy scheme she had hatched.

Now I understood Wiggins's trepidation that I might revert, leave behind the Heavenly graces of charity and patience, succumb to anger, dislike, and disdain. To be utterly frank, I had decided opinions when I was on the earth. I was quick to make up my mind about people.

Oh, all right, I was a good hater, and that's a bad thing.

When we arrive in Heaven, one of our first duties is forgiveness. No grudges are permitted. I'd passed that test with flying colors.

Well, perhaps not with exceedingly high marks.

However, I passed. For those who might think less of me, consider this: How many on earth have grudges they gnaw with the pleasure dogs give to old bones? Well, then. They, too, may find that entry exam a challenge. Before crossing through the Heavenly portals, I forgave everyone.

But that was in Heaven.

To go back to earth and maintain such magnanimity was, I'm afraid, expecting a bit much.

I gave myself a mental shake. I desperately wanted to make this visit to earth a picture-perfect exercise as an emissary from the Department of Good Intentions. If so, I must suppress all negative feelings about Kay Clark and convince her I wished her well. "Kay . . ." I forced a smile which didn't feel genuine, but hey, I was making the effort. "I'm here to help you."

She blinked again, as if she might will away my presence. "This is crazy. You are definitely dead. You've been dead for years. You and Bobby Mac went down in the Gulf." Kay glanced at the broken vase and debris-littered ground. "There's the vase. Or what's left of it." She looked down at the gun in her hand. "The gun's real."

"Much too real. Put that pistol in your pocket." I'd developed quite a firm voice when I taught high school English.

Numbly, she dropped the gun into her pocket and glared at me. "I feel like I'm standing here. Maybe I'm not. If you're dead, I must be dead." Her eyes narrowed. "You can't be here, and besides, you'd be ancient and you look younger than I do."

"Of course I look younger." I did not say this pridefully. I simply stated a fact. "That's one of the joys of Heaven." I hoped Wiggins didn't feel I was revealing too much. However, I had to convince Kay that she was alive, and I was, well, dead. "Age doesn't matter in Heaven. Those who died too young find full flower. Those worn by illness or despair once again move with ease and grace. They are at their best and brightest. That is the criterion, to be your best and brightest whenever in life that may have occurred. Your choice. One of my happiest years was twenty-seven. That's the me you see."

There wasn't a handy alabaster pillar to reflect me, but I was confident the crimson tunic and gold trousers were a perfect foil for flaming red hair. I would emphasize that I was merely taking an innocent pleasure in the lovely fabric. Heaven knows I eschew vanity.

"If I'm alive, you are not standing there." She tugged at an earlobe. "So why do I hear you?"

"Watch closely." I disappeared. I counted to five, reappeared. For good measure—really the change wasn't intended to be spiteful—I transformed the tunic to emerald green and the trousers to brilliant white. White sandals, too, of course.

Kay blinked several times. She touched fingers to her temple. She took an experimental hop. "I'm not hurt, so how can I be dead? Besides"—her tone was dismissive—"if Heaven is like the terrace of The Castle, I want my money back." She shot me a look of undisguised distaste. "Obviously you are a figment of my imagination. Although why I'd draw you of all people out of my subconscious is one for my psychologist." She paused, gave a gurgle of laughter. "Now that I think of it, maybe you're part of the baggage I've carried since I slammed out of the mayor's office, jumped in my car, and left Adelaide in my rearview mirror. Did you know the mayor made a pass at me? I suppose he'd heard the rumors about Jack and thought I'd be a nifty entry in his black book. I saw you on the way out. Your face had a decided prune look. You and all the other virtuous ladies of the town had decided I was a vixen. Actually, I doubt you and your friends were quite so ladylike in your terminology. I can't wait to tell my psychologist. She's always insisted that almost everyone has ghastly repressed memories except for me and I might be better off if I started repressing stuff. Finally, I have a repressed memory for her. But it's weird that you popped to the top of my mind just because I had a close call. Okay." She blew out a breath of relief. "I'm alive and I'm nuts, but that's fine. Anyway, since you're imaginary, I'm not going to waste any more time with you. I've got things to do." She started for the steps.

I grabbed her elbow. "What do I have to do to get your attention?"

She jerked her arm away, her face strained. "Those felt like real fingers."

"Kay Clark, listen to me." I shook my head in exasperation. "You haven't changed since you were working on the *Adelaide Gazette* and hell-for-leather to break up Jack Hume's marriage." Poor Virginia Hume. Sweet, gentle, kind, shy. What chance did the wren have when a macaw strutted onstage?

Kay's thin face was abruptly still. Her eyes were deep pools of sadness. And anger.

I didn't evade her gaze. Despite the passage of many years, we both remembered our last encounter. I had been, if possible, even more impulsive then than now. Virginia was the only daughter of Madge Crenshaw, my best friend. It was past ten on a hot summer night when Madge called, crying out her anger and despair over Virginia's unhappiness. " . . . that awful girl's chasing Jack. I tried to talk to him but he slammed out of the house. Virginia's heartbroken."

The minute I hung up the phone, I snatched my car keys and raced out of the house. I drove straight to Kay Kendall's apartment and knocked on the door.

She'd faced me, young and beautiful and defiant.

When I finished, she'd stood straight and tall, her face deathly pale. Her lips had trembled. I'd scarcely heard her low voice. " . . . you don't know . . . you don't know!" The door slammed shut.

There was no door between us tonight, but there were memories and heartbreak. Her eyes held mine. "All my fault?"

I didn't speak. I suppose my cold gaze told her my opinion.

"I was nineteen years old. He was twenty-seven. I came here"—

she pointed up at The Castle—"to interview his father, J. J. III, about a rumor that Hume Oil was for sale. I met Jack in the main hallway as I was leaving." There might have been a quick sheen of tears in her eyes. "I was so young. I didn't know how much love hurt. I didn't know . . ." She gave an impatient shake of her head. "He was the handsomest man I'd ever seen." She spoke without emphasis, stating a fact. "Being near him made everything sharper, brighter, faster. Did I chase him? No. Suddenly he was everywhere I went. I left town, went to Dallas. He came after me." Her face was suddenly sad. "Every time he walked into a room, it was like the Fourth of July, but I would have gotten away if Virginia hadn't died." Her eyes probed mine. "Did the ladies of the town blame me for her death and Sallie's, too?" Her gaze was somber. "Why do I ask? Sure, everybody blamed me and Jack." She shook her head. "Jack and I didn't create Virginia's demons. He tried to help her. His dad tried. Did you know Jack's dad had insisted on Virginia and Sallie coming to live at The Castle? He'd been down to see them in Houston. He wasn't anybody's fool. He was crazy about the baby. That's the only reason Jack was in Adelaide that summer. He spent very little time here after Hume Oil moved its headquarters to Houston. Of course, his dad still called the shots from Adelaide. But that one summer, Jack was here. He got away as often as he could. He was in Dallas the night of the accident."

I remembered his absence. "We'd all heard that he was in Dallas. With you." Everyone had talked, of course . . . *running after that girl . . . poor little Virginia . . . his fault . . . was it really an accident?* . . .

"He was with me." Kay spoke as if from a far distance, as if she were observing shadowy figures dimly seen in a dusky lane. "I told him I wouldn't see him again. And then the call came. Virginia's car went into the lake on a bright, sunny, beautiful afternoon." There was pity and sadness in Kay's dark eyes. "Virginia was drunk. As usual."

"Virginia?" I remembered sweet slender Virginia and her beguiling blue eyes and gentle smile. My shock must have been evident in my face.

"Did you know her headaches and the days she spent in bed were because of vodka?" The honesty in Kay's voice was unmistakable.

I didn't want to believe Kay, but I'd lived long enough to understand that people we think we know well often hide destructive secrets.

Kay spoke quietly. "Hardly anyone knew. Jack. His dad. His sister. I don't think Virginia's mother knew, or perhaps she refused to see. Virginia was always pretty and kind, a sweet, good-natured, pathetic drunk."

I looked at Kay and saw beyond the mature woman who faced me now. I saw the girl of nineteen, beautiful and accused. I remembered myself that night, angry, my voice hard. "Why didn't you say anything the night I came to see you?"

Her dark brows drew down in a fierce frown. "Did I owe you an explanation? And how could I talk about Virginia? The family was trying to help her."

I made many mistakes during my lifetime. Here was another, even if lately realized. "I'm sorry." I wished my words could make a difference, but nothing I said now would erase that night.

Her face twisted in a sardonic smile. "I'll save your apology for a therapy session. Apparently, my subconscious likes you better than I do. But that encounter with you was the least of my concerns after Virginia and Sallie died. I had too much else to deal with then. Jack was devastated. He blamed himself for the accident. He said he should have put Virginia in a hospital and made sure that she wouldn't be out alone with Sallie. But he never expected what happened. Of course"—and now her tone was bitter—"the generous ladies of Adelaide had the answer, Virginia drove into the lake because of Jack and me. The reality? Virginia drove into the lake because she was too drunk to drive and she made a wrong turn on the way to the park with Sallie."

The photograph in the *Gazette* had been heartbreaking, water spilling out of the convertible as the winch pulled the white car to the surface of the lake.

Kay's thin hands tightened into fists. "Virginia didn't commit suicide. She would never have hurt Sallie. Jack didn't matter to her. She shut him out after Sallie was born, but she adored Sallie. So did Jack. When Virginia and Sallie died, Jack was lost. It was the only time I ever knew him to be lost. Until—" She drew a sharp breath. "Why should I tell you any of this? You aren't here, and I've got plenty to deal with."

"Skulduggery." I spoke firmly.

She came back from the past, gave me a disdainful stare. "I would never have expected you to be quaint, Bailey Ruth."

I felt a flicker of outrage. Kay Clark might not be a scarlet woman who had tried to steal another woman's husband, but she was definitely infuriating. The night I'd made a plea for Virginia, Kay hadn't revealed the truth. I realized now she'd been hurt by the town's suspicions, but she had refused to defend herself. Was she driven by pride? Or was she a woman who would always go her own way without any thought to the effect of her actions on those around her? Now she was doing everything in her power to send me packing.

I was tempted to disappear and let her deal with whatever forces she had unleashed.

. . . on *the earth, not* of *the earth* . . .

Did I hear the whistle of the Rescue Express in the distance?

I spoke quickly. "When I was sent here to help you, I was told there was skulduggery afoot. If you prefer more up-to-date language, let me put it this way. You are in a big mess, and unless you want your attacker"—I nodded at the remnants of the vase—"to get away with murder—yours—you need to listen to me. I was dispatched to save you and I'm going to do it." Whether she liked it or not. I felt pugnacious as all get out. Kay affected me that way.

"You save me?" She flicked me a glance of disdain. "I don't need your help. Thanks, but I know what I'm doing. I don't need a guardian angel."

"Stop." I held up a commanding hand. "I am not an angel. Heavens, no. Angels are a separate order of being. I'm an emissary."

She shrugged. "Angel, emissary, what difference does it make?"

This was not the time to argue theology. I lost patience and snapped, "In case you haven't figured it out by now, I am a ghost." Wiggins had to understand that sometimes language must be clear.

"Ghost?" She raised an inquiring eyebrow. "I guess you are a ghost of times past, that's for sure. Whether you're here or not, angel, ghost, or devil, please whisk back to wherever you came from and leave me in peace. Now that I know I'm on the right track, I'll take it from here."

I despised lack of clarity in speech when I was an English teacher. *Right track. It.* I wanted specificity.

"Take what where?"

She looked blank.

"You say you are on the right track and you will take *it* from here. Take what where?"

"You seem singularly uninformed for a so-called ghost." She made a shooing gesture, as if I were a bothersome fly.

"It's a good thing"—I hoped I didn't sound waspish—"that Heaven doesn't hold grudges, or I would be gone. In a heartbeat. Look, we need to talk." I gestured at the shattered vase. "Why is someone trying to kill you?"

Her smile fled as she stared at the debris. In the moonlight, her face looked suddenly older. She drew in a quick breath.

I patted her shoulder.

Kay stiffened. "You are not here." The words were evenly spaced, but her voice was strident. "I haven't had that much to drink. Two glasses of champagne at dinner. That's nothing. I am perfectly sober. Maybe I need a drink. I've got to get my head on straight. Maybe if I talk the situation out, I'll know what to do next." She flicked a quick glance toward me. "That must be why I'm imagining you. All right. My subconscious will be my guide." She began to pace. "I found a note on my pillow. But not a billet-doux this time." Her face softened. "Jack wrote lovely pillow notes. I still have them. This wasn't that kind of note, but I was thrilled. I knew I was getting somewhere."

Kay reached into a pocket.

I was wary, prepared for the gun.

Kay lifted out a square of white cardboard, read aloud: "'Be on the terrace at midnight in the cul-de-sac. I know what happened to Jack.'"

Interesting. I asked eagerly, "What happened to Jack?"

Kay lifted startled black eyebrows in surprise. "You don't know about Jack? My subconscious must have gone on vacation after calling you up. You can't be a good sounding board if you don't know what's happened."

"I know you are engaged in a foolhardy and"—I jerked a thumb at the wreckage—"dangerous scheme."

"Scheme." She considered the word and gave an approving nod. "You better believe it, honey. I've got a scheme, and that pile of dirt"—she jerked her thumb—"proves I was right. I knew things were breaking my way when I got the note. I suspected something would happen." She patted her pocket. "That's why

I brought a gun. But"—she looked up at the empty pedestal—
"somebody outsmarted me."

"When I got to the balcony—"

She looked sardonic. "You flew, of course."

I tamped down my immediate flare of irritation . . . on *the
earth, not* of *the earth* . . . With an effort of will (Wiggins, are you
applauding?), I was pleasant. "Not exactly. It's more immediate
than that." I disappeared, zoomed up, stood on the balcony ledge,
reappeared, and looked down on Kay. I was clearly visible in the
light from a lamp. I waved, then reversed the process. In another
instant, I stood before her.

Her eyelashes fluttered.

The instantaneous switch from ground to balcony to ground
obviously dazzled her. What fun.

She pressed fingers against her temples. "Hallucination. That's
all that it is. Maybe champagne isn't good for me."

I was impatient with her dogged rejection of my presence.
Time was fleeting and action was essential. I began again, firmly.
"When I reached the balcony, no one was there. I heard a door
shut, but I was too late to see anyone. Maybe the police will be able
to find some evidence."

"The police." She spoke in a considering tone, then gave an
abrupt head shake. "I don't think—"

"Excuse me, is everything all right?" The puzzled call came
from the upper terrace.

Kay's expression was grim. "Everything's just super, Laverne.
Come on down." She turned the flashlight toward the steps.

CHAPTER THREE

I disappeared.

Kay drew in a sharp breath.

"Don't worry. I haven't left. We'll talk later." My whisper was intended as a reassurance.

Regrettably, Kay stamped her foot. "I've got to stop imagining things."

A tall, thin woman with dark hair in a coronet braid descended the steps. She walked majestically, as if pages might be to the left and right of her strewing flowers. She was either someone of importance or someone who wished to appear important. She was dressed all in black, a rayon blouse with a fringe and a billowing black skirt. A sharp nose and thin lips dominated her bony face. "Has there been an accident? I heard a huge crash. I thought something had happened in the garden, and I should go and see."

Kay's smile was grim. "Did you indeed? Where's Ronald?"

Laverne ignored the question as her gaze swung back and forth, searching the shadows. "Where did that woman go?"

Kay's eyes widened. "You saw a woman?"

Laverne's stare was haughty. "Of course I saw her. However, I have no intention of intruding upon your meeting. I came down because I heard a big crash. What happened?"

Instead of answering, Kay swung the flashlight toward the heap of dirt and broken porcelain. A portion of broken marble bench protruded from the debris.

Laverne's lips parted. A hand touched at her throat. She was either shocked or a fine actress. Her gaze rose.

The emptiness of the pedestal was obvious in the moonlight.

"No wonder the sound was so loud." She turned back to Kay. "How could that huge vase fall?"

"I don't know what made the vase"—there was an appreciable pause—"fall. In any event, no harm done." Kay glanced at the broken bench. "I suppose someone can check the pedestal tomorrow. I don't see that there's anything we can do tonight. Accidents happen."

I was stunned. What was Kay thinking? She knew the vase's fall was no accident.

Laverne's sharp gaze studied Kay.

Kay's lime green jacket was dirt-streaked. The right knee of her slacks was torn.

Laverne looked concerned. "Where were you when the vase fell?"

Kay's smile was grim. She pointed at the heap of dirt and broken pottery. "Ground zero. Luckily, I was able to jump out of the way."

Did Kay believe she'd jumped? Was she actually convinced I was imaginary?

Kay bent and snagged a clod of dirt. She threw it into the pond with so much force the frogs were startled into silence. "I'm not dead." She sounded buoyant.

Laverne looked puzzled, as well she might. "Was that woman here, too? Where is she now?"

I didn't like the way the conversation was going. Could I count on Kay being discreet?

I slipped behind Laverne and swirled into visibility.

Kay saw me, of course. How could she not? I cupped my hand near my ear as if holding a telephone, mouthed, "Call the police."

Kay stood as if turned to stone, her oval face shocked into immobility.

Laverne looked uneasy. "What's wrong?"

I pointed with a peremptory finger at my make-believe phone and mouthed, "Call 911." It was a shame neither Laverne nor Kay apparently had a cell phone with them. Most people seemed to be tethered to them at all times, but I understood a cell phone might not be essential for a late-night walk in the garden. I didn't want to appear prideful, but I was au courant with new technologies after my previous visits to Adelaide as a Heavenly emissary. I knew about computers, too. However, I make no claim of expertise there.

Kay appeared shaken. She wavered unsteadily. Eyes wide, she looked past Laverne. "You aren't there." She spoke with angry emphasis.

Laverne took a step forward. "Are you ill?"

I lost patience. I would have liked to stalk up to Kay and give her a good shake. Instead, I disappeared and turned toward the silent, dark house.

One of the delights of ghostly peregrinations is the ease of transport from place to place. Picture a destination and there you are.

I stood in total darkness. However, I have great faith in my comings and goings. I never doubted I was in the study of The

Castle. It was no great gamble to will myself there. What mansion didn't have a study? What study didn't have a telephone?

I lifted my hand in search of the wall switch and flicked it up. I went straight to the desk, picked up the handset, punched 911. I glanced at the ship's bell clock on the mahogany desk. Twenty minutes before one A.M.

"Adelaide Emergency Services."

"There's been an attempted murder near the pond on the south side of The Castle." I didn't bother with an address. Everyone in Adelaide knew The Castle. "Intended victim Kay Clark survived. No trace has been found of the attacker."

I daintily replaced the handset.

As I expected, the telephone immediately rang. I didn't answer, of course. Someone would hear the peals and respond. I smiled in anticipation and spoke aloud: *"Laissez les bon temps rouler."* I hoped Wiggins was impressed by my French.

I popped back to the garden.

Kay darted back and forth near the pond, calling out. "Where are you? Where did you go?"

Laverne hesitated, then spoke sharply. "Kay, I'm here. I haven't gone anywhere."

Kay glared at her. "I know you're here."

I swooped next to Kay, tapped her on the shoulder.

She stopped and stiffened.

I murmured, "The police will be here—"

A siren wailed.

Kay looked haunted.

"Oh, good, here they are. I think I'll watch from the parapet. See you later." I couldn't resist a parting shot. "You might—or might not—see me."

I landed on the third-floor balcony and sat on the ledge overlooking the drive. The fire truck was the first to arrive, lights flashing. A patrol car and ambulance slammed to a stop within another two minutes. Lights flared in rooms on the first and second floors of The Castle.

The firemen waited next to their truck. The paramedics jumped lightly from their van. A chunky, middle-aged policeman, flashlight in one hand, thudded up the broad front steps to the massive entrance. A lithe policewoman, hand near her holster, followed. Her eyes swept the porch and then she turned to gaze at the drive. Her partner held a finger to the doorbell. "Police. Police." His shout was loud and imperative.

The front porch lights came on as Kay and Laverne hurried around the side of the house. Kay was in the lead. Her expression was a mixture of shock and wariness.

The front door opened. A small woman with faded blond hair clutched at the lapels of her seersucker robe as she stepped onto the porch. Her voice lifted in fear. "What's happened? What's wrong?"

An older woman stepped carefully to the doorway, hand on the lintel. She stood with her face slightly turned as if trying to hear. She had strong features, a broad forehead, jutting nose, and firm chin. The porch light glittered on exceedingly thick-lensed eyeglasses. She had an aura of authority. "Diane, what has happened?" Her dressing gown was a deep mauve.

A plump woman hurried up the steps from the driveway. She had obviously dressed hastily in a wrinkled blue cotton top and jeans. Her auburn hair needed a trim. She might once have been pretty, but her rounded face now sagged, marred by deep-set lines and a defeated look. She stepped onto the porch. She was followed by a young woman in a light cotton robe. Tawny hair hung loose on her shoulders.

A stocky man in his late forties with silver hair and a Vandyke beard edged onto the porch past the older woman. He wore a

short-sleeved seersucker shirt and tan trousers. He looked immediately toward Laverne. I pegged him as the Ronald of whom Kay
had inquired. His gaze at Laverne was curiously intent.

Last to arrive was a young man with thick brown hair and
a broad, tanned face. He blinked sleepily. He was shirtless and
barefoot in worn jeans.

The young woman and young man immediately glanced at
each other, then quickly averted their gazes.

A muscular EMT with matching dragon tattoos on his fore-
arms climbed the steps. "Anyone injured?"

At the bottom of the front steps, Kay held up her hand. "Wait
a minute, everyone." She looked toward the EMTs. "No one's
hurt. We don't need you." She looked at the helmeted and coated
firefighters. "Or the fire truck."

His face grim, the officer at the door looked down at her.
"What's going on? We got a 911 call about attempted murder."

"Murder?" The faded blonde swung around to glance at each
in turn, then faced the policemen. "Everyone's here."

Laverne pushed past Kay. "Go look on the terrace. A vase fell
from the balcony and almost hit Kay. But who called the police?"

Exclamations sounded: "That must be what I heard." "For
God's sake, Kay, what were you doing on the terrace?" "How
could a vase fall?" "I heard a crash." "Did someone push it?"
"That's ridiculous. Nobody could knock one of those vases over."

Another siren sounded. An unmarked sedan pulled up behind the patrol car. Police Chief Sam Cobb swung out and walked
swiftly toward the house. He hadn't changed much since I'd last
seen him: heavyset, fiftyish, with grizzled hair and a blunt face,
domed forehead, bold nose, square chin.

Cobb moved fast for a big man. He thudded rapidly up the
steps. "Burton?"

The patrolman stood straight. "Nobody's hurt, Chief. We received a call claiming there was attempted murder." He pulled a notebook from his pocket. "The intended victim was named Kay Clark."

"I'm Kay Clark." Kay hurried up the steps. "I can't imagine who made that call." Her smile was full of charm. "There's obviously been some confusion. All of us"—she gestured at the group on the porch—"are fine. I suppose it was a prank call. Possibly the vase was toppled by a vandal. In any event, there is no need for any of you"—she waved her hand at the assorted vehicles—"to be concerned."

Chief Cobb was firm. "A 911 call came from this number and it requires investigation. I'm sure all of you"—he looked from the middle-aged blonde to the older woman with the thick glasses and air of authority—"will be cooperative."

The older woman, who obviously didn't see well, turned toward the sound of his voice. "We are happy to cooperate. I am Evelyn Hume. How can we assist you?"

"With your permission, we want to check the site from which the vase fell. If someone could show us?"

Evelyn was crisp. "Kay, since the call to the police apparently concerned you"—there was distinct reproof in her deep voice—"perhaps you will be kind enough to escort the gentlemen to the balcony. Diane will switch on the outside lights." Evelyn Hume turned back to Chief Cobb. "Since the hour is late and the crash of the vase caused no harm, I'm sure that the rest of us will not be needed."

Chief Cobb frowned. Obviously, he would have preferred to speak with the occupants of the house tonight. However, he had no clear evidence of crime, and he was dealing with one of Adelaide's most prominent families.

After an instant of silence, he said gruffly, "A search of the grounds will continue. If the results of the investigation indicate that the fall of the vase was not accidental, I will pursue the investigation tomorrow."

Lights now fully illuminated the balcony. Chief Cobb studied the empty pedestal. He spoke rapidly to a slender young officer who made quick notes. "Possible chisel marks apparent on the pedestal. No cement particles on balcony. Vase may have been loosened earlier, resulting debris removed. Hammer and chisel likely needed. A crowbar may have been used to tip the loosened vase." His gaze swept the balcony. "No tools on balcony. Fingerprint and film the site."

"Yes, sir." The young officer hurried toward the stairs.

Chief Cobb looked at Kay. "Did you call 911?"

"I did not. I have no explanation for that call. I assume the call was made in error." Her expression was bemused, a woman obviously puzzled.

I was indignant. She appeared determined to block any investigation into the attack on her.

Cobb drew a small notebook and a pen from a back pocket. "The call came from the house. Who's staying here tonight?"

Kay folded her arms. "Since the call was in error, I fail to see the point of your question."

"It's a misdemeanor to place a false 911 call. Until the origin of the call is explained, the investigation will continue." His gaze was unrelenting.

Kay shrugged and spoke rapidly, as if in a hurry to answer and be done with his questions. "Evelyn Hume. Diane Hume, James's widow. Diane and James's son, Jimmy. Laverne and Ronald Phillips, friends of Diane. Margo Taylor, the housekeeper, and her daughter, Shannon Taylor, occupy a small cottage on the grounds."

"Why were you in the garden?"

"I read late. I wasn't sleepy." She sounded relaxed and untroubled. "I decided to take a stroll."

Cobb looked both suspicious and puzzled. "Were you alone?"

"Yes. I walked down to the second terrace. It was lovely in the moonlight. I paused by the cul-de-sac that faces the pond. I heard a noise. I was turning to see and the vase landed behind me. My lucky night."

Cobb glanced at her torn slacks. "How did you rip your slacks?"

Her eyes flared a little. If she'd faced the balcony and fallen forward, she would have been hit by the vase. "Everything happened so fast." She made a deprecating gesture. "I suppose—yes, I think I was turning to look up and I realized something was falling and I whirled and stumbled toward the pond."

"Did you see anyone on the balcony?"

"It was dark."

"When you came to the front porch, you were with a tall, thin woman in black."

"Laverne Phillips. She heard the crash and came to see." The tension had eased from Kay's body. She knew the interview was almost over. Laverne Phillips had seen me with Kay, but I supposed that Kay doubted the police would speak to Laverne. Or, if they did, Kay would deny Laverne's claim of a redheaded woman. After all, the police would find it hard to prove I had been there. Kay obviously was willing to gamble.

Cobb flipped shut his notebook. His face creased in thought as he looked toward the steps leading down to the garden. "The balcony seems to be a site for accidents." His gaze swung to Kay. "Were you here the night of June sixth?"

Kay's face was somber. "No. I was at home."

"Where is home, Mrs. Clark?"

"Dallas."

"What brought you to The Castle?"

He could not have been as eager as I to hear her answer. If only I'd been more attentive when Wiggins had briefed me.

Her lips moved in a faint smile. "Business."

He waited.

She met his gaze in silence.

How maddening.

"Very well." His words were clipped. "Get in touch if you remember anything helpful." He turned to walk away.

I seethed. Kay was not only foolish, but an ungrateful wretch. Refusing to tell the police that someone had toppled the vase placed her, in my view, in further danger. I'd saved her once. Who knew if I could manage to save her again?

If I'd been visibly present, I knew my eyes would be glinting and my lips pressed tight. But I wasn't visibly present. So . . . I took two quick steps and plunged my hand into the capacious pocket where she'd dropped the note found on her pillow.

Kay made a gurgling sound in her throat. She seized my wrist.

Chief Cobb turned to look. His eyes widened.

As we struggled, she listed to her right. To an observer, Kay's posture was odd.

"Let go," she hissed.

"Mrs. Clark?" The chief took a step toward her.

She yanked herself upright, but maintained her tight grip on my wrist. "Sorry." She was breathing fast. She made an effort to move forward, but I braced my feet against the balcony floor. She continued to appear strained. "I'm a bit unsteady. Shock."

Chief Cobb took a step forward. "Can I help you?"

"No." The word was forced between breaths. Kay twisted free and used both hands to shove me.

I lost my balance, but I had the note.

She flung herself in pursuit of the folded sheet and grabbed the note. As she whirled toward the railing, she tore the paper into tiny pieces and threw the particles out into the night. Her chest heaving, she faced the chief. "Sometimes I have trouble breathing. Asthma, you know. That accounts for my unsteadiness and . . . and the choking sounds. If you'll excuse me, I'll go to my room."

Chief Cobb's massive face was a study in disbelief.

No doubt he was trying to reconcile what he had seen with what she had said. The note had been small. The movement of her hands could have been a flutter of distress. The pieces of paper were now well disposed of.

"If you're certain you are all right . . ." Cobb spoke slowly, his gaze bewildered.

"I'm fine. Thank you." She strode past him.

Reluctantly, I gave her an unseen thumbs-up. She was a worthy oppo—oh. I must not align myself against her. Unless forced to do so by circumstances beyond my control.

Chief Cobb and I gazed after her as she walked swiftly toward the steps leading down to the garden. Whatever he thought, he surely realized that there was more to this evening than met the eye.

As for me, I was willing to cede the first round, but I wasn't through. Kay wanted a verdict of accident. I had no idea why she had made that decision. I was determined to engage the police. An active investigation of attempted murder would protect Kay. Keeping her safe was my priority. For me, that goal had neared the status of a search for a unicorn. However, I would not be thwarted by obdurate, stubborn, impossible Kay Clark.

My eyes narrowed in consideration. No tools had been found on the balcony. Tools were kept in a workshop. One quick thought and I again found myself in total darkness. I slipped my hand over the wall and turned on the lights. Any handyman would have been thrilled with the collection of tools in The Castle workshop.

Tools were arranged in niches or holders on one wall. I spotted a collection of chisels and hammers and three crowbars of varying size. The tools appeared clean and shiny, but I would expect no less in a well-kept tool room. There was nothing to suggest any of these tools had been used to loosen the vase, but nothing to show they had not. I chose a claw hammer that had a nice heft and a moderate-size chisel. In my nonvisible state, I didn't have to be concerned with fingerprints.

However, burdened with tools, I had to transport them through actual space. I could no longer envision a destination and immediately arrive. Turning off the light, I opened the workshop door and stepped outside. I was near the garages. The Castle blazed with lights. Flashlight beams danced in the garden.

The tools should appear to be well hidden, yet I wanted to place them where they'd be easily found. Moreover, I hoped to put the tools inside the house. I hadn't forgotten the sound of that closing door. I wanted the police to look very hard at the occupants of The Castle.

I moved from shadow to shadow, edging ever nearer the garden.

The stark glare of a flashlight swept over me. I wasn't there, but the crowbar glittered silver.

I dropped to the ground.

"Hey, Joe. Something moved over there near the mimosa."

Heavy footsteps moved cautiously nearer. "Police. Hands up. Police."

Three flashlights cut bright swaths near me. The searchers held the flashlights to one side to avoid providing a silhouette.

Keeping the tools barely above the ground, I retreated, escaping those seeking beams by inches. My heart was thudding by the time I reached a huge oak with a massive trunk. I rose. The tools hidden by foliage, I watched the police officers below. As the search of the lower terrace continued, I zipped, still hidden by trees, to the front of the house.

In my absence, the fire truck and ambulance had departed. The chief's car and several cruisers remained in the drive. The brightly lit porch was empty. Happily, the front porch wasn't visible from the terrace. I found the front door closed and locked. I placed the tools on the welcome mat and moved through the wooden panel. Once inside, I turned the lock, opened the door, retrieved the tools, closed and locked the door.

A low-wattage yellow bulb burned in a wall sconce. Otherwise, the hallway was dim. The stairs stretched up into darkness. I wondered how well the occupants were resting after the late-night interruption.

In a mirror on a sidewall, the crowbar, chisel, and hammer appeared to dangle in space.

The door at the end of the long, marbled hallway began to open.

Hurriedly, I looked around. A massive oak cabinet sat beneath the mirror. I opened the second drawer, the one at eye level. If the drawer had been locked, the situation would have been perilous. Fortunately—good work by Wiggins?—the drawer easily slid out. I stashed the tools inside.

Kay stepped into the hallway, carrying a tray with a carafe and a plate covered by a napkin. A late-night snack? Perhaps she would share.

At the foot of the stairs, she flipped several switches and started up.

I opened the drawer a few inches and pulled out the shiny tip of the crowbar. Anyone going out the front door in the morning would be sure to notice.

Now for a chat with my recalcitrant charge.

CHAPTER FOUR

Kay's bedroom was enchanting. I wondered if all the guest rooms at The Castle were this grand. The terra-cotta walls matched the tiled floor. A collection of Roseville pottery filled a bamboo cabinet. Photographs decorated the walls, Oklahoma scenes all: a gusher, Wiley Post and Will Rogers standing by the *Winnie Mae,* Maria Tallchief in *The Fire-bird,* the Cherokee alphabet, the château-style Henry Overholser Mansion in Oklahoma City, a Black Angus bull, an eagle wheeling in the sky.

Kay Clark sat at a fruitwood desk, a tray to one side. Her eyes narrowed, she studied an open file, pen in hand.

I was abruptly starving. However, I always try to be mannerly. "The roast-beef sandwich looks wonderful. May I have a half?"

Kay's head jerked up. She gazed all around the room, her dark eyes wide with shock.

"Oh, come on, Kay. We're in this together." I tapped the desk next to the tray. "Surely you don't mind sharing."

She stiffened. Without a word, she pushed the tray nearer the edge of the desk.

I took her action as an affirmative. I picked up a half. Only a half, mind you.

"Mmm. This is almost Heavenly." I made the modification in the interests of accuracy. Though not divine, Oklahoma beef is by far the best in the world. "I especially like the mustard."

"Colman's," she muttered, her dark eyes huge as she watched the sandwich disappear.

"May I have some Fritos?"

"Whatever." She averted her eyes as I scooped up a handful.

"Thank you. Now." I daintily used a paper napkin to brush my fingers, dropped it into the wastebasket by the desk.

Abruptly, Kay pushed back her chair, which thudded to the floor as she stood. She turned away and paced toward the windows.

I reached down, righted the chair. "Kay, please. Look, if it makes you feel better, here I am." I swirled into being. I saw my reflection in a mirror framed by ceramic parrots studded with turquoise. Perhaps the scarlet tunic and gold trousers were a bit much. The tunic swirled into ivory and the trousers into turquoise.

Kay placed her fingers over her eyes, then slowly dropped her hands. "My psychologist probably won't even charge for my next session, not after I tell her about you. Go away."

I folded my arms. "Not until you're safe."

Her face creased in thought. She strolled back to the desk, settled in the chair. She picked up the other half of the sandwich, took a bite. "I don't remember eating the rest of it." Her tone was uneasy.

"I ate it." I'm afraid I was impatient.

"Sure. Next thing you know, I'll be tap-dancing with a frog."

She looked warily about. "If I see a frog, I'll know I'm nuts." Not spotting any stray amphibians, she finished the sandwich, slumped back against the seat. "But I keep seeing you." The pronoun wasn't said with affection. Her gaze slid toward me, swerved away. "I guess I *am* nuts. Maybe I should go to bed. But I have to think." She drew a notebook near, began to write.

I moved the tray out of the way, perched on the edge of the desk. "What happened to Jack?"

Her head snapped up. "I'm not only nuts, I've got amnesia. That weird figment of my imagination, Bailey Ruth Raeburn"— her tone was brittle with indignation—"doesn't even know what's happened!" She shook her head forcefully. "Okay, my subconscious is telling me something. Maybe I need to look again at what I know about Jack's fall. Maybe my subconscious is onto something. Maybe I missed something." She flipped to a fresh page, muttered aloud as she wrote.

I disappeared.

Kay took no notice. I suppose if she didn't believe what she was seeing, she wasn't surprised when she didn't see it.

I read her notations with interest.

1. Jack's body was found at the base of the balcony steps on Sunday morning, June 7. Although there was multiple trauma, the medical examiner said death resulted from a broken neck.

2. Time of death was estimated at some time after nine P.M. the previous evening. At the end of a dinner party, he had announced his intention of taking a stroll on the balcony to smoke a cigar. Since his arrival from Kenya three weeks earlier for his father's funeral, it had been his custom to end each evening on the balcony with a cigar and a glass of brandy.

3. A postmortem offered no explanation of the fall. The physician noted that he was in his early sixties and in excellent health, but sudden dizziness could not be ruled out.

4. A police investigation concluded the death was an accident. The balcony was dimly lighted and possibly he had misjudged a step and fallen.

I tapped on her shoulder. "Why not an accident?"

Kay quivered, but refused to glance behind her. She wrote in her distinctive script:

5. Why not an accident?
    A. Jack was an accomplished athlete in excellent condition. Why would he fall down steps?
    B. He had jogged Saturday afternoon, returned to The Castle shortly before six P.M., showered, dressed.
    C. Dinner was at seven. In addition to family members and Ronald and Laverne Phillips, dinner guests included Alison Gregory and Gwen and Clint Dunham.
    D. Jack drank one glass of wine at dinner and carried a glass of brandy to the balcony. He was sober when he died. This was confirmed by the autopsy.
    E. Jack had excellent night vision. The possibility of an accident or sudden illness is remote.

6. Why murder?
    A. Jack had returned to The Castle for his father's funeral. It was his first visit from Kenya since the death of his brother, James, five years earlier.
    B. During the earlier visit, he stayed for only a few days. This time he had spent several weeks in Adelaide. His e-mails indicated concern about what he had discovered since his return.

Kay's face suddenly crumpled. She wiped away tears and took a deep breath. She pulled out the desk drawer and picked up an ebony case. Game animals in mother-of-pearl designs made the lid exquisite. Kay opened the box and picked up several sheets of paper.

I read over her shoulder. The e-mails were addressed to her. I noted the dates and subject lines. "Why did he print out his e-mails to you?"

She shook her head. "I think I am completely losing it. Why doesn't one part of my mind know what I know in the rest of my mind? He didn't. FYI, I brought these e-mails with me, but I'm keeping them in a box with Jack's papers that I found in the room when I arrived."

I scanned the sheets.

Sent: May 30, 11:05 P.M.
Subject: Déjà vu all over again

Just like time travel. The Castle hasn't changed since I was here in '86 for James's wedding. Or for his funeral five years ago. Poor old James. He died too young. I wasn't back long enough then to get much of a glimpse of the old place. At the wedding, I was still young enough to think I could see someone across a crowded room and everything would change. You were married to Bob. I hadn't met Helen yet. Anyway, I didn't have eyes to see much on that trip. This time it's different.

Dad's funeral was kind of fun. He was an engaging old reprobate. I guess my years in Kenya have made me mellow.

I visited Sallie's grave. She's been gone so long. Virginia never meant for her to die, but she took my princess with her.

Wish you were here. J

P.S. You used to like adventure. Come home to Kenya with me.

Sent: June 3, 4:03 P.M.
Subject: The Castle

Placid on the surface, nasty things bubbling beneath. I may
need to stay for a couple of weeks. I guess the old man must
have lost his grip to let things get to this state.

I'd take a tangle with a rogue elephant anytime. Instead,
there's Diane and her leeches; Evelyn, who can't see and
may be blind in other ways as well; Margo, who'd like my head
on a platter; Shannon, who's flattering the hell out of me; and
Jimmy, who wants to break my neck. Maybe a little competi-
tion will make him realize what a neat girl Shannon is. She
and I have had a swell time together. She's made me feel like
a kid again. However, she's starting to be too interested in
me. I'm going to have to tell her she's great and I want to be
good friends. But there's no good way to say you don't love
someone. She's still young enough to believe in love at first
sight. She's a gorgeous, sweet girl, but I'm old enough to be
her father.

The only thing that keeps me sane is knowing I'll get back
to Kenya. Come with me, Kay. I promise you a good time.
Lake Nakuru in moonlight. Flamingos massed in a tapestry of
pink against blue-green water. Every time I see them, I know
God has a sense of humor. Nobody wants brackish water,
but it's the slimy algae that draws the flamingos. I'll take you
out to see a leopard munch on a carcass he's pulled up into
a tree and gazelles more graceful than ballerinas. Bougainvil-
lea. Flamboyant trees. Rocky hills. Open grasslands. Yellow-
barked fever trees. And you and me, far, far from cities and
crowds. I know you loved Bob and I'll never forget Helen, but
we're fated, Kay. You and me finally together. You've got to
write the book.

Sent: June 5, 5 A.M.
Subject: Shock of my life . . .

Someone slipped a photograph underneath my bedroom
door last night. I have to find out what it means. If it turns out
to be true . . . God, the lost years.

I'll find out.

What will I do? I'd like to smash heads. And this, on top of
all the rest. When they say you can't go home again, maybe
they mean you damn well better not. But I'm here and I intend
to set everything straight. I'll see if Paul Fisher can help.

J

"What do the e-mails mean?"

Kay didn't look toward the sound of my voice. After all, if she
was talking to herself, what would be the need? She stared at her
list.

7. In the space of three weeks, Jack learned something that meant
   he had to die. His acquaintances in Adelaide were limited to
   those living at The Castle and a handful of other people.
   A. Evelyn, his older sister. She never married and has always
      lived at The Castle. Evelyn is legally blind. Perhaps
      because of her poor eyesight, she tries to dominate every
      gathering, every situation. I sense that she resented Jack's
      years in Africa and her role as caregiver to their father.
   B. Diane Hume, his brother's widow. In her late forties,
      Diane is nervous, anxious, and easily upset. James lacked
      his sister's strong personality and his brother's daring
      nature. Shy and reclusive, he taught biology at Goddard
      College and spent most of his time painting birds. His
      hero was George Sutton, the University of Oklahoma
      naturalist famous for his bird paintings.

C. Jimmy Hume. He reminds me of Jack when he was young. Jimmy finished high school a year early and attends OU. He's a geology major and will likely go to work for Hume Oil when he graduates. He rock-climbs, surfs, spelunks, and never met a dare he wouldn't take. He visited Jack several times in Africa. He's crazy about Shannon Taylor.

D. Shannon Taylor. The daughter of The Castle housekeeper, Margo Taylor, Shannon will be a freshman at Oklahoma State this fall. She helps out at The Castle in the summer. Evelyn's companion is the wife of a Goddard professor and they usually spend the summer in France. While the companion is gone, Shannon drives Evelyn. Shannon and Jimmy have been dating on and off since middle school, but when Jack arrived at The Castle, Shannon was dazzled by him.

A smile transformed Kay's face. Despite the traces of tears, she looked rueful and amused and understanding, a woman with a long view and a generous heart. "I could have told Shannon." In the margin of her notepad, she sketched a heart with an arrow. Across the heart, she wrote: *Women*. She tagged the arrow: *Jack*. Kay leaned back in the chair still smiling. "He couldn't help it. The man was magic."

Kay pulled a laptop toward her, flipped up the lid. In only a moment, a striking picture filled the screen. The background was mesmerizing, falls tumbling behind him in a feathery spray of white, but despite the magnificence of thundering water, the man in the foreground dominated the photograph, thick silver hair, broad forehead, strong nose, high cheekbones, chiseled chin, full, sensuous lips. He was in safari garb, topee hat, khaki shirt and shorts, boots. A patch covered his right eye. An angry red scar curled down one cheek. Whether it was his expression of barely leashed intensity or the way he stood, or something more, the image radiated vigor and recklessness and the make-me-any-bid challenge of a gambler. Beneath the vitality, there was also an underlying gravity, suggesting he had been tested in many arenas and was sadder and wiser for his experiences.

I'm not sure I would have recognized him. After his wife and daughter's death, Jack had left Adelaide as a very young man with coal black hair and smooth features. He'd returned as an older man whose scarred face and confident bearing reflected adventures in a dangerous environment.

"While he's asking me to leave my world behind and move to Africa, he's breaking a college girl's heart. Like he wrote, there's no good way to say thanks, but no thanks." Kay's smile fled. She picked up her pen, added to the note on Shannon.

8. Was Shannon distraught enough over Jack to have wanted him dead?

   E. Margo Taylor. The housekeeper's face looks hard as granite at any mention of Jack. Was she angered by her daughter's pursuit of him? Or did she think he was taking advantage of Shannon?

   F. Laverne and Ronald Phillips. Laverne claims to be clairvoyant. Diane consulted her several years ago in Dallas. Laverne insists she is in contact with James Hume. Diane begged her to come to Adelaide and live at The Castle. Every Wednesday night, they hold a séance. It's all nonsense, of course, but Diane believes every word. Neither Laverne nor Ronald is likable. Laverne tries to be a grande dame, but she's all theater and no substance.

Ronald is like a fancy lapdog, always deferring to her, talking about her "gift."

"Oooh." I knew I sounded appalled. "Heaven doesn't approve."

Kay's expression was a mixture of disdain and perplexity. "What is with my subconscious? Séances may be stupid, but I doubt they rank as immoral. I had no idea I was such a prig."

Prig! I reached out and gave her arm a sharp pinch.

"Ouch." Kay looked at her arm. "Maybe I need a nightcap." She popped from the chair, walked to a wet bar. As she filled a tumbler with ice, I put another glass next to hers. With scarcely a pause, she scooped more ice. "Sure. The more the merrier. Me and my little helper." A line of single-serving bottles included Scotch, bourbon, and gin. She poured Scotch and added club soda.

I opened a little gin bottle.

She watched as a bottle of tonic water was lifted and poured. "I loathe gin and tonic."

"I don't," I answered sweetly. I carried the drink across the room.

Determinedly ignoring the moving glass, Kay stalked back to the desk. "Maybe I wasn't supposed to take a break. In fact, I don't need a drink." She turned, marched to the sink, dumped the contents of the glass, and returned to the desk. "I freaking hope when I figure out what happened to Jack, my mind gets its groove back." She slammed into the chair.

I took a sip. The glass tipped.

She covered her eyes with one hand.

"If it makes you feel better . . ." I swirled back into being.

She dropped her hand and swept me with a hostile glance. "At least you're better-looking than Poe's phantasms."

"Faint praise is worse than no praise at all." I took another sip. "Excellent gin."

She tapped her fingers irritably on the desktop. "Okay. I get the message. I'm missing something. Obviously, I won't be rid of you until I figure out whatever it is I haven't figured out."

"I'll help." I pushed a hassock near the desk, settled on it. "How did you manage to be invited to stay here?"

"I didn't know Jack had died. I kept e-mailing to no answer. I knew something was wrong. I called. It was the day of Jack's funeral." Her lovely face was stricken. "I ended up speaking to Diane. She told me he'd fallen down the balcony steps. I kept pressing her. I suppose I sounded incredulous. She kept talking about an accident. I remembered his e-mails. I knew he'd been murdered." She snapped her fingers. "I knew it like that. It didn't take five minutes on the phone with Diane to know she was a patsy. I told her Jack had asked me to come this week and make plans for a book I was writing about him. I asked her if I could go ahead and come, that I'd promised him about the book. She agreed." She looked around the lovely room. "I'm in the room where he stayed on his visit. It's as near to him now as I'll ever be. What happened tonight proves I was right. Someone pushed him, and someone's going to pay."

"Why didn't you tell the police someone tried to kill you tonight?" My tone was both sharp and puzzled. She knew and I knew she had been lured to the cul-de-sac and the vase had been pushed. Yet she'd done everything in her power to prevent an investigation. Now that I realized she suspected Jack Hume was a murder victim, I felt bewildered. "What were you thinking? What's to keep the murderer from trying again?"

Her combative, on-top-of-everything pose slipped. She lifted a shaky hand, as if to push away my words, but fear glimmered in her eyes. She knew she'd missed death by an instant. "Don't you understand? If the police questioned people, everybody would be scared. Some of them might not be willing to say anything about Jack. He blew into town and started upsetting applecarts. Nobody would admit they'd quarreled with him or were angry with him. As long as no one knows he was murdered, they'll answer my questions. I can find out everything that's been going on."

I was exasperated. "The murderer won't be fooled."

She brushed back a tangle of dark hair. "That's the gamble I have to take. But it may not be a gamble now. When no investigation is begun, it will be obvious I haven't told the police anything about Jack's death. The murderer will know I don't have any idea who killed him."

"There's a small problem with that."

She massaged one temple. "Okay, subconscious, give me a hint."

I didn't mind telling her and she could take my appraisal as an internal warning if she wished. "You plan to ask a lot of questions. If you start to find out what led the murderer to push Jack, you'll be at risk again. This murderer seems to like accidents. If you discover too much, there may be another 'accident' and this time you may not survive."

"I won't tip my hand. But someone knows something that will lead to the murderer."

I looked at her with growing admiration. She was exposing herself to danger. She was gambling with her life. But I understood. "You must have loved him very much."

Tears filmed her dark eyes. "For so long. And yet I always knew that we were better apart."

"However"—I was crisp—"Heaven doesn't want you to be at risk. I have a proposition."

Her smile was crooked. "A message from one corner of my mind to another? Damn laborious." She clamped fingers to her temples. "Come on, mind. All together now."

I persevered. "Go home. Leave the detecting to me. If you stay here, you will be in danger if you get too close to the murderer."

"Hey." She bristled with indignation. "I can't believe I heard that." She shook her head. "I've been called a lot of things, but I've never been called a coward. Especially not by myself." The emphasis on the pronoun was marked.

I felt uneasy about Kay's mental confusion. Perhaps she would cope better if I disappeared. I swirled away.

She didn't even blink.

I returned.

Kay's gaze was steely. "Stuff yourself back into some far crevice of my brain. I'm here and here I stay." She spoke fast and hard. Perhaps she felt that was the only way to communicate with the part of her mind that she credited with my appearances. Her gaze never left my face. "Tonight accomplished two things. The note on my pillow and the crash of the vase prove Jack was murdered. My acceptance of the vase as an accident should reassure everyone, maybe including the murderer, that I'm here because Jack hired me to write his life story."

I was skeptical. "He doesn't sound like the kind of man who was that self-absorbed."

Now Kay massaged both temples. "Will you keep quiet? You know—or you should unless my subconscious has completely lost its marbles—that story is pure fiction. He wanted me to write a book about his camp near Lake Nakuru: Five-Star Safaris, Jack Hume, Victoria Falls specialist. So, I'm perfectly safe. I'm a non-fiction writer, specialty biographies, most recent title a biography of Jerrie Cobb. I'm telling everybody here that I need information about Jack's last days in order to write the end of the story, then I'm traveling to Kenya. I can find out everything about what happened before he died. Plus the attack on me may give some clue to the identity of the murderer."

She drew the pad near, began to write.

9. The note was placed on my pillow after I went downstairs for dinner at a quarter to seven. Any member of the household (Evelyn, Diane, Jimmy, the Phillipses, and Margo and Shannon) could have put the note there. Dinner guests were the family, Alison Gregory, Paul Fisher, and Gwen and Clint Dunham. Everybody but Fisher was at The Castle the night Jack died.

Kay looked pleased. "I asked Diane to invite them since I understood Jack had seen all of them during his visit. Alison Gregory has a gallery and Evelyn buys artwork from her. They are also quite good friends, Alison being no dummy." Kay's tone was dry. "The Dunhams live next door and are longtime family friends. I asked Diane to include Paul Fisher because Jack may have talked to him about the photograph someone slipped beneath his door. Anyone who was at dinner could have pushed the vase. It would be easy for either of the Dunhams or Alison to return. I don't include Paul as a suspect because I understand he wasn't in Adelaide the night Jack died. I'll check that out to be sure."

I wasn't convinced. "Someone in the house pushed the vase. I heard a door close when I reached the balcony."

Kay shrugged. "Maybe. Maybe not. If a dinner guest left the note in my room, it would be easy to hurry up to the third floor and unlock a French door on the balcony. The Castle is old-fashioned. There's no alarm system. Later, someone could have approached the house, climbed the balcony steps, pushed the vase, then escaped through the house to avoid being seen in the garden. There are many ways out of the house on the ground floor."

I glanced again at the list. "What do you know about the dinner guests?"

She sighed in relief. "That's why you're haunting me. I need to find out whether Jack had a connection to one of them. Nobody was very forthcoming tonight. I don't suppose it escaped anybody's notice that they had all, except Paul, been at The Castle the night Jack died. The conversation was pretty stiff. Alison Gregory talked about a traveling exhibit of Impressionists at the Oklahoma City Art Museum. No matter what I asked her, pretty soon she got back to the exhibit. I learned more about Monet than I ever wanted to know. As for the Dunhams, they had very little to say. She's a blonde with exquisite bone structure. She's been beautiful all of her life. Tonight she was distant. Polite enough, but clearly wishing she were elsewhere. Her husband's big and burly and looks like he's outside a lot, a ruddy face. You would have thought the art exhibit up in the City was the most fascinating thing Gwen Dunham had ever heard about. I did manage to ask how well she knew Jack. She looked surprised and murmured she thought they'd met years ago, but her memory wasn't too clear. Her husband just shook his head."

Suddenly Kay yawned. She looked at the clock. It was shortly after three A.M. She yawned again. "I've done all I can do."

I understood. A near escape from death had sent her adrenaline sky-high. Now the adrenaline had drained away and she was exhausted.

Kay pushed back the chair, walked toward the bed, turning off lights. She kicked off her shoes, and fully dressed, she dropped onto the bed.

I think she was asleep before her head hit the pillow.

I struggled, too, with fatigue. Being in the world is physically tiring. Appearing and disappearing consumes enormous energy, though I didn't think I would get any sympathy from Kay. I rubbed scratchy eyes. Before I slept, I wanted to explore the papers left behind by Jack Hume.

The ebony box still lay open on the desktop, next to Jack's e-mails. I lifted out the contents one by one. A passport. I opened it, saw a photograph of Jack Hume. I flipped through the pages. He was indeed well traveled, visiting London and Paris several times each year as well as many of the African countries adjoining Kenya. His only recent visit to the United States coincided with his arrival in Adelaide. There was a packet of letters from Kay. I did not read them.

A thick legal document turned out to be the trust provisions of his father, John J. Hume III. A handwritten sheet in masculine writing was tucked inside along with two business cards. The sheet was the beginning of a letter to Kay. The sheet wasn't dated.

> *Hi, Kay,*
>
> *Too late tonight to call you. Paul explained the provisions of Dad's estate this afternoon. All the trusts are set up, equal shares for Evelyn, me, and Jimmy. Surprised the hell out of me. I guess the old man really had mellowed. Maybe my coming back for James's funeral made a difference. Maybe using the inheritance from Mom and making a go of my company in Kenya pleased him, even if he was mad as hell that I blew off Hume Oil. Who knows? Anyway, the Hume fortune will last at least another couple of generations. Everything will ultimately come to Jimmy since Evelyn and I don't have kids. None of it matters a damn to me, anyway. I want to get back to the bush. I hope you . . .*

Apparently, Jack had started the letter to her, then tucked it in the legal folder, intending to finish it later. I studied the business cards. On thick white stock with black printing:

PAUL FORBES FISHER, ESQ.
FISHER, BENTON, AND BORELLI, LLC
201 W. MAIN STREET
ADELAIDE, OK 74820
580.333.7942

The second card was a soft cream with dark blue lettering:

ALISON GREGORY
GREGORY GALLERY
104 WISTERIA LANE
ADELAIDE, OK 74820
580.333.6281

The second card carried a brief notation on the back: *2:30 P.M.*
Leonard Walker.

The last item in the ebony box was a computer printout en-
titled *Hume Estate Artwork.* I scanned several single-spaced pages,
a list of paintings, statuary, silver, and any other artworks in The
Castle. The evaluations startled me. A painting by Gainsborough
was valued at $640,000. My oh my.

I checked to see if anything was tucked between the pages of
the list or the copy of the estate provisions sheets.

In Jack Hume's final e-mail, he was upset because a photograph had been slipped beneath the door of his room. What photograph and where was it?

Tomorrow I would ask Kay.

I replaced the items in the order in which I'd found them. Jack
Hume's letter about his inheritance indicated that no one in the
Hume family needed money, making it unlikely that Jack had
been murdered for his estate.

Kay was focused on what Jack had discovered in his three

weeks at The Castle that made his murder essential. Tomorrow I would try again to convince her to leave the investigating to me.

I checked her bedroom door. It was locked. However, I propped a chair beneath the handle. It never hurt to take precautions.

I disappeared and whirled through the wall into the hallway. I began to explore, seeking a suitable guest bedroom. Who would ever have thought I would spend a night at The Castle?

I had some difficulty in making a choice, finally opting for a truly dramatic guest room with white walls, white rugs, and a spacious four-poster bed with a white spread. White is such a nice background for a redhead.

Of course, I could better appreciate the contrast if I appeared. I swirled into being. White shorty pajamas were perfect . . .

"Oh, dear. Harumph." A hurried clearing of his throat announced Wiggins's arrival. "Bailey Ruth, please." There was a touch of embarrassment in his voice, but I didn't miss the underlying stern tone.

Quick to observe the proprieties, I changed to a sky blue blouse and white linen trousers with the most fetching white sandals. I took a deep breath and looked in the direction of his voice. I wished he would appear. I suddenly empathized with Kay Clark. Dealing with an unseen presence was unnerving.

Moreover, I knew I was a ghost in trouble, fighting for my mission.

CHAPTER FIVE

I t is better to give than to receive. Especially if trouble is on the way. Before Wiggins could scold, I beamed and clapped my hands in appreciation. "How nice of you to come. I'm sure you want to know the latest developments."

"I know the latest." His voice had a curious strangling sound. "Appearing, always appearing."

I suspected an accusatory forefinger was at this moment pointed at me. I increased the wattage of my smile, clearly a woman confident of her actions. "Everything is working out splendidly!"

"Working out?" There was a note of uncertainty and possibly a flicker of hope.

I almost felt a moment of compunction. Really, men are such lambs, always responding readily to concrete statements.

"Definitely." I was tempted to break into "Everything's Coming Up Roses," but decided not to push my luck. "Kay thinks I'm imaginary. So, should I need to appear, no harm done. She won't believe I'm there."

I continued to beam in the approximate direction of his voice. I wished he weren't so averse to being visible. "Of course, tomorrow—today actually—I'll try again to convince Kay to leave the investigating to me. The wisest course would be for her to leave Adelaide."

"That will be wonderful." Relief buoyed his voice. "Your mission will be done. The Express can pick you up this afternoon."

Perhaps I was too clever by half. My high-wattage smile felt fixed. "I'll do my best to persuade her to depart, but there are ramifications." My face grew grave.

"Oh?"

I spoke quickly. "Others may be at risk. Kay is my primary responsibility, but I need to discover the reason for Jack's murder." I gave my husky voice a portentous vibrato. "Until then, no one at The Castle may be safe."

"Unfortunately"—Wiggins sounded somber—"I have a similar feeling. In the department, we are not privy to the innermost thoughts of those on earth. Only God knows. However, when I checked your file, I felt most uneasy. Though possibly your predilections might be the source of my discomfort. And"—his voice was dour—"I find it discouraging that you arrived at your post unaware you were here to protect Kay Kendall Clark. I most specifically"—great emphasis—"advised that you were perhaps unsuitable considering your attitude toward Kay. You assured me"—now there was a put-upon note to his voice—"that you were absolutely capable of discharging your duties. That moment in the garden when each recognized the other was not a scene I like to dwell upon."

I refused to be daunted. "All missions have their ups and downs. Why, you yourself when last in Tumbulgum"—at the conclusion of my previous visit to earth, Wiggins had admitted a deviation from the Precepts when he had been forced to intervene in a mission in that remote Australian community—"realized that despite the best of intentions, at times one does what one has to do. In this instance, I will emphatically carry out my duties with a brave heart and a clear conscience."

"Well put." He was hearty.

Dear Wiggins. So easily deflected from the matter at hand.

I looked soulful. I caught a quick glimpse in the mirror. Perhaps the world lost a great actress. Truly, I appeared as noble as Portia in the famous painting by Millais.

"Bailey Ruth, do your best."

I stood straight as a soldier with a battlefield commission. Until I was sure he was gone. Then I gave a whoosh of relief. In any event, I'd better work fast and hope Kay Clark turned out to be as stubborn as I thought she was. It was essential that I speak with her privately in the morning. I thought for a moment, then popped to the kitchen. I turned on a light, found a notepad near the telephone, and composed a message. I left the note on the kitchen table. Upstairs in Kay's room, I used a sheet from her notepad, wrote quickly: *Breakfast will arrive at eight o'clock. Await further instructions.* I propped the note on the lavatory in Kay's bathroom and returned to the guest room.

Possibly I fell asleep even more quickly than Kay. A clear conscience affords that luxury.

My eyes popped wide. I'd had only a few hours' sleep, but I was eager to get a glimpse of the inhabitants of the house. When they are alone, many people's demeanors differ profoundly from that exhibited when in the company of others. Also, I needed to check on the not-quite-hidden tools.

With no fear of observation while in the bedroom, I chose to be visible. In the luxurious bathroom, I was enchanted by the huge white marble shower designed without a curtain or glass door. Absolutely Heavenly. As the water pelted, I recalled the household members as they gathered on the porch last night:

Evelyn Hume—Tall, imposing, a commanding figure. Dark hair streaked with silver. A long face with a determined jaw. A deep, imperious voice.

Diane Hume—Faded blonde. Dresden-fine features marred by a lost look in her blue eyes and anxious lines at her eyes and mouth.

Jimmy Hume—Tall and well built. Bright blue eyes. Wiry, short-cut brown hair. Squarish face set in a dark frown.

Margo Taylor—Frowsy auburn hair. Unsmiling. An aura of discontent.

Shannon Taylor—Young and pretty, blue-eyed, brown hair with gold highlights, her expression withdrawn and sad.

Laverne Phillips—Coronet braids. Dark eyes. Thin nose. Bony face. She tried to appear important, but came off as theatrical, a shopgirl pretending to be personage.

Ronald Phillips—He, too, seemed to be playing a role, the husband of a great woman. I wondered what was behind his unctuous manner and perfectly styled silver hair and beard.

Stepping out of the shower, I enjoyed the fleecy softness of the towel. Once dry, I disappeared and chose my clothing. Before departing, I materialized long enough to glance in the bedroom mirror, an extravagant, full-length affair with a white limestone frame. My copper-bright hair shone. An azure blouse complemented white slacks and sandals. My green eyes sparkled, my freckled face was eager. I was ready.

I checked to be sure there was no evidence the room had been used. I'd made the bed, of course. The bathroom had a plentiful supply of towels, so one less would not be noticed. I folded my damp towel. I'd drop by The Castle laundry room on my way out.

I disappeared and stepped into the hall, making sure no one was about to observe the floating towel. I gently closed the bedroom door and thought: laundry room. To move an object required me to traverse the distance rather than immediately arriving. I floated—floating is such fun—down the hallway to an inconspicuous door. I opened it to find the interior stairs meant for the domestic staff. A dim light midway down revealed a narrow passageway and steep steps. I found three narrow doors at the bottom of the stairs. Dimly, I heard a dog barking excitedly.

The first door opened. "Walter, what's wrong with you? What's on the stairs?"

A yipping bundle of golden fur scrambled up the steps, nails clicking, in a wriggling frenzy of excitement.

"Shh." I reached down to pet.

The dog lunged, yanking the towel from my other hand.

I grabbed one end, held tight.

A joyous growl sounded. The dog pulled, his claws scrabbling on the uncarpeted stairs. What could be more fun than tug-of-war first thing in the morning?

"Walter, what are you doing?" Margo sounded exasperated. She stood at the foot of the steps, glaring upward. "Hush. You'll wake everyone up." The door evidently opened into the kitchen. The scent of coffee and bacon beckoned me. I let go of the towel.

Walter slid down several steps, dragging the towel with him.

"Give me that towel." Margo bent, but the dog bolted past her into the kitchen, the towel dragging behind him.

I sighed. Now there would be the Mystery of the Damp Towel on the Service Stairs. Wiggins felt strongly about unexplained incidents that might prompt speculation of otherworldly intervention.

Looking on the bright side—I hoped Wiggins would do so as well—now that I wasn't burdened with the towel, I was free to carry out my plans.

I had a decision to make. Although Kay's refusal to involve the police likely put her in greater danger, I understood her reasoning. As long as those with whom she spoke—with the exception of the murderer—remained unaware that Jack Hume had been pushed, they likely would answer whatever questions Kay asked.

However, if the tools I'd so cleverly placed in the drawer in the oak cabinet were discovered, it was inevitable that the police would be summoned and a thorough investigation begun on the sabotage of the vase.

I am rarely indecisive. Did I play Kay's game? Or did I try to involve the police in hopes of protecting her? If the former, I must move quickly, retrieve the tools, place them in the tool room.

I popped to the main hallway. Shadowy openings at either side near the front door led to the living and dining area. I looked at the massive cabinet.

The second drawer was closed. I reached out, pulled.

The tools were gone.

I'd expected the first person through the hallway this morning to see the glint of the crowbar in the light from the wall sconce and immediately raise the alarm. The police would be summoned.

Someone had indeed walked past and been attracted by the silvery glint, but no alarm had been raised.

Either a murderer had walked this way or someone willing to protect a killer.

· · · ·

In the workshop, the spaces for the crowbar, hammer, and chisel remained empty. The tools could be in the pond or hidden in dense vegetation. I'd been outwitted. I had no idea when the tools had been taken. Yet I felt almost certain they must have been discovered early this morning. Who had been up early?

I left the workshop and rose in the air to survey the surroundings.

Evelyn Hume walked down the stairs from the terrace. Her fingertips slid smoothly down the stone balustrade. Her silver-streaked dark hair was pulled back in a bun. She looked cool and attractive in a gray chambray blouse and slacks. As I watched, she reached the terrace, turned, and walked without hesitation to the cul-de-sac.

I dropped down beside her, near enough to see the grim set of her face. The thick lenses of her glasses magnified her milky eyes.

Despite the bright morning sun, the cul-de-sac was dim, shadowed by the tall, thick evergreens on three sides. There was light enough to see that the vase had been blue porcelain. Light enough also to recognize the great force of the vase's impact. The vase had shattered into large pieces, spilling clods of dark rich dirt. There was still the scent of gardenias, though the blossoms were already browned and wilted.

It was only as Evelyn moved slowly forward, her steps cautious, that her poor vision became apparent. As the toe of her right shoe encountered debris, she stooped to pick up a shard of pottery. Her lined face was brooding, intent.

She held the broken piece for a moment, then dropped it. As she turned away, she reached out, touched a prickly evergreen. As soon as her shoe grated on the flagstones, she swung to her right, walked unerringly toward the marble stairway.

Had she come to the cul-de-sac to confirm the fall of the vase? Did she find it hard to believe that a huge porcelain vase, securely in place for many years, would topple of its own accord? Or was her early-morning inspection more sinister in intent? Was she a thwarted murderer hoping that there would be no suspicion raised about the vase's fall?

I watched as she climbed the steps. After one initial brush with her hand at the base of the steps, she climbed with confidence. I didn't know why she had visited the cul-de-sac. However, it was obvious now that poor vision was no obstacle to Evelyn Hume's going anywhere she chose. Would she have noticed the not-quite-hidden tools? The old Spanish cabinet was on the way to the front door. Did she customarily reach out to touch the cabinet to confirm her distance from the door? Had her hand encountered the cold steel tip of the crowbar?

I didn't know.

However, Evelyn Hume's poor vision was no proof of her innocence. She could easily have walked up behind her brother on the balcony, pushed him to his death, and slipped away in the darkness, just as her hand might have gripped the crowbar that tipped the vase last night.

I glanced up at the balcony. A silent observer watched as Evelyn reached the terrace and moved purposefully toward a side door.

I landed a few feet from Ronald Phillips. His silver hair was stiff from hair spray and his Vandyke perfectly trimmed. He was natty in a blue polo and blue-and-white-striped seersucker trousers. Ronald was too much of a dandy to be attractive to me. Nor did I care for the cunning look on his face. He reminded me of a ferret. As Evelyn disappeared, he moved swiftly and lightly, his steps making little sound, to a French door.

I followed him through a ballroom to the main stairway and down to the second floor. He turned left and walked swiftly to the end of the hallway and opened a door.

Laverne sat at a desk midway across the room. She watched as he stepped inside. There was no warmth in her gaze. A lamp revealed a face with all imperfections concealed by makeup. She, too, was fully dressed. Despite the heat, she was garbed all in black, a rayon blouse, polished cotton slacks, leather sandals. "Where have you been?"

He gave a satisfied smile. "Here and there." He had a light tenor voice. "Evelyn's worried. She was down there nosing around the broken vase."

Laverne's narrow face was abruptly expressionless. "Where were you last night?"

He smoothed his beard. "Out for a cigarette. It's damn stupid I can't smoke in here."

"You know how Diane feels about smoking." Laverne's tone suggested this was a familiar reply to an oft-stated grievance.

His face twisted in a sneer. "This place has absorbed plenty of cigarette smoke. And enough whiskey to supply a whorehouse." His smile was wolfish. "I've got more stuff for James's spirit to talk about, thanks to the historical society. The ladies there think I'm wonderful. I take them Godiva chocolates. They can't wait to help me find stuff. Yesterday I looked at microfilms about James and Diane's wedding. I even got some pix. Did you know Jack was part of the wedding party when James and Diane got married?"

She waved a long thin pale hand in dismissal. "Diane didn't like Jack. She only wants to hear about her husband."

Ronald rocked on his feet, the quick movement of a man with too much restless energy. "James will have lots to say."

Laverne's dark eyes were alert. "What are you doing, Ronald?"

His smile was reckless. "Looking around. I like to know what's going on. I'm good at putting two and two together."

Her hands clenched. "You'd better be careful."

"Don't worry about me. I always land on my feet." His eyes

gleamed. "Maybe you're the one who should be careful. You went down to the garden last night." His gaze was sharp.

"I heard that crash. You weren't here."

He took a step toward her. "I was here." His light blue eyes were cold, commanding. "Neither of us left the room until you went out to see about the noise." He took two quick steps, seized her arm. "Where was I?" His voice was silky.

"Here. With me."

He nodded in satisfaction, loosed his grip. "I've been thinking about tonight's séance. Who knows what you might hear from the great beyond." He smiled and turned to leave the room.

As the door closed behind him, Laverne's tight fists slowly opened. She flexed her fingers. Her face looked bleak. And frightened.

I almost whirled outside again, but decided to check the floor for other occupants. In a large bedroom, one wall contained sports trophies inscribed with Jimmy Hume's name. The room had a comfortable, masculine appearance with brown plaid drapes and a brown rug with geometric black squares. A copy of a thriller lay open on a brown leather couch. The bathroom was still steamy. Jimmy had apparently showered and dressed and left not too long ago.

Two doors down, I found Diane Hume. This room was clearly feminine, white-and-gold French Provincial furniture, a gold Persian rug, and a plethora of knickknacks, including Chinese lacquered boxes, Hopi dolls, crystal bowls, and gleaming brass animals.

Diane arranged peach-colored dahlias in a cut-glass vase. On top of a marble table, gardening gloves rested in a basket with traces of dirt and remnants of stems. She wore a loose blue blouse and designer jeans with mud-stained knees. The anxious lines smoothed out in her face as she gently rearranged the blossoms.

When she was satisfied, she placed the vase behind a framed photograph in the center of the tabletop. She gazed at the arrangement for a long moment. She started to turn away, then picked up the silver frame. She sat in a small gilt chair and looked down at a man's face.

He seemed familiar to me, dark hair a trifle overlong, long oval face, high bridged nose, dark eyes, well-formed lips. His gaze was remote, as if he listened to faraway music.

"Oh, James." Her voice wavered.

I understood the familiarity. This was Jack Hume's younger brother. The resemblance was there, but James's portrait had no hint of the vigor and engagement in Jack's picture by the falls.

Diane's eyes glazed with tears. "James, you need to tell me what to do. You will, won't you? But I can't tell Laverne. I'm too afraid . . . Maybe"—her tone was feverish, intense—"you can send me a message I'll understand."

In the front hall, the grandfather clock struck the quarter hour. I supposed breakfast was served at eight. I still had fifteen minutes to find Jimmy. I checked the first-floor rooms, all of them silent and dim, then zoomed outside and hovered above The Castle. I spotted Jimmy on a huge stretch of grass below the second terrace. The Millie No. 1 pump jack rose and fell in a steady rhythm.

Jimmy addressed a golf ball. He swung an iron back, then down through the ball and forward. The ball hooked to the left.

I stood a few feet away. There was no joy in his practice. His face was drawn in a tight, grim frown. He hit the balls, one after another, with ferocity. If he had skill, it was lost in the fury of his swings. Usually, the balls hooked.

Finally, he glanced at his watch, yanked up a golf bag, and flung three irons into it.

The crowbar, hammer, and chisel would have fit easily into the bag.

He walked with his head down, oblivious to the chitter of starlings and the low cry of mourning doves. On the terrace, he hesitated, then swung toward the rear of The Castle. In a moment, he was looking through a window into the kitchen. His young face was taut with unhappiness, his gaze uncertain, his lips pressed together.

The Castle kitchen was impressive, everything up-to-date, with granite countertops, gleaming silvery appliances, stone floors. Daffodil yellow curtains framed the window. Shannon emptied the contents of a juicer. Fresh orange juice glistened in a clear glass pitcher. She worked swiftly, competently, but her expression was distant, as if she were far away, where no voice could reach her.

Jimmy took a step toward the door, then, with a mutter, swerved and disappeared around the side of the house.

Inside the kitchen, several platters waited on a counter. Margo's face was flushed with exertion. She retrieved the last few strips of bacon from a skillet, dropped them onto a paper towel. "You'd better take that tray up."

Shannon looked irritated. "As if I don't have enough to do to get the buffet in place. Why can't she come down to breakfast like everybody else?" Shannon added a napkin to a tray and condiments, including jam and ketchup.

I nodded in approval at a plate with bacon and sausages, scrambled eggs, a Danish, toast, and coffee. The note I'd left last night had requested that breakfast be delivered to Kay's room at eight A.M.

Shannon's face twisted in resentment. She turned to pick up the juice pitcher.

I used the tongs to add more bacon and eggs. I slipped an extra plate beneath the first.

"Maybe last night upset her." Margo gestured toward the window. "I went out to look this morning. She must have been terrified."

"Too bad the vase didn't hit her."

"Shannon." Margo's voice was sharp.

"I don't know who she is, coming in here and acting like Jack belonged to her." Shannon's hand shook as she poured juice. "And she insisted on staying in his room."

"I suspect she knew him better than anyone here." Margo's voice was dry.

"Jack didn't care about her. I know who he was sneaking around to see." Tears brimmed in Shannon's eyes, spilled down her face. She gulped back a sob as she grabbed the tray and hurried to the door to the back stairs. She opened the door, left it ajar.

Margo's eyes burned. "He isn't worth your tears. He was . . ." Her words were lost in the clatter of Shannon's shoes on the uncarpeted stairs.

I was waiting inside Kay's room when the knock sounded on the hall door. From the bathroom, I heard the splash of the shower. I called through the panel. "Leave the tray on the floor. I'll get it in a minute." I'm quite good at mimicking voices.

I waited a moment, eased open the door. As soon as I heard the door to the service stairs close, I retrieved the tray and closed the door. As I placed the tray on a table near the window, I hummed "Oh What a Beautiful Morning."

The extra plate was perfect. I found a glass at the wet bar

and poured half the juice in the tumbler. As for silverware . . . I shrugged, picked up the spoon. Kay could make do with the knife and fork. I fixed the plates share and share alike, each with bacon, sausage and eggs, half a Danish, and a piece of toast. I replaced the plate cover over Kay's portion.

Would it be remiss to begin without her? I called out, "If you don't mind, I'll start before the eggs are cold."

Kay appeared in the doorway of the bathroom, pulling on a terry-cloth robe. She looked at the table and the settings. Slowly she lifted her hands, covered her eyes, waited a moment, let them fall.

"Delicious." I added a dash of ketchup to my eggs. "Thanks for sharing." I lifted a spoonful of eggs.

Her eyes dark, her face strained, she stalked to the table. She pawed the air, bumping my arm.

The spoon tipped and the eggs fell. Fortunately, they landed on my plate. "Don't be rude." I retrieved the eggs. "I'm here. I'm not going anywhere. Get used to it." In case Wiggins was attuned, I added, "Please."

She uttered a sharp, short expletive, then grimly sat in the opposite chair. "A spoon in the air. A floating glass of juice. I thought a good night's sleep would clear up my mind."

Apparently, floating cutlery and glasses unnerved her. "I'm sorry." I appeared. This morning I chose a floral-swirl print shirt, blossoms in rose red and hydrangea blue, and white cotton trousers. I spared a quick glance in the mirror, smoothed a vagrant red curl. "Eat your breakfast. You need food for strength. We have lots to do today."

She grabbed the Danish, took a bite, poured a cup of coffee. "How did breakfast get here?"

"I put a note in the kitchen, requesting a tray for you."

"A note. Like the note I found in the bathroom. Now I'm writing notes I don't remember writing." She darted a wild look toward the door, clearly dismayed that a note had been left in the kitchen. She shook her head and began to eat, ignoring me.

I finished and poured a cup of coffee into a mug from the wet bar. Mmm, excellent coffee. "I don't believe I've told you about the tools. You see, I thought you made a mistake in preventing an investigation." I described my clever arrangement of the tools in the cabinet by the front door last night and their subsequent disappearance. "Anyone in the house could have found and removed them."

She was thoughtful. "My mind is all screwed up. I didn't want the police. No way I would have put tools out to be found." She brightened. "Of course I wouldn't. That's why they disappeared. My mind is making up for that nutty idea." Suddenly she looked forlorn. "Why do I keep having these thoughts?"

I gazed at her without warmth. She had to be one of the most stubborn women I'd ever encountered. "Have you ever thought about Zen?"

She flung down her napkin. "This has to stop. Okay, mind, listen. I will not be diverted. Hush. Now."

I sighed. "I am not diverting you. I want to find out who pushed Jack ASAP, so I can leave you in my cosmic dust. If you'll hush, I'll let you in on what I discovered while you were relaxing in a hot shower." I ticked off the occupants of the house, one by one. "This morning Evelyn was on the upper terrace, checking out the vase. Ronald Phillips surreptitiously watched her from the balcony. When Ronald returned to their room, he and Laverne had a curious exchange. Diane cut fresh flowers this morning and talked to her dead husband's picture. She's desperately worried about something. In the kitchen, Margo and Shannon talked about Jack. Jimmy practiced hitting irons on the third terrace."

Kay spread marmalade on her toast. She gave me a defiant glare. "Big deal. People are up and around. So?"

My eyes slitted. "Has anybody ever told you that you have a smart mouth?"

Her grin was immediate and delighted. "This is more like it. Let's level with each other. You don't like me. I don't like you. Why don't you take a hike?"

I opened my mouth, grabbed my temper, pressed my lips firmly together. I managed to sound pleasant when I spoke. "Actually, it should be the other way around."

She crunched bacon and quirked an eyebrow.

"You are lucky to be alive this morning, thanks to my timely intervention. I understand—and I'm sure Heaven does as well—that your motive in coming to Adelaide was admirable. You believed Jack's death was murder. The note on your pillow and the toppled vase prove you were correct. However, now that I am here, the wise course is for you to leave. You can be assured I will continue to investigate."

She swallowed the bacon, took a deep breath, and spoke through gritted teeth. "If I have two personalities, I guess I have to communicate with the asinine part of my brain that's imagined you. Get this straight. I'm not going anywhere until I know what happened to Jack."

I was tempted to give her a high five. I'd hoped she would refuse to leave. I needed her presence in order to approach the possible suspects.

I needed . . .

Wait a minute. I felt overwhelmed by remorse. What I needed or, to be more accurate, what I wanted was unimportant. Kay's life was all that mattered. I hadn't been dispatched by the department to find a murderer. I'd been sent to protect Kay, yet my excursions this morning were all about discovering what had happened to Jack Hume.

"Kay, this is foolish." Just because I heard the siren call of the chase was no excuse to put her in further jeopardy. "Heaven is concerned about your safety or I wouldn't be here. I truly will do my best to find out what happened to Jack, but you must leave."

"Get a life." She took another bite of sweet roll.

Kay Clark was a fighter. I suppose she felt that I (or a negative aspect of herself) was challenging her courage. "Kay . . ." I heard the difference in my tone. For the first time, I moved away from my irritation with her. Instead, I wanted to help the weary, grieving woman who faced me with an indomitable light in her eyes.

She looked as immovable as the tank battery for the Millie No. 1.

Her decision meant that if she were to be kept safe, I must discover the identity of the murderer.

Have I ever shared the truth that I am moved by impulse, not logic? I felt dimly that perhaps this was the course of events Wiggins desired. Was his mind serpentine enough to have known that my actions would strengthen Kay's resolve and she and I together would be bound to investigate? It was as if I heard a distant bugle call to charge.

Impulse was all very well, but I must harness my proclivity for quick action and think logically. Kay had come to Adelaide because of Jack's e-mails. That's where she started and that's where I must start. "In Jack's last e-mail, he said a photograph had been slipped under his door. Where do you suppose he put it?"

She looked perplexed. "I don't know." She nodded toward the desk. "All of his papers seemed to be in the ebony box. There was only one photograph and it can't be the one he mentioned."

I was surprised. "There's no photograph in the box."

Her gaze was sharp. "How would you know?"

"I studied the contents last night."

She pushed back her chair and hurried to the desk, returning with the box. She opened it and quickly thumbed through the contents. "That's weird." She shot me a suspicious glance. "You're messing with my mind. Where did you put the picture?"

"Do not succumb to paranoia. Why would I take a photograph?"

"Why not? You write notes . . . I mean I write notes . . . I wouldn't take the picture . . . why would I do that?" She jumped up, rushed to a dresser, opened drawers, fumbled through lingerie and clothing. "I want that picture. Maybe I put it in my things to take home." She rushed to the closet.

I followed, leaned against the doorjamb. "Tell me about the picture." I used my most soothing tone.

She glared. "Don't talk to me as if I'm demented."

I shrugged and returned to the table. I poured another cup of coffee.

Finally, she dropped into the chair opposite me. "I found a photograph in the ebony box of Jack in his cap and gown when he graduated from high school. He was incredibly handsome and young." Her smile was tremulous. "That's the attraction of youth, the innocence, the lack of foreknowledge. He didn't know how many times his heart would be broken, how much life could hurt. Not then."

"Was that the only photograph in the box?"

"The only one. It can't be the photograph he mentioned in his e-mail. That picture upset him. I don't understand why anyone would take the graduation picture." Slowly her face changed. "Maybe someone else wanted to remember him when he was young."

"That could be why."

"I understand." Her voice was soft. "Anyway, I don't know what picture he was talking about in that e-mail. Either he put that picture somewhere and I haven't found it or someone re-moved it before I looked in the box." She glanced toward the door.

Either was a possibility. I reassured her. "Let's not waste time worrying about a photograph. We know he was shocked and upset, both by a photograph and the circumstances he'd found at The Castle. It's up to us to find out what he did and when. I can help."

"It would make me feel better if you disappeared." Kay reached for another piece of toast. "Come on, sometimes you're here and sometimes you aren't. Wouldn't you like to disappear?" Her tone was coaxing.

"Then you'd be upset when I picked up my coffee mug. Thanks, but I'll remain visible for now. In any event, I'm not important." Actually, everyone's important in Heaven, but I hoped my modesty would charm her. "What matters is finding out who killed Jack. When you interview the people Jack saw, keep these points in mind: Evelyn Hume has no difficulty moving quickly and quietly around The Castle. Ronald Phillips picks up Hume family background at the historical society, like Jack being in James's wedding, and feeds the facts to Laverne for the séances. Laverne is either afraid for him or of him. She lied last night when she told you they were together when she heard the vase crash. Diane Hume's hoping for guidance from her dead husband, but she's afraid to tell Laverne what she wants to know. Jimmy Hume hit golf balls like he was killing snakes, then glared through the kitchen window at Shannon Taylor. Shannon got upset talking about you and Jack. She said—" I hesitated.

Kay licked a smear of marmalade from one finger. "Nothing Shannon says about me would come as a surprise. Go ahead."

"She said, 'Jack didn't care about her. I know who he was sneaking around to see.'"

"Poor kid." Kay's voice was kind. "Jack turned her down, so she's convinced he had to be involved with someone else. That's not true. He was focused on problems, not another woman. He was magic"—her lips trembled a little—"and he was honest. In his next-to-last e-mail, he wanted me to come home with him. He wouldn't have urged me to come to Africa with him if he'd plunged into a passionate affair."

I saw confidence in her face as well as sorrow.

I wondered if she was missing something important, something powerful in Jack's last days, because she didn't believe he would betray her. I hoped she was right, but I wasn't certain.

Kay was confident of her analysis. "The question about Shannon is whether she was angry enough by his rejection to wish him dead."

To me, Shannon's anger was a separate question from whether she was right or wrong in connecting Jack to another woman.

We could argue this possibility another time. "We'll keep an open mind."

"Open?" She made a sound similar to a strangled snort. "My mind's as full of holes as Swiss cheese. Maybe"—she brightened—"I can push you out."

"Maybe." My tone was encouraging. She might feel better if she clung to the pathetic hope that I would depart. "For now, we're working together. I suggest you start your research with Evelyn."

She finished the sweet roll, poured another cup of coffee. She'd almost emptied the cup when her gaze slid toward me. "Why Evelyn?"

Kay might insist I didn't exist, but she wasn't going to take a chance on missing out on a good piece of information, whether from me or her subconscious.

Our relationship might be rocky, but, like it or not, Kay and I were going to be a team. I gave her an encouraging smile. "Older sister. Younger brother. The years of separation don't matter. No one knows anyone better than a sibling."

I disappeared.

CHAPTER SIX

Evelyn Hume sat at a stone table on the upper terrace in the shade of a cottonwood. As Kay approached, Evelyn's head turned in the direction of the footsteps. The silvered dark hair drawn back into a tight bun emphasized the gauntness of her face. The family resemblance was evident, the same strong features as her brother Jack, but with no glimmer of charm or humor.

"Good morning, Evelyn." Kay stood next to the table. "If its convenient, I'd like to visit with you about Jack."

"That's why you're here, so I suppose now is as good a time as any." Evelyn inclined her head. "Please join me."

Kay sat on the opposite side of the table and opened her laptop. The breeze stirred Kay's tousled black hair. Despite her informal clothing, a pale yellow cotton top and beige linen slacks, she looked capable and confident. Her dark eyes were bright with intelligence.

Evelyn gestured toward the cul-de-sac. "I wondered if the unfortunate accident last night might cut your visit short."

Kay's eyes narrowed, but her reply was swift. "I plan to stay until I have the material I need for the book. However, I promise to work as quickly as possible. I don't want to take advantage of your hospitality."

"I believe it was Diane who invited you to stay here." Evelyn's tone was dry.

Kay looked wary. "I hope you don't mind."

Evelyn shrugged. "This was Jack's home as well as mine and James's." The milky eyes behind the thick lenses of her glasses reflected no emotion. "How may I help you?"

"What is your earliest memory of Jack?"

The question clearly surprised Evelyn. It was a long moment before she replied. "I was eight when he was born . . ."

Kay's skillful questions pierced a hard shell of time and distance.

Evelyn's words came more quickly, painting a picture of a younger brother colored by both admiration and jealousy: " . . . reckless . . . fearless . . . quick to be kind . . . stubbornly honest . . . much too attractive to women . . . ruthless when he made up his mind . . . selfish . . . he thought of himself before others. Jack left it to me to take care of our father." Her grievance was clear. "Then, when he came home for Dad's funeral, Jack was disruptive." Her glance at Kay was cold. "It was obvious there was something between him and Shannon Taylor. That made Jimmy angry. Jimmy had always thought very highly of his uncle. But not now." Evelyn sighed. "Jack upset Diane and the Phillipses as well. I'm afraid you won't get positive reports about his last visit."

"Jack wanted the book to tell the truth, whatever I found. I need to create a framework for Jack's final days, talk to everyone he saw. The conversations, whether ordinary or remarkable, will touch readers because he had no idea that his time was so short." Pain flickered in Kay's eyes. "Of course, the focus of the book will be his years in Kenya. However, his ironic death in a fall down the steps of his childhood home has to be chronicled. This will be my only opportunity to interview those who spent time with him during his final days."

"I see." Evelyn sipped her coffee. "I don't know how helpful I can be. I wasn't keeping a record of his activities. He had various conversations with those living at The Castle." There was a satisfied look on her face. "His hostility to Laverne and Ronald Phillips reduced Diane to tears one evening. Jimmy, sweet boy that he is, came to his mother's defense. I thought for a moment Jimmy and Jack might come to blows. Of course, Jimmy was furious about more than that discussion. I saw the Phillipses scurrying back to the house one morning and they both looked out of sorts. Jack looked furious as he came inside behind them."

I bent near Kay and whispered in her ear.

After an instant's start, she asked smoothly, "As Jack's sister, I'm sure you had insight into his moods. Was there a change between the day he arrived and the day of his death?"

There was a look of disdain on Evelyn's aristocratic face. "In some ways, there was no change. As always, there were women. I have no doubt Jack at one time knew Margo better than he should. If a man and woman—" She broke off. A tiny flush touched her cheeks. "I was sensitive to his behavior. Since Margo is in our employ, I expected him to refrain from inappropriate behavior. I was chagrined to realize he was attracted to Shannon and that was even worse. A young girl! I spoke to him sharply. He insisted the interest was on her part, not his. But he was in and out of his room at odd hours in the night. I almost spoke to him again, then I decided time would solve any difficulties. That last day, I was again troubled. He told me he was delaying his departure, but he wouldn't tell me why." For an instant, her lips tightened. "Despite what Jack said, Margo's daughter certainly spent a great deal of time with him. Jack always treated women as if their conquest was a sport."

I saw the flare of Kay's eyes. Quickly, I reached out and gave her arm a sharp pinch. No matter how she felt about Jack, this wasn't the moment to challenge his sister.

Kay's arm jerked.

Evelyn didn't react. Obviously her sight was not only blurred but was also myopic.

Kay glanced at her arm, gave a tiny shake of her head. She gazed at her hands. Both rested lightly on the keyboard of her laptop. I feared she was wasting time thinking about her occupied hands and the momentary discomfort of her arm, refusing to accept that she had not, in an aberrant moment, pinched herself.

I leaned down, hissed in her ear. "She said in one way there was no change. In what way was there a change?"

Woodenly, Kay asked, "In what way was there a change in Jack's demeanor?"

"Saturday. The day he died." Evelyn looked disdainful. "Make no mistake, I don't believe in presentiments, despite the nonsense Laverne spouts. Jack certainly didn't have otherworldly imaginings that he was doomed. Far from it. He looked tough and determined and deeply angry. Jack was terribly upset. I doubt anyone else was aware. But you are quite right. He was my brother and I knew. I saw a hardness in his eyes that I'd only seen twice before. Once when Virginia and Sallie died. Once when he told Dad he was leaving Adelaide. I went to his room and knocked. When he came to the door, I asked him what was wrong. He gave me an odd look and shook his head. 'Nothing you can help, Evie. But thanks.' He closed the door. That was the last personal conversation we had."

I whispered again in Kay's ear.

This time she took my instruction in stride. Without hesitation, she asked, "Did he renew old acquaintances in Adelaide?"

Evelyn shrugged. "I have no idea who he saw when he was around town. Possibly you might ask Shannon." Her smile was sardonic.

Kay nodded. "I'll talk to Shannon." She glanced down at her notes, then, her voice encouraging, she said, "I suppose you and Jack had a great deal of catching up to do."

I nodded my unseen approval at Kay's question.

Evelyn's milky eyes narrowed. "Jack left his family behind. The burden of caring for my father was left to me. Jack spent his life running away from his failures, from the death of his first wife, from the responsibility for Hume Oil, from his country. He was a great disappointment to our father."

"He spoke with affection for his father in an e-mail to me."

I thought Kay was generous in her interpretation of Jack's comment about his father's funeral.

Slowly, Evelyn's face softened. "I thank you for sharing that with me. In some respects"—her tone was grudging—"I believe Jack regretted his dismissal of his past. We had a very genial conversation one morning. He evinced great interest in some of the family heirlooms." For the first time, she sounded enthusiastic. "We spent more than an hour walking the hallways, talking about some of the art our mother had collected. She was a woman of great refinement and taste. We have a Holbein, several Reynoldses, a Chase, a Metcalf, and two Rockwell paintings." She made a spreading gesture with her hand. "And many others. Mother also collected Cherokee artworks. Jack was very attentive."

Kay smiled. "I'm glad you have that happy memory."

Evelyn took a quick breath. "Being Jack, he had to ruin the moment. He blamed me"—there was a quiver of fury in her voice—"for Laverne and Ronald Phillips. As I told him"—the words were harsh—"I do not control my brother's widow. This is her home as well as mine. If she chooses to invite charlatans to share it with her, it isn't my place to object." Her thin lips pressed together, then, unexpectedly, flared in a grim smile. "Besides, fools deserve to reap what they sow."

Stone steps led down to a cavernous basement. Kay's footsteps grated on the stairway.

Shannon Taylor came around a pillar, clutching an armload of sheets. Golden brown hair framed an appealing round face with bright blue eyes, a snub nose, and a trace of dimples in smooth cheeks flushed from heat. She looked surprised and not pleased. She stared at Kay with no hint of friendliness.

Kay's face was kind. "I hoped you might have a moment to visit with me."

"I don't know if that's in my job description." Her tone bordered on rudeness. "I'm the laundress today."

Kay walked nearer. "Let me help. Those look clean. I'll fold."

Shannon shrugged. "They're hot."

Kay strode around the pillar and moved to a dryer with an open door. She carried another mound of hot sheets to a folding table. "I didn't know The Castle had such a huge basement."

"There's a lot that the family and guests never see. Or probably even know about. Mom is in charge. She arranges for the cleaning service that comes twice a week and a landscaping company that does the grounds."

"Everything is certainly well kept. Your mother has done an excellent job." Kay folded quickly, efficiently. "Evelyn suggested I visit with you. You know about the book I'm writing."

"Why talk to me?" Shannon's voice was ragged. "What's the point?"

Kay's voice was pleasant. "I hope you can tell me something about Jack's last days, the people he saw, what he might have said about them."

Shannon whirled toward a heavy-duty washing machine, blindly picked up clothes from a basket, dropped them into the machine, added soap. "When he first came, he was so much fun. Then Mother told him to keep away from me. Like I was some kind of stupid kid. He was nice after that, but he avoided being alone with me. I know he liked me. He really did." Tears streaked her smooth cheeks.

Kay started a second stack of clean towels. "I'm sorry." Her voice was gentle.

Shannon's face creased in hot, unreasoning anger. "Don't patronize me. I know all about you. You were one of his old flames." She emphasized the adjective, made it ugly. "Maybe you think he still cared about you. I can tell you he didn't. I followed him Friday night. He sneaked out of the house." She looked miserable and defiant. "I was watching the windows of his room, and when the lights went out, I waited by the side of the house. I thought he was coming out for his car. But he looked around and I could tell he didn't want anyone to see him. Of course, he was sneaking. She's a married woman. I guess that didn't matter to him. He met her in the gazebo by the stream. I saw his face in the moonlight. He was angry. She paced up and down, up and down. I tried to get close enough to hear, but Diane's old cocker spaniel came running up and yipping. They heard the noise and she came down the steps and ran toward the path to her house. I saw her in one of the garden lights. Then Saturday night at dinner, he called her Gwen as if the name meant nothing to him. She acted like she hardly knew him. But people don't quarrel like that unless they are lovers." She turned and ran sobbing toward the stairs.

I swirled into being. I chose a lime green blouse with a dramatic flared collar and cropped twill slacks. Multistrapped leather sandals matched the blouse. Summer clothing is always cheerful, especially when fresh and new. No ensemble could be fresher or newer than mine. I am not claiming superiority in appearance. That would be too much *of* the earth. I smoothed a sleeve, marveling in the silky feel of the cotton.

Kay didn't react to my physical presence. She stood in the middle of the gazebo, hands on her hips. "I'm going to talk to Jimmy next."

Sycamores shaded the gazebo, but offered little respite from the heat. However, I like hot weather, and I adore the rasp of cicadas. "Gwen Dunham is more important."

"Who's in charge?" Kay demanded.

I smiled. "Heaven." I spoke the simple truth.

Kay did not smile.

I observed her with a kindly expression. "Even your fine bone structure lacks charm when your features are set in what can only be described as mulish obstinacy."

She ignored me and paced the perimeter of the gazebo, muttering to herself, "Idiotic imagination. Why do I keep seeing her?"

"Because I'm here." I pirouetted, humming "I'm Looking Over a Four-Leaf Clover."

She faced me, her gaze resistant. "You insisted we come out here. What is this supposed to tell me?"

Her refusal to acknowledge me made conversation difficult. Truth is always the best policy. Sometimes truth is even believed. "I want to discuss our next step, and I'm tired of being invisible.

As I've told Wiggins, I'm not at my best when I'm invisible."

"Certainly it's important you be at your—" She broke off, stared. "Wiggins?"

"My supervisor. Let's leave it at that."

"Oh, no. Come on, Bailey Ruth, level with me."

Since Kay never believed what I said, I saw no harm in explaining the Department of Good Intentions, the old-fashioned train station, and the Rescue Express.

She listened with flattering attention.

" . . . so you see, you've been specially chosen for protection."

"Yeah. I'm special. I'm so special my mind is splintering." Her tone was morose. She looked warily about. "Is Wiggins lurking around, too?"

I sincerely hoped not. "Not usually. He permits his agents great independence. Normally I wouldn't dream of appearing." Are you listening, Wiggins? "But it's such a lovely morning." Besides, I might know I was wearing a stylish outfit, but I liked to see it as well. I dropped my gaze to my sandals. The shade of green was glorious, almost translucent, like sunlight spearing through green glass.

I gave Kay a reassuring smile. "You'd like Wiggins."

"I'm sure I would. The more the merrier."

"Sarcasm isn't becoming."

She cuffed the side of her head. "Now I'm scolding me. All right, redheaded brain wave. What's your plan?"

"You need to talk to Gwen Dunham."

"Oh." Her huff was derisive. "Dumb idea, brain wave. You're caught up in Shannon's romantic nonsense. Even Jack couldn't sweep a woman into a passionate love affair in the space of three weeks and reach the point of dramatic scenes. Besides, scenes weren't his style. He was too cool for that." There were memories in her eyes, not all of them good.

"Shannon saw them quarreling."

Kay shrugged. "Shannon probably saw what she wanted to see. I'll talk to Gwen Dunham, but she's not high on my list. As far as I've been able to figure out, she scarcely knew Jack. Actually"—she looked grim—"Shannon ranks close to the top. Nobody loves—or hates—like a twentysomething. How hurt was she by Jack's turndown? And how angry? I want to talk to her mother, see what I can find out. After that, I'll—"

Footsteps sounded on the gazebo steps.

Both Kay and I swung to look.

I'd been engrossed in our conversation. Wiggins would not see that fact as an excuse. He would point out that my stubborn habit of appearing had now come home to roost.

Diane Hume reached the top step. Sprigs of blond hair poked from beneath a huge straw hat. The cuffs of her long-sleeved smock were tucked into gardening gloves. She carried a straw basket brimming with cut flowers. "Kay"—Diane's voice was high and breathless—"that police chief is here. He's talking to Evelyn. He wants to see you. Oh." She gave me a shy smile. "Hello."

Kay looked slowly from me, back to Diane. "You see her?" The words were unsteady.

Diane looked surprised. "Did I come at a bad time? I didn't mean to interrupt. I didn't know you were having a private meeting. What do you want me to tell that policeman?"

I felt I had no choice. It was time to seize the moment. Was I being led? Possibly I'd underestimated Wiggins's openness to innovation. Perhaps he was coming around to my view. Sometimes an emissary had to be onstage. In two quick strides, I reached Diane. I offered my hand. Oh. I took an instant to redo the polish. Pink is much more summery than red. "Hi, I'm Francie de Sales, and I just arrived."

I hoped the patron saint of writers approved of my nom de plume.

Kay made an inarticulate noise somewhere between a gasp and a moan. "Francie . . ."

I gave her a sharp nod. I had no intention of being identified publicly as Bailey Ruth Raeburn. There's a memorial column for me and Bobby Mac in the cemetery by St. Mildred's with *Serendipity* chiseled on the hull of the dearest carving of a cabin cruiser and the inscription: *Forever Fishing*. I doubted anyone from The Castle hung out at the cemetery, but a ghost can't be too careful. I hoped Wiggins admired my quick thinking.

Kay stared with huge and rounded eyes.

What an unfortunate moment for her to grapple with the reality of me.

Diane scrambled to pull off a glove. She looked at me with the kindly friendliness of a puppy. "I'm Diane Hume."

I smiled as we shook hands. "Kay's told me about you and how welcoming you are. She is so appreciative. You'll have to forgive her. Such a shock. A huge tarantula jumped toward her just a moment ago. She's always had a thing about tarantulas."

Diane darted frightened looks around the gazebo.

"An Oklahoma Brown Tarantula. *Aphonopelma hentzi.* Don't be concerned. A very docile spider. Huge. With those dear furry legs. I dropped him over the edge of the gazebo. I have a great admiration for spiders. Don't you?"

Diane gazed at me in awe. "Not really." Clearly she wanted to be agreeable, but there were limits.

Kay stared at me, too. Awe did not describe her expression. Horror perhaps came nearest.

"Anyway, it's lovely to be here." I leaned forward, spoke confidentially. "I'm Kay's assistant. She asked me to join her. I do fact-checking, that sort of thing." I had no idea if writers had assistants, but if I didn't know, I doubted Diane knew. "Kay's main effort will be in Africa, of course. She's eager to be on her way there, so she's asked me to help round up the information in Adelaide. I can be a help." I waved my hand. "Running around, talking to people." I turned to Kay. "Such a shock. That tarantula. After you speak with the police chief, perhaps you might want to go to your room and rest. I can take care of the interview with Gwen Dunham."

"I'm fine." But she made no move to go.

Diane looked earnest. "Francie, would you like to stay with us? It might be more convenient for you and Kay."

I beamed. "That would be wonderful." I wished Kay would stop looking like she was marooned on a ledge twenty stories above the street. "Thank you."

Diane turned to Kay. "I suppose you thought it was too late to invite Francie to stay last night. Laverne was sure she saw you speaking to someone in the garden."

Kay's tone was dazed. "Last night. Yes. It was late."

Diane's face squeezed into a commiserating frown. "I can't believe how that vase fell. Wasn't it awful that you and Francie were standing in the one place where it would land. Why, Laverne said it was almost as if it were meant." Diane looked at me. "You'll meet Laverne. She's the most wonderful woman. She has insights from beyond this world."

Kay gave a ragged laugh. "I don't think Laverne has a monopoly on otherworldly insights."

"We're concerned with the here and now." My voice was sharp. "Right here and right now."

"Oh, yes, ma'am, Bai—"

"Diane." I spoke with the vigor of a tour guide and in a sense possibly that was my role. "Kay tells me you have an exquisite sense of atmosphere. You are the perfect person to give us a perspective of your brother-in-law's last few days on earth. You and I can visit while Kay goes up to the house to talk to the police."

Kay shot me a strained glance and walked down the steps in a daze.

I hoped she didn't appear stiff and tense when she met with Chief Cobb.

When I turned back to Diane, she was edging toward the steps. "I'm right in the middle of weeding. There are red spiders in my marigolds."

I moved right alongside her. "Spider mites. That can be such a problem. Lady bugs are the answer. Put out some sugar water for them. I will only take a minute of your time."

She stopped at the bottom of the steps, pleated the garden gloves. "I don't know how to say this, but I don't want to talk about Jack. I mean, Kay is very nice. I didn't expect her to be so nice and I know this book matters to her, but I'll tell you the truth."

I remembered Wiggins's appraisal of Diane. *She has a sweet nature.* There was a childlike openness about her.

"I don't think Jack was a very nice man. He wanted me to send Laverne and Ronald away." Her voice trembled. "Laverne is my rock. Why, she's told me all about James and how he is and that he loves me but he wants me not to hurry to come. He says there's no time in heaven—"

I was glad to know Laverne had one point right.

"—so he wants me to be here to help Laverne and Ronald because they can see through to what's real and true and I should contribute what I can to their foundation. Jack was just downright ugly. He said he was going to find out where the money went and put them in jail, but I talked to Paul, and what I have is mine and I can do anything with it that I want and Jimmy's share belongs to him, so there wasn't anything Jack could do. But he made me so upset and Laverne and Ronald said they'd have to leave if he kept accusing them of bad things. I couldn't bear it if Laverne went away." Tears spilled down her face. "I'd rather die." She whirled away and ran blindly toward the house.

I looked after her. Would she rather die? Or would she rather kill?

I waited until Diane was out of sight to disappear.

On the balcony, Chief Cobb and Evelyn watched in silence as Kay climbed the steps.

Kay managed a smile. "Good morning." There was the faintest hint of inquiry in her voice.

Chief Cobb's heavy face looked determined. "I appreciate your joining us, Mrs. Clark."

Kay nodded, but said nothing.

Cobb's brown eyes glinted with irritation and, possibly, a hint of respect. "As I explained to Miss Hume, a study of photographs by our expert suggests that a tool was used to loosen the vase. He believes it would have required a crowbar to leverage the vase from the pedestal."

"That is shocking information." Evelyn's tone was grim.

Kay appeared unruffled. "Really." Her voice lifted in a tone of amazement. "Why, who would have thought such a thing could happen? It sounds like vandalism."

I was afraid she was overdoing her ingenuous response a trifle.

Evelyn bent her head, apparently listening intently. Her expression was alert.

Cobb cleared his throat. "Mrs. Clark, you were in the garden when the vase fell. Apparently, you narrowly escaped being crushed. Do you think it is likely the vase's fall at that precise moment was a coincidence?"

Kay gave a cool smile and turned her hands palms up. "I wouldn't know what else to think."

"Really." He drew out the word in a sardonic mimicry. "Mrs. Clark, why were you in the garden?"

She hesitated for an instant, then said smoothly. "I was meeting with my assistant, Francie de Sales. She'd just arrived in town." Kay glanced at Evelyn. "Diane has very nicely invited Francie to stay at The Castle."

"Oh?" Evelyn turned her milky gaze toward Kay.

Kay was suddenly voluble. "Francie and I met in the gazebo this morning. Diane stopped to visit and she saw at once that Francie and I could be in closer contact if Francie stayed here. I truly appreciate her generosity and yours." She smiled at Chief Cobb. "Francie will be in and out."

Uh-oh. I knew Chief Cobb well enough to be certain he would ask to talk to Francie. Kay had no way of knowing that the chief and I had met before, though he hadn't known me as Francie de Sales. I thought fondly of my previous appearances as Officer M. Loy and family friend Jerrie Emiliani.

"Is Miss de Sales available? I'd like to speak with her."

Kay looked uncertain. As well she might. "I'm not sure when she'll be back. She went to get her luggage."

On the spur of the moment, that wasn't a bad ploy.

Cobb nodded. "Ask her to call me, please."

Whew.

"I will."

"Now, about your conference with her in the garden last night: Who knew about that meeting?"

"No one." She sounded utterly confident. And believable.

Wiggins knew, of course. Oh well, she was speaking the truth as she understood it.

Cobb folded his arms. "I understand you are in Adelaide to write a book about Jack Hume. Has it occurred to you, Mrs. Clark, that someone might not want you to write that book?"

Her gaze was unfaltering, her voice convincing. "Chief Cobb, I'm quite sure no one pushed a vase from that pedestal because of the book."

Again, she spoke the truth. A murderer pushed the vase to hide a crime.

"And"—she spoke brightly—"speaking of the book, it's time I continued my research." She turned and started down the steps.

Chief Cobb stared after her, eyes narrowed, face hard.

"I suppose this concludes your questions." Evelyn spoke pleasantly, but firmly. "I consider the matter closed now. We won't make a complaint. Further investigation isn't necessary. The destruction of the vase may have been vandalism. But"—her tone was silky—"experts are often wrong. Thank you for your good efforts, Captain." Evelyn, too, turned away and moved down the steps.

CHAPTER SEVEN

Kay slid behind the wheel of a canary yellow Corvette convertible with the top down; her eyes flicked uneasily here and there.

I settled comfortably in the soft leather seat. "Are you looking for me?" It's nice to be missed.

She stiffened. "You."

"Me."

She glared at the passenger seat. "I don't know which is worse, seeing you or not seeing you."

The chief's car pulled around Kay's. He gave her a half-angry, half-worried glare. I warned, "Let's wait until the chief's car is out of sight."

Kay was surly. "I'm surprised you didn't appear on the scene and tell him everything."

I didn't intend to share with Kay my determination to avoid

the chief. He had seen enough of me on previous visits to suggest an otherworldly link. Wiggins had been upset. Wiggins would be proud of me if I avoided the chief.

"Don't sound bitter, Kay. I'm going along with your plan."

"I can't stand hearing a voice out of nowhere." Her tone was hot. "If you're here, be here."

Always happy to oblige, I swirled into being. In my new role as Kay's assistant, I sought to appear more businesslike, a crisp white blouse with a flared collar, cream linen trousers, white leather flats. I pulled down the visor and glanced into the mirror. Ah, just the right amount of green eye shadow. Not, of course, that I am prideful about having green eyes. Green is as green does, but green does better with a little accent.

Kay reached out, tapped my sleeve with her forefinger. "Okay. I'm convinced. Diane saw you. But you come and go." She spoke in a whisper. "I have my own personal ghost. Ghosts . . ." She had a faraway look. Abruptly, she sat up straight and turned to me. "All right. Level with me. Who killed Jack?"

It was the last question I'd expected. "How should I know?"

She was impatient. "Don't play games. You hang around. You see things. You know things. Who pushed him?"

"I wish I knew. For one thing, I wasn't here yet. Besides—"

"Stop right there. You claim you're here from Heaven, right?"

I nodded.

"They know everything in Heaven. All I need is the name. Then you can pop back there and I'll take care of everything." She waved a hand as if Heaven were somewhere near.

I couldn't fault her assumption, but she didn't understand the rules. I had a quick memory of Precept Seven: *Information about Heaven is not yours to impart. Simply smile and say, "Time will tell."* Surely this was an exception. "Kay, only God knows. And, as I understand it (I will admit my comprehension was perhaps not at the highest level), when people on earth aren't following God's will, their thoughts are hidden. All that is known is their outward attitudes and the results of their actions."

"I get it. Whoever pushed Jack is keeping quiet and the only thing I can do is nose around." She frowned. "So what good are you?"

"I'm here to keep you safe." I gave her a reassuring smile.

"Why?"

I looked at her, my eyes widening. "I have no idea." Why, indeed?

"There are people in trouble all over the place. Why do I have a special angel—"

I was firm. "Not an angel. Ghost. *G-H-O-S-T*."

"Angel, ghost, agent, emissary, whatever. Why me?"

"Maybe because you're so difficult." I'm afraid I sounded testy. "Heavens, I don't know. Maybe years from now, somewhere down the road, there's something important you're going to do or say. Maybe there's a great big celestial lottery and your number came up." I rather liked that idea. God clearly was a gambler. He'd certainly taken a flier on creating Earth.

"If it weren't for the honor, I'd be just as happy if you returned to . . ."—she took a deep breath and forced out—"Heaven."

"When my task is done." I'd never analyzed how or why the recipients of aid were selected by Wiggins. Did files simply appear in Wiggins's office? The ways of Heaven are, of course, Heavenly. I urged Kay, "Remember 'The Charge of the Light Brigade.' " My years as an English teacher sometimes prompted a literary reference.

Kay looked at me blankly.

" 'Theirs not to reason why, theirs to do and die.' "

"You are so last century."

Kay had a talent for offending me. I snapped, "You may not be this century for very long if I fail. Now let's go."

"Go where?"

I was beginning to feel like an old Abbott and Costello routine, but I wouldn't share the thought with Kay. "Wherever you were going." I waved my hand.

She ran her fingers through her dark hair in a gesture of exasperation. Her unevenly cut hair appeared even more casual and youthful.

I brushed back a curl. "I really like your haircut. Would you mind if I tried that style?"

"Bailey—"

"Francie."

She tried for a smile, but it took great effort. "Let's try not to talk for a while. I feel like I'm in the middle of an old Abbott and Costello movie and I should say, 'What style?'"

I felt much more warmly toward her. "I won't say a word." At least until I had something cogent to offer. "Where are we going?" Surely a simple question was permitted.

"Paul Fisher's office. Jack said ugly things were bubbling beneath the surface at The Castle. Paul might know." She pushed the brake and reached out to punch a button. The motor purred to life.

"Oh. That's clever. No key."

She opened her mouth, closed it.

"I know. So last century."

"You said it, not me." There was a burble of laughter in her voice.

She started to shift, then looked in the rearview mirror.

A bright red Lexus curved into the drive and jolted to a stop near the front steps. A strikingly attractive blonde climbed out.

In her mid-to-late thirties, sleek Jean Harlow–bright hair (I liked the last century) gleamed in the sunlight. She was one of those perfectly put together women who always drew every eye, especially those of men. She ignored the front steps and walked swiftly around the corner of the house.

Kay jerked a thumb in that direction. "Hey, you can make up for your generally irritating ways. Do your disappearing act. Follow her. That's Alison Gregory. She was here last night and Jack had one of her cards. She's made a fortune selling this, that, and the other to Evelyn. Find out what's going on."

The enormous cottonwood still shaded the stone table on the terrace. A vagrant breeze rustled the shimmering leaves. From her chair, Evelyn Hume looked toward the sound of Alison Gregory's shoes on the terrace.

Alison was midway to the table when she stopped to look up at the empty pedestal. Her gaze traveled down to the three-sided enclave of evergreens. From her vantage point, the great mass of debris was hidden by the evergreens, but clumps of dirt and pieces of vase were visible. She whirled and stalked toward Evelyn. "I came the minute I got your message. That vase can't have fallen. I'm telling you"—she spaced the words for emphasis—"the vase absolutely could not have fallen. The balance was perfect. I placed a slight glaze around the base to prevent erosion, but the stability of the vase was maintained by its weight and design. There is no way that vase could have fallen." She stood beside the table, face flushed, hands outflung.

Evelyn was crisp. "No one is blaming you. I want your expert judgment. Please go up on the balcony and examine the pedestal."

"I don't need to go up on the balcony. The only way that vase could come down is by someone using a tool." She mimed gripping, jamming, and pushing down. "It's criminal. That vase was Chinese porcelain. What barbarian did this?"

"Sit down, Alison." Evelyn's hand wave was peremptory. "The police claim a vandal was at work. Unfortunately, Kay Clark was in the garden, apparently standing in the cul-de-sac, and she barely managed to avoid being crushed. She was there very late at night, conferring with her assistant, who had just arrived in Adelaide." There was a singular lack of conviction in Evelyn's voice.

Alison's face reflected a cascade of responses: surprise, wariness, suspicion. "It's odd the vase came down when someone was standing in the cul-de-sac." There was the faintest hint of a question in her voice.

Evelyn spaced the words for emphasis. "That's why it's important to be clear that the vase's fall was an accident. I'm sure when you oversaw the installation of the vases, you directed that every precaution be taken to assure their stability. Now, if you find evidence of, say, erosion, despite the application of a sealant, we can inform the authorities and insist that the matter be dropped."

Alison's head turned to look up at the pedestal. Her white-gold hair glistened. I judged she likely spent quite a bit of money on her hairdresser.

"I'm confident you can find an excellent replacement." Evelyn's voice was smooth. "Perhaps an antique porcelain. We might replace all of the vases. That would be an interesting project."

And such a lucrative one.

Evelyn added casually, "I've always depended upon your good taste. You've done an excellent job of reframing some of the finest paintings. I think several others might be enhanced by a change. Perhaps we might consider some Baroque frames in the upper gallery."

I could almost see dollar signs dancing in Alison's blue eyes. She spoke quickly. "I'm always happy to help improve the setting for pieces in your collection. I'll take a look at the vase. I should have examined everything before I spoke. I was remembering how carefully the vase was installed. But time does pass and weather can affect stone." Alison walked swiftly toward the steps to the balcony.

A hint of movement behind the cottonwood caught my eye.

In the shadow of the huge trunk, Ronald Phillips watched Alison climb the steps. His mouth twisted in a sardonic smile. He soundlessly clapped as if in admiration of a performance, then turned and stepped lightly, making no sound, to a line of evergreens. He was natty in a green polo and white linen slacks.

I followed him to the front of the house. He hummed as he walked up the front steps. I thought I recognized the tune. Oh. Of course. "Happy Days Are Here Again." How last century.

Inside, he bounded up the stairs and walked swiftly to his and Laverne's room. His thin lips curved in a satisfied smile.

I flowed into the combination bed and sitting room. Laverne huddled in one corner of a lime-colored sofa with a faintly pebbled fabric. She clutched a bright orange cushion and stared unseeingly toward chrome bookcases filled with books too evenly aligned, books meant for decoration, not enjoyment. As the door clicked, she drew in her breath and turned to look.

Ronald flung himself into a chair opposite the sofa and gave a bark of laughter.

She stiffened, her eyes wide with apprehension.

He gave her a contemptuous glance. "Pull yourself together."

She lifted long, thin fingers to clutch a gold chain. "I talked to Diane a little while ago."

His good humor fled. "What have you done?"

"I told her we needed to go home to Dallas, that Jenny was sick—"

He was up and out of the chair, gripping her arm and pulling her to her feet. They stood close enough for a lovers' embrace, but there was no love, only fear and anger.

I sensed this was a long-standing pattern. There was no physical abuse, but emotional control.

"Tell Diane"—the softness of his voice was chilling—"the Great Spirit has assured you that Jenny is going to be fine and your duty is to remain here, that you sense turmoil and danger which can only be warded off by summoning the Great Spirit. You have been bombarded by fragments of thought, but one thing is clear. The Great Spirit must be invoked tonight for protection. Otherwise, Death"—he smiled with relish—"will walk these halls again."

"I get such dreadful headaches." Her voice was faint. "I can't do the séances anymore."

"You will perform tonight. If you do a good job, we'll go and visit Jenny." The tightness of his grip eased. He patted her shoulder. "I've got a few more things to check out. Isn't this Diane's afternoon with James?"

Laverne looked at him with pleading eyes.

"Don't make me mad."

Her hands clenched. She nodded.

"When does she go?"

"At four."

He looked pleased. "Plan on meeting her. You can tell her James has been talking to you. I'll have everything worked out by then. The Great Spirit's going to put on a good show tonight."

His smile was wolfish as he turned toward the door.

Kay had turned off the car motor. Her fingers drummed on the steering wheel.

I dropped into the passenger seat. "I haven't been gone that long. Have you ever heard about the stressful effects of a type A personality?"

Her eyes narrowed as she punched the button. "When I want mental-health advice, I'll ask my shrink. What took you so long?"

"Ronald Phillips eavesdropped on Evelyn and Alison." I described the scene in Laverne and Ronald's bedroom.

She gave a low whistle of surprise. "Laverne moves majestically around The Castle and he follows like a well-bred lapdog."

"Fake." I was crisp. "He's the puppeteer."

"What do you think he's up to?" Her tone was considering.

"He said, 'The Great Spirit's going to put on a good show tonight.'" I had a feeling of foreboding.

Kay gave a hoot of laughter. "They'll make Diane pay double. Sounds like fun."

"Kay!" My tone rebuked her.

She shot a wickedly amused glance toward the passenger seat. "I forgot, you don't take kindly to the afterworld. Isn't that a bit of a double standard, lady?"

"Absolutely not." My reply was hot. "I am an official emissary of the Department of Good Intentions, sent to achieve goodness. Psychics and fortune-tellers purvey nonsense to the credulous for their own profit."

"Go, girl. I like a woman who will slug it out. As for psychics, et al, I agree with you, even if you sound like you have vinegar in your mouth."

Had I sounded acidulous? Possibly. But that wasn't the point. "We should discourage Diane from engaging in the occult."

"Lots of luck on that one." Kay's expression was abruptly compassionate. "Threatening to cut her lifeline to James turns her into a shrew."

I remembered the gazebo and Diane's passionate defense of Laverne.

Kay glanced behind her, backed up, then wheeled the car toward the street. "I've got places to go and people to see." The Corvette burned out of the drive. "But"—and her tone was almost admiring—"your coming and going may turn out to be helpful. What did Alison want?"

My hair streamed behind me. I liked speed. I recalled the exhilarating plunge down one of Adelaide's biggest hills when I was here for a spot of Christmas intrigue. As then, I couldn't resist a whooping, "Yee-hah!" If you've never given a Rebel yell, you don't know how to have fun.

Kay gasped and the Corvette swerved. "What's up with you?" Her voice was both shaky and exasperated.

"Riding shotgun, sweetie, and having a blast. As for Alison, it's a shame I didn't have a camcorder. The Adelaide police carry them as part of their equipment."

Just for fun I appeared in full police regalia, black-billed blue cap, long-sleeved French blue blouse, French blue trousers with a darker blue stripe, a nameplate for Officer M. Loy—my tribute to Mryna Loy—holster, gun, belt with flashlight, and a camcorder.

After one swift glance, Kay stared straight ahead. "Has anyone ever told you showing off is poor form?" The Corvette slowed to the speed limit.

I didn't think it was showing off to swirl into a more summery outfit. Besides, Adelaide is a small town and a police officer riding in the passenger seat of a yellow Corvette would definitely be noticed. This time I chose a hand-painted silk georgette blouse and pale pink slacks.

Kay glanced again. "Nice blouse."

"Thank you."

"Why did you wish you had a camcorder?"

We were almost downtown. "I wish I had a recording of Evelyn and Alison's conversation." I described Evelyn's not terribly subtle offer of profit for a verdict of erosion at the base of the vase and concluded, "As soon as Evelyn dangled the bait of replacing the vases, Alison did the Texas two-step quicker than a firefly flickers. Tell me about Alison."

Kay turned into a parking lot behind a small redbrick building with black shutters. "Clever, smart, on the make. Jack called Laverne and Ronald Diane's leeches. I'd describe Alison as Evelyn's leech, albeit a suave, sophisticated, savvy leech." She eased the Corvette beneath the shade of a sycamore.

"It doesn't surprise you that Alison would be willing to adjust her opinion to suit Evelyn?"

Kay was sardonic. "Does the sun rise in the east? The surprise is Evelyn. Either she's protecting herself or someone else."

"Who would she protect?"

Kay looked thoughtful. "Possibly Jimmy. She's fond of her nephew. I'd say no one else in the house matters to her at all. Maybe it's all much simpler. Maybe she's trying to deflect scandal from the family."

"The Humes"—my voice was dry—"have always had a talent for scandal."

"Not Evelyn." Kay slipped out of the car.

I disappeared.

Her dark brows drew down in a tight frown. "Will you either be here or not?"

"The two of us together would intimidate any man. Use your charm with Paul Fisher. I'm sure you have some."

She shot a hostile look where I had been. "As Charlie Chan said, 'Assistants should be seen, not heard.'" She strode toward the entrance.

I called after her, "So last century." As she opened the door, I added sweetly, "Charlie also said, 'Charming company turn lowly sandwich into rich banquet.'"

She looked back. "Touché."

My intent was to pop directly to Paul Fisher's office. I wanted to see him when he considered himself safe from observation. Private faces revealed character. Are the brows drawn in a frown? Is there sadness in the eyes? Does the expression show meanness or generosity?

I felt no need to hurry. Kay must first speak with the receptionist. I paused to enjoy once again the rasp of cicadas. When I was growing up in Oklahoma, we called them locusts. A biology teacher explained they were not locusts, but insects of another order. Whenever I heard cicadas, I felt even younger than my chosen age of twenty-seven. I was ten again and running barefoot through freshly cut grass with its distinctive scent, sunlight hot on my skin, living gloriously and heedlessly in what seemed to be the never-ending sun of summer.

"'Mind, like parachute, only function when open.'" Wiggins's voice was gruff. I might even describe his tone as anguished. "Bailey Ruth, when will you stop and think?"

Without taking time to reflect, I blurted, "Too much thinking is deleterious to mental health."

His riposte bristled. "That's not Charlie Chan."

"Of course not." Had I made that claim? "That's Bailey Ruth Raeburn." Possibly I had a future in some great salon of intellectual conversationalists.

"Umph. Not bad. But you're distracting me from my point. If you hadn't appeared in the gazebo, you wouldn't have been seen by Diane Hume and now the fat's in the fire."

"It's much too hot to picture a lump of fat sizzling in flames."

"Bailey Ruth, focus on the matter at hand. You. Visible you. Contravening Precepts One, Three, and Four." His voice rose and a splatting sound suggested fist hitting palm.

A girl walking a golden retriever stopped and looked around, seeking the source of the scolding voice. No one was visible in the parking lot. The teenage dogwalker's gaze swept up, down, back, forth.

Wiggins and I hovered unseen about fifteen feet above the hot, still parking lot.

"Precept Six." The exclamation seemed torn from Wiggins's heart.

At the shout above her, the girl's head jerked up. She gazed at sycamore limbs quivering in the breeze. With a squeal, the girl turned. Pigtails flying, she bolted up the sidewalk with the dog.

When the girl and dog were out of sight, and, of course, earshot, I tried for a light touch. "Don't worry. She'll probably decide she heard a car radio." The street was empty of traffic.

"From an imaginary car? From an invisible car?" Wiggins's volume increased with each word.

"These things happen." I hoped he was in an accepting mood. "Dear Wiggins, don't you always feel there's a purpose? Perhaps that sweet girl will be led to a life of creative imagining. Why, this moment might mark the beginning of a career as a novelist. She may—"

"Bailey Ruth."

"Apoplexy doesn't become you, Wiggins." I hoped I sounded more chiding than critical. Men are very sensitive. "Besides, quivering with distress isn't good for you. Now, let's talk about outcomes. Everything is happening as it should." Sounding positive can have the most amazing effect in a combative situation. "If I hadn't appeared in the gazebo, Kay would not have been forced to introduce me to Diane and I wouldn't have been invited to stay at

The Castle. I attributed the fortunate moment to you. You are always one step ahead of your emissaries, smoothing the path, foreseeing obstacles, creatively amending protocol when necessary. Even though becoming visible is anathema"—I was fervent and clearly in agreement—"to emissaries, sometimes we must appear *in* the world in order to discharge our duties. Since Kay's safety is paramount, my visible presence at her side in The Castle will afford her great protection. Wiggins, you were brilliant to think of it!"

"Greater protection?"

"Absolutely." I was almost there.

"I don't recall thinking that at all."

"Your mind is full of important duties! You can't be expected to remember everything, certainly not a minor deviation from business as usual. I thank you for your trust." My voice held a hug. "Kay thanks you. And now, to work."

"Bailey Ruth!"

I chose to ignore his call. After all, Wiggins must surely applaud emissaries who hewed to duty despite impediments.

Paul Fisher's office reflected a man comfortable with himself, an old oak desk, a couple of easy chairs with somewhat worn plaid upholstery. A black Lab rested on a window seat. I wondered how many clients felt less threatened by their legal troubles the minute they saw the silver-muzzled old dog, his adoring dark eyes fixed on his master. Fisher was lean and lanky. His angular face had a faintly quizzical expression. He was likely in his early sixties, tall, fit, and tanned with sun-bleached hair. " . . . expect to see you at the deposition next week." He reached for a legal pad, made quick notes. "If that's a firm offer, I'll see what my client thinks. I'll be back in touch." He drew a box around a figure. "Sure, Rob. Maybe something can be worked out." He hung up and punched his intercom. "I'm free, Martha. I'll see Mrs. Clark now." He reached up, smoothed his untidy hair, and stood. There was a youthful eagerness in his gaze.

Oh, of course. They'd met at dinner at The Castle.

The office door opened.

Paul came around the side of his desk to greet Kay.

She walked toward him, slim hand outstretched. She was strikingly attractive, layered short dark hair, deep-set, intelligent brown eyes, slim straight nose, generous mouth, firm chin. Her close-fitting black sheath dress with a white bamboo pattern emphasized her excellent figure.

As their eyes met, I became aware of that ages-old, evernew, always-indefinable magic connection between a man and a woman.

Oh, my.

CHAPTER EIGHT

S orry to have kept you waiting." His voice was pleasantly deep. His eyes told her he was acutely aware of her presence.

"You are very kind to see me without an appointment." The words were mundane, but her gaze responded to his.

He still held her hand. "What can I do for you?"

She gave him a quick smile. "I'm hoping you can help me with some research." She pulled her hand free. "I'll try not to take too much of your time."

He pointed at the chair nearest his desk. "The springs are better in that one. Martha's been after me to redecorate."

I popped out to the waiting room. Martha was a plump seventy with a mound of white hair and bright blue eyes in a face wrinkled with good humor. I returned to his office.

Kay sat lightly in the chair. She drew a small notebook from her purse. "Jack had your card among his papers. Had he consulted you?"

Paul settled in the other easy chair, the one with presumably inadequate springs. In my day, lawyers wore dark gray or blue suits, white shirts, and tastefully striped ties. He looked athletic, muscular, and very attractive in a light blue polo and tan slacks and black loafers. "I was not"—he spoke precisely—"representing him in a legal matter."

"I'm eager to know whatever you and he discussed. Everything Jack did while he was in Adelaide is important to me."

His quizzical look was pronounced. "How does that information fit into a book about his life?"

"Some of the information will be important. Some won't. His life ended here. Readers may gain a particular insight if they know what mattered to him in his final days. Why did Jack come to you, if not for legal counsel?" Her gaze was intent. His careful answer had caught her attention.

Paul looked thoughtful. "I was his oldest friend. He trusted me."

"He trusted me as well. I hope you will, too."

Paul looked toward a wall filled with framed certificates and photographs. One pictured a football team in a formal pose. "He was my quarterback."

That simple sentence told Kay everything she needed to know about Jack and Paul. When Jack turned to Paul, Paul helped him, not as a lawyer, but as a long-ago teammate.

The lawyer reached over to pick up a green folder from his desk. I hovered behind his shoulder.

Paul opened the folder. "Jack came to see me a few days before he died. He didn't want to go back to Africa until he was sure everything was right at The Castle. He felt responsible for the well-being of his sister and his brother's widow." Paul glanced at an index card. "He asked me to obtain information for him about Alison Gregory and Laverne and Ronald Phillips."

I was abruptly alert. There were two more names on that card that he hadn't mentioned.

"Alison Gregory." Kay repeated the name, made a note on her pad.

Paul's tone was warm. "That was easy duty. As I told Jack, I've known Alison for years. She played tennis with my wife. Alison was a huge help when Mindy was sick. Alison took her for some of her chemo treatments. She was there for Mindy right up to the end." He glanced away.

"I'm sorry." There was sincerity and understanding in Kay's voice. "My husband died two years ago."

They exchanged glances, understanding that each had experienced loss and that memories mattered.

She brought them back to the comfortable office. "Why was Jack interested in Alison?"

"Jack said Evelyn was considering becoming Alison's partner. That surprised me. Alison's very independent. I asked Jack if he was sure and he said maybe he'd misunderstood, but he wanted to know the financial status of her gallery, just in case. That would reassure him, even if nothing ever came of the proposal. He wanted a dossier on Alison. That was easy to put together. Alison grew up here, but she's quite a bit younger. She was Alison Frazier. She has a degree in fine arts from SMU. Her folks owned an upscale clothing store. They did fine until her father died. Her mother ran the store well enough, but she let the insurance lapse. A fire wiped out the store. Her mother wasn't able to rebuild. When she died, the money was all gone. Alison was an only child and she'd grown up having everything she wanted. Her degree was useless for a job that would make money. She ended up in Dallas, working for an art dealer. That's where she made her contacts in the art world. She married a trust-fund cowboy, E. J. Gregory the Fourth. The marriage didn't last. She took the settlement and came back to Adelaide and opened a gallery. She has contacts in Dallas and Mexico City. I got the names of some of the private collectors she deals with. She often brokers private sales of big-deal art. I nosed around, got financials on her. She's made a bundle, no outstanding debts, good reputation in art circles. Evelyn Hume is her best client. Evelyn collects Mexican and American art. Evelyn's awfully proud of a Frida Kahlo self-portrait. I thought it looked pretty dingy and lifeless, but I'm no art critic. Anyway, Jack didn't see why Alison wanted a partner if she was solvent. I was able to reassure him. Gregory Gallery has lots of cash in the bank. She's a great supporter of the art department at Goddard, often exhibiting student work. She's thick with one of the full-time faculty, Leonard Walker. Some people think they are very close."

"How did Jack react to your report?"

"He thanked me, said that seemed like good news."

"And Laverne and Ronald Phillips?"

Paul looked amused. "A different breed of cat altogether. I confirmed Jack's suspicions. Laverne Phillips had a shabby little office in a strip shopping mall in Gainesville. You know the sort of thing: 'Psychic Readings, Private Consultations.' When I see that kind of setup, I wonder how anyone can be sucked in. If the 'psychic'"—his tone put the noun in quote marks—"knows so much, why isn't the office upscale? You'd think applying a little of that savvy to the futures market would make a hacienda in Acapulco small change. Of course, any rational person knows the answer. It's bogus. Certainly, Laverne Phillips is bogus, but Diane is convinced that Laverne is her personal portal to the afterlife. Not long after James died, Diane was on her way to Dallas and she saw the sign and stopped." Paul looked sardonic. "I can imagine the scene, Laverne delicately probing, 'You are clearly suffering. Perhaps the spirits can bring you comfort,' and Diane prattling about James and The Castle and how lonely she was. Diane wasn't Laverne's first victim. A Gainesville woman's daughter filed a lawsuit, claiming her mother had been swindled. Laverne paid back some money and the suit was dropped. Who knows how many others she's fleeced."

Kay's hand was poised above her notepad. "Do you have the Gainesville victim's name?"

His eyes narrowed. "I thought you were trying to round up information on Jack's last days."

Kay was bland. "I want to see if he contacted the Gainesville woman. If he did, that conversation will give readers a wonderful example of his determination to protect the family."

Paul slowly nodded. He thumbed through some papers. "Helen Cramer." He added the address and phone.

Kay wrote rapidly. "Anything else?"

"I gave Jack plenty of ammunition to use against the Phillipses. Basically, Diane rescued Laverne and Ronald. He's a ne'er-do-well with a checkered work career—car salesman, insurance agent, radio DJ. He'd lost his latest job selling vacuum cleaners and was on his last week of unemployment. They were behind in their house and car payments. Now they're on easy street with more than a hundred thousand in the bank." He grinned. "You can take that as an educated guess."

Later I could explain that enigmatic statement to Kay. It's a good-old-boy world in Adelaide. I was confident that Paul, as a high school football hero, had faced no difficulty in getting an unofficial report on Laverne and Ronald's bank account.

"Did Jack confront the Phillipses?"

"I don't know."

Kay was brisk. "I'll find out."

He looked skeptical. "I doubt you'll get much out of them."

Kay was confident. "People like to offer their side of a dis-agreement. That will be my approach. Inclusion in a book may be tempting. What I discover may or may not be useful. I never know where I may find an important fact or impression that will give life to a piece. That's why I explore every possible source." Kay glanced at her notebook. "When did you last talk to Jack?"

"The day he died. He wanted to see me, but I was on my way to the City for a golf foursome. I stayed for dinner. Jack and I planned to get together the next day. I found out about his ac-cident when I got home. The dinner ran late, and I didn't get in until almost eleven. There was a message on my phone from Evelyn."

"How would you describe Jack's mood when he talked to you Saturday morning?"

"Not good." Paul sounded regretful. "He told me he had some unpleasant tasks facing him and he intended to deal with them as soon as possible." The lawyer kneaded a cheek with knuckles. "Maybe that's why I wasn't surprised that he'd died. I thought maybe he was furious with someone and saw that person in the garden and started down the steps too fast."

His words evoked a picture of a man caught up in powerful emotion.

"When he came to your office, did he say anything about a serious disagreement with someone?"

"He was disgusted by Laverne and Ronald's free rein at The Castle and upset when I told him I didn't think there was any legal approach that could be taken. Otherwise, he confined our discussion to obtaining information."

If I had been a cartoonist, I would have drawn a balloon above the lawyer's head with this message: *There are many different ways to tell the truth.*

Kay wrote swiftly in her notebook, then looked up. "I don't want to overlook anyone who might have spoken with Jack those last few days. I understand the Dunhams, next-door neighbors, were at dinner the night Jack died. What can you tell me about them?"

Paul's expression didn't change. He placed his fingertips together in a careful, precise tepee. "Native Adeladians. Clint has an insurance agency. Gwen is active in AAUW and League of Women Voters. She and my wife worked on a bunch of committees together. You might ask Diane. Gwen is her good friend. I believe they go back a long way. I don't know if Clint and Jack had ever met. Diane would know."

"I'll do that." Kay closed her notebook. "Did Jack mention anything else to you?"

I watched the lawyer carefully.

He didn't hesitate. He'd been practicing law for a long time and he knew how to play a hand. "I wish I knew something more that I thought would be helpful." He sounded sincere. He placed the closed folder on his desk.

I studied him with great attention. The card in the folder had also contained the names of Gwen and Clint Dunham. Surely that indicated they also had been the subject of an inquiry by Jack. If so, the lawyer had not shared that information with Kay.

She stood, held out her hand. "I appreciate the information you've given me."

He rose and came nearer.

She didn't move away.

He looked down into her face as if seeking an answer to an unasked question.

She looked up, her dark eyes intent.

He took her hand.

Again, their handclasp marked an instant of connection far beyond polite leave-taking.

"I'll see you again." He spoke decisively.

She gave him swift, appealing smile. "I hope so."

He walked to the door, held it for her. He closed the door behind her, moved to his desk chair, and sank into it. He reached for the folder and placed it in the lower right drawer of his desk, his face drawn in a troubled frown.

As the Corvette roared from the parking lot, I debated whether to tell Kay about the Dunhams. I decided to wait. I had every intention of looking at that file. A fragile connection had been made between Kay and Paul. I wouldn't destroy it heedlessly. There might be a good reason for Paul's reticence.

I hoped Wiggins was pleased by my thoughtfulness. Did I feel an ethereal pat on my shoulder?

"Wiggins—" I clapped my fingers to my lips.

The car swerved. Kay's hands tightened on the wheel. She shot a glance toward the passenger seat. "I thought maybe you weren't here. You usually aren't quiet."

"The less said the better," Wiggins boomed. "Oh, bother. Remember, Bailey Ruth, silence is golden!"

Kay turned a startled glance toward the passenger seat. "Where did that come from?"

"Watch the road." I reached over to push the wheel to the left. The Corvette barely missed a parked FedEx truck.

She looked straight ahead, her shoulders hunched. The Corvette turned on a back road. "I heard a man's voice. He spoke to you." Her tone was accusing. "Where was he? Where *is* he?"

"Not to worry. You should be honored. That was Wiggins, my supervisor." Wiggins no doubt was embarrassed that he had spoken aloud in Kay's hearing. I was sure he'd departed. I would encourage him when next we spoke. One mistake does not a disaster make. I was living proof. Ghostly proof? Whatever. "Wiggins doesn't take a direct part in most missions." It wasn't necessary to explain that perhaps the oversight was for me, not for her. Everyone likes to feel special. I decided it might make Kay feel more comfortable if she could see me. I appeared.

She shivered. "One ghost I can take. Two is more than my mangled sensibility can tolerate."

"You have such a nice way with words."

She shot me a look of pure loathing. "Look, Bai—"

"Francie. You don't want to make a mistake at The Castle."

"You're still coming to stay?"

I decided to overlook her clear lack of enthusiasm. "With a song in my heart." I paused, grinned. "I know. Soooo last century." I thought I detected a quiver of amusement on her face. Possibly we might forge a better relationship.

I gave some thought to my visit, selecting clothes and accessories and personal items, then informed Kay. "My suitcase is in the trunk. You might see if I could be put in that lovely white room. That's where I stayed last night. It's very convenient to yours."

"Oh, sure, I'll ask. Let me know if there's anything else you'd like." Her tone was just this side of churlish.

"I don't want to be a bother."

"No bother. Nothing I'd rather do than make you as comfy as possible." The car picked up speed.

My feeling of bonhomie eroded. However, I resisted responding in kind. I hoped Wiggins was even now adding a star to my file. "Is Gregory Gallery near The Castle?" I knew this old part of town well and we were retracing our earlier route.

"Gregory Gallery?" She sounded abstracted.

"Alison Gregory. Surely that's where we're headed."

"Bai—Francie, you may ostensibly be my assistant, but please leave the tactical planning to me."

I don't like to be patronized. However, I made my tone quite reasonable. "Jack specifically sought information about Alison Gregory's financial status. There was a time noted on the back of her business card and a name. That suggests he made an appointment with her."

Her head jerked toward me. "How do you know about the business card?"

I didn't bother to answer. If she was so smart . . .

Her face screwed up in dismay. "That gives me the willies. You've been creeping around—"

"I never creep." Absolutely not. I float.

"You know what I mean. You were there, but I couldn't see you and you pawed around in the desk."

"Please." It was my turn to patronize. "Let's focus on what matters."

The Corvette curved into the front drive. "Let's do that very thing," she snapped. "Alison Gregory's a side issue. Jack didn't find out anything to derail Evelyn's plan to buy into the gallery. What matters is the background of Laverne and Ronald Phillips. I'm going up to my room and do some calling."

Sometimes it's better to remain aloof from controversy.

I disappeared.

The Corvette squealed to a stop. Kay looked above, around, and behind. "Come back here. What are you going to do? Where are—"

Diane Hume stepped from the shadow of an elm. Eyes wide, she stared at Kay.

"Are you all right?"

Kay punched off the car. She managed a strained smile. "I'm fine. Sometimes"—she swallowed hard—"I practice questions before I talk to people. I asked myself, 'What are you going to do?' That helps me organize my thoughts." Kay slammed out of the car, headed for the front steps.

Diane hurried to catch up. "That's a wonderful idea. I'll try it. 'What are you going to do?' Why, I already feel more empowered. That's what Laverne urges me to do. Open up and be empower—"

The front door shut behind them.

In my experience as an emissary, I'd learned that clothes and accompanying articles such as a purse with customary contents could be imagined into existence. Perhaps . . . I squeezed my eyes shut and imagined the most fetching red Corvette convertible—not, of course, that I wished to imitate Kay, but the ride was exhilarating.

I opened my eyes.

No red Corvette gleamed in the drive of The Castle.

Oh, well. It never hurt to try. Instead, I thought Gregory Gallery and there I was.

Built of golden adobe in the style of Santa Fe, Gregory Gallery drowsed in the shade of cottonwoods. Water splashed from a fountain of brilliant red-and-blue-patterned Talavera tiles. A bell tinkled as I turned the oversize iron knob and pushed the hand-planed, sugar-pine door.

The entryway opened to a large, rectangular room. Cleverly spaced lights plus natural light from skylights illuminated paintings mounted on pale lemon walls.

Alison Gregory moved gracefully toward me. Her cool blue eyes swept me, likely tallying the price of my hairdo, makeup, and wardrobe. The sum must have been adequate for a customer. I was glad I'd chosen the silk georgette blouse. Perhaps she admired the pale pink of the hand-painted flowers against the lime background. Her smile was welcoming. "May I help you?"

I smiled in return. "I hope so. I'm Francie de Sales."

A graceful hand was extended. An emerald glittered in an elegant gold filigree setting. "Alison Gregory. Welcome to Gregory

Gallery." Her handshake was cool and firm. "Are you looking for a particular kind of painting?"

"I wish I were." My voice was admiring. "That's a striking scene." I gestured at a painting of Indians on horseback against the backdrop of granite buttes.

"Thomas Moran." She spoke as if he were an old friend.

"Remarkable." My gaze swept the displayed paintings. "Your gallery is very impressive. No wonder Evelyn Hume plans to become your partner."

Utter surprise widened her eyes. "I beg your pardon?"

"Oh?" I showed confusion. "That was my understanding. Jack Hume told a friend that Evelyn hoped to become a partner in the gallery. Wasn't that what he discussed with you?"

Her face was suddenly unreadable, smooth and controlled. "What do you have to do with the Humes?"

"I'm Kay Clark's assistant. She asked me to visit with you for her book about him. He had an appointment with you. I doubt there's much that would matter for the book, but she didn't want to overlook you since he'd made a special note about seeing you. I hope you can spare a few minutes to tell me about your meeting."

"I'll be happy to do that, though I doubt my conversation with him will be of interest to you." She gestured toward an alcove. Well-worn leather furniture looked comfortable. "Come sit down."

We faced each other across a rough-hewn pinewood coffee table. Several art magazines rested on the table.

She relaxed against the soft leather, crossed her legs, and locked her hands around one knee. Even in the fairly dim light of the alcove, the emerald glowed grass green. "However, I first want to make it clear that you have received false information about my gallery. Evelyn Hume and I have never discussed going into partnership." She spoke briskly, but pleasantly. "Evelyn is a dear friend and a valued customer, but she isn't interested in being my partner, nor have I ever suggested a partnership to her. I own Gregory Gallery. I run Gregory Gallery. That's the way it is and that's the way it's going to be."

It was my turn for surprise. "I see." Though, of course, I didn't. "Definitely there is a mix-up. Jack told a friend he was interested in the gallery's business performance because Evelyn was considering a partnership."

"How odd." She stared toward the stuccoed wall, her eyes narrowed in thought. "I don't see why he wanted to know about the gallery . . ." It was as if she were speaking to herself. " . . . unless he was taking that route to see if I was trustworthy." She gave a decided nod. "I suppose that had to be his reason. The Humes"— and she was both admiring and critical—"always look at the bottom line. I suppose he was vetting me to decide if he could trust me. He did come to see me for a specific reason." She gave me a searching look. "I don't suppose there's any harm now in revealing our conversation."

I felt close to discovering something important. The mixture of hesitancy and reluctance suggested she knew something of a matter that had been important to Jack Hume.

"He wanted to talk about Evelyn. On a personal level. Evelyn"—the gallery owner's smile was quick and unaffected—"comes across as a curmudgeon. In reality, she's kind and sensitive. She is passionate about art. And"—she looked grave—"about family. That was the problem. Jack approached me because I am one of Evelyn's closest friends. In fact, when he came to the gallery, I wasn't surprised. He'd made a special effort to be friendly to me. One evening at The Castle, he asked me to tell him about some of the artworks. He wanted to be able to talk to Evelyn about the art and, as he put it, he'd spent most of his life in a rough-and-ready place and he wasn't an art connoisseur. I realized when he came to the gallery"—she waved her hand at the magnificent arrays of paintings—"that he'd used art as an excuse. What he really wanted to talk about was Evelyn."

She brushed back a strand of blond hair, sighed. "Their situation was sad. Evelyn was angry with him. She felt that he'd neglected the family, that he'd hurt their father deeply. She especially resented the fact that her brother didn't come home when his father was dying. Oh, he came for the funeral. But Evelyn told him, I'm afraid not very kindly, that he'd come too late. He didn't come home to Adelaide to see his father one last time." She pointed at me. "He sat in that chair and asked if I thought there was any way he could reach her. He said, 'My sister hates me. If she had the chance, I think she'd shoot me. I don't want to go home with that on my conscience.' "

My sister hates me. If she had the chance, I think she'd shoot me.

The words, spoken in Alison's soft, quiet voice, seemed to hang between us.

"What did you tell him?"

"Nothing new. Maybe there's nothing new in the world when it comes to love. And hate." She looked pensive. "We've all made mistakes with people. I never had a sister or brother, but I know when I've hurt someone, the best words are 'I'm sorry.' That's what I suggested he say to Evelyn: 'I'm sorry.' He came to see me the afternoon of the day he died. He didn't know he had so little time left. He wanted to make things right with his sister. I hope he had a chance to tell her. But I won't ask Evelyn. If he didn't, it will only grieve her."

I shook my head. "I'd consider telling Evelyn. If she doesn't know, you might bring her great comfort. And certainly, this is material that will add depth to the book."

"You may be right." She sat straighter on the couch. She looked poised to rise, making it clear that the interview was at an end, that she was a businesswoman, that she had matters to deal with.

I stood and smiled. "Thank you so much for your time."

She walked with me to the door.

As I pulled the door open, sunlight flooded the entryway. She stood with the grace of a model. I admired her indigo trousers and zebra-print blouse, the zigzag blue stripe evocative of a shimmering Caribbean lagoon. Large crystals glittered in a summery golden bib necklace. She might have been any well-to-do woman on a lovely summer day except for a hint of weariness in her smooth face.

I paused. I'd forgotten one point. "Jack had made a note about Leonard Walker."

Something moved in her blue eyes. Wariness? Fear? Or was she simply surprised? Her reply came slowly. "Leonard Walker? I can't imagine—oh." She shook her head. "I'd forgotten. When Jack and I talked about paintings one evening at The Castle, he asked about local artists. He said he had a photograph of his late wife and he wondered if he could commission someone to paint a portrait for him. I must have suggested Leonard. He's in the art department at Goddard."

CHAPTER NINE

I didn't bother going to the campus. It had never been my experience that academics spent much time in their offices and certainly not during the summer. I disappeared and zoomed to a nearby dress shop. An empty office provided a phone book. I found Leonard Walker's address.

I felt no need to hurry, so I wafted through the shop to see the clothes. Oh, yes. Very nice. I changed into a salmon rose-print blouse and cool gray trousers, then arrived on a shady street near downtown with well-kept bungalows from the 1930s. The modest homes were unpretentious, charming, and livable. I immediately applauded Walker's taste.

I waited until the mailman walked away to become visible. I admired the crisp white of the heavily timbered front-porch gable, then climbed the shallow front steps. The shingled wood exterior was painted a soft sea green. The gleaming mahogany front door featured an opaque oval glass inset with a daylily incised in the center.

I rang the bell and faintly heard a distant chime.

Cicadas rose to a crescendo, dropped away, began again. In the moments between their songs, I heard the poignant cry of mourning doves and the rustle of magnolia leaves. But the house lay silent.

I rang again.

Possibly Leonard Walker was out of town. The mention of his name had apparently surprised Alison Gregory. I had only her word for Jack's question to her. Had he really sought an artist to create a painting of his late wife? Or had Jack been interested in Walker for another reason?

I only knew for a fact that Leonard Walker's name had been written on the back of Alison's business card, his name and a time.

I pressed the bell again.

Suddenly the door swung in. A tall, stocky bear of man with a mane of golden hair filled the doorway. He gave me an admiring glance from dark brown eyes. He was handsome in a bohemian way, a blue work shirt loose over cotton shorts, a single earring, a gold-link necklace. "Yeah?"

I introduced myself. "I'm hoping for a moment of your time. I'm gathering information on Jack Hume for a book and apparently he was in touch with you before he died."

He looked blank. "Hume?" He sounded puzzled.

"I understand he wanted to commission you to paint a portrait of his deceased wife from a photograph."

"Oh. Yeah. Dude in his sixties." He lifted his heavy shoulders, let them fall. "He never got back to me."

"He died in a fall."

Again he shrugged, though this time he added a commiserating shake of his head and the thick blond hair rippled. "Sorry about that. Anyway, he came to see me a couple of weeks ago, I never heard back. That happens. People change their minds. So, I can't help you."

The door closed in my face.

I walked swiftly down the sidewalk. I waited until I was screened by trees to disappear. In an instant, I was inside the house. The living room enchanted me: a copper flying pig hung from a thin wire, a tulip vase adorned a cherry-and-ebony cabinet, and everywhere there was distinctive Stickley furniture, cabinets, chairs, and end tables, as well as Queen Anne and Chippendale armchairs.

Walker was in the kitchen. He picked out a can of Coke from the refrigerator, flipped the top. He looked relaxed. It didn't appear my visit was lingering in his mind.

I floated about the house and found his studio. A large easel sat in the middle of the room. Paint splotches marked the old wooden floor. Canvases leaned against the walls, some finished, some not. The strong scent of turpentine and linseed oil cloyed the air. Mussed paint rags overflowed from a wastebasket, littering the nearby floor. A studio easel held a half-finished oil painting of a golden retriever. A photograph of a dog was clipped to the top right of the easel. In the clear north light, there was an uncanny resemblance between the photograph and the painting of the large blond dog holding a pheasant firmly in his jaws. The oval palette on the nearby table was splotched with varying shades of oil paint.

Footsteps sounded. Walker came in and picked up his palette, looked at the painting, lifted his brush. He added several dots of orange to one paw, then stroked the bristles against the canvas. The fur looked amazingly lifelike, shining in sunlight. His face folded in a frown of concentration.

I left him at work. Outside, I moved out of sight of the house, stepped into the shadow of a willow, and, after a careful look about, appeared long enough to look at my watch. Of course I have one. Heaven doesn't stint on details. I changed from a silver case and black leather strap suitable for Kay Clark's research assistant to a stylish Swatch, the bull watch. This had nothing to do with Pamplona. This had to do with Black Angus bulls in Pontotoc County, Oklahoma. It was a quarter after twelve. Paul Fisher's office should be empty. I disappeared.

I turned on the light in Paul Fisher's office. My stop would be brief. As a widower, I doubted he went home for lunch. I felt a pang. Was he even now settling into one of the four booths at Lulu's? I was starving. However, I resisted the impulse to pop to Lulu's for a heavenly hamburger. Lulu's is an Adelaide institution. More important, Lulu's serves delectable, sizzling hamburgers with freshly chopped onions, crisp lettuce, and real tomatoes, not those bright red but tasteless greenhouse products. I could picture my hamburger, the bun fresh and hot and seasoned from a slap-down on the grill. In a minute, perhaps . . .

I dropped into Paul's chair, opened the lower right drawer, and picked out the green folder. I looked at the square white card:

> *6/3*
> *Alison Gregory*
> *Laverne and Ronald Phillips*

There was a space and in a different ink, black, not blue, was written:

> *6/5*
> *Gwen and Clint Dunham*

The folder contained several sheets of paper. I found information on Alison Gregory and Laverne and Ronald Phillips. The lawyer had accurately reported his findings to Kay. The last sheet had the names of Gwen and Clint Dunham at the top. Instead of a summary of information, this sheet listed three questions.

Wedding date?
Birth of son?
Hairbrush?

I turned the sheet over. The other side was blank. I looked again at the questions. There were no answers given. I went carefully through the folder. There was no further mention of the Dunhams. All of the other material pertained either to Alison Gregory or the Phillipses.

Three questions asked on June 5; no answers given. Or, at least, no answers had been recorded in this file. Jack died the night of June 6. Quite likely Paul had not had time to make any inquiries.

In addition, Paul had deflected questions about the Dunhams to Diane, saying that Diane and Gwen were close friends. Was that intended to be helpful or was it a subtle attempt to maneuver attention away from Jack and the Dunhams?

I replaced the folder in the drawer. Just in case, I flipped through the other files. This apparently was Paul's personal drawer. Folders contained income-tax statements, home-, car-, medical-, and life-insurance policies, the Paul Forbes Fisher REV. Trust, deeds, and Ameritrade quarterly reports.

I had difficulty replacing the files. I reached inside and felt an obstruction at the back of the drawer. My fingers touched a slick material. Something covered with plastic wrap had apparently slid forward when I picked up the files.

My fingers closed around the oval lump. I pulled it out, intending to replace the files, then drop the object behind them as Paul must have done. I stared through clear plastic wrap at a man's silver-backed hairbrush with the initials *RPD* ornately engraved.

I didn't disturb the wrapping. I placed the hairbrush on the desk as I returned the folders. I started to shut the drawer, then stopped. If I took the hairbrush with me and Paul discovered its loss, he might sharply question his elderly secretary. I could not put her character in jeopardy. If I didn't take the brush, there was always the possibility that the lawyer might dispose of it. Or return the brush to its owner. However, he had no reason to believe anyone would ever become aware of the brush. Perhaps he had decided the brush, whatever secret it held, might be safest tucked behind his folders.

Reluctantly, I reached to the back of the drawer and slid the brush sideways behind the folders. It was now as he had left it. I hoped the brush remained where it was. Whatever happened, I knew Jack Hume very likely had brought the brush to Paul and I could describe, very accurately, the bright silver back and intricately engraved initials: *RPD*.

RPD . . .

On the second floor of the public library, I wafted through the staff offices until I found one momentarily unoccupied but with the computer on. It was the work of only a moment to find what I needed. Gwendolyn Marie Parker and Clint William Dunham were married at the First Baptist Church on August 11, 1990. Ryan Parker Dunham was born April 23, 1991. *RPD* . . .

. . . .

The Dunhams' stone, clinker-brick, and oak-beam house was a small version of an English manor house. Slate shingles glittered on the steep roof and terra-cotta pots adorned the chimney. The dark green of thick ivy emphasized the brilliance of red shutters. The lawn was a green pelt. A maroon Lexus was parked in the shade of spectacular pink, white, and red flowering crape myrtles.

Inside, I heard the distant sound of a piano. I flowed through the house, admiring the living room with a white marble chimney piece, hand-beaten copper vases, a rosewood whatnot with a collection of porcelain birds. In the dining room, stained-glass windows with a heraldic motif of a metal visor in the center of a blue-and-gold design overlooked a rectangular mahogany table. Balloon-backed chairs repeated the design in blue-and-gold tapestry.

At the end of the hall, I entered a long room. Chintz-covered easy chairs, a large-screen television, and a wet bar provided a homey atmosphere. A bricked wall suggested this room was a later addition.

A slender woman sat at a grand piano. Her hands moved lightly as she played "Clair de lune." The mood and movement were mournful. She looked cool and summery in a light blue cotton blouse and a leaf-print-pattern blue-and-silver sarong skirt. Softly curling blond hair framed a face with the beauty of classic features: smoothly rounded forehead, wide-spaced blue eyes, narrow nose, perfect lips curved in a hint of a smile. She had the kind of beauty made famous long ago by Grace Kelly.

My gaze swept past a wall with an English hunting scene and stopped at a knotty-pine wall covered with family photographs that followed a little boy from toddler days to college. I saw the boy and the woman seated at the piano as they had changed over time. The woman who held him when he was little smiled down at him adoringly, a mother's look of passionate love. The little boy's father had an open, blunt face that had improved with age from a rather vacuous expression when he was young to a tolerant, genial middle age. Family pictures, the three of them smiling and happy, included sitting on the top rail of a wooden fence, skiing, playing tennis, boating, birthdays, dances. I studied the photos with a prickling of shock.

I stepped back, scanned the wall. Across the top of the wall was a series of studio photographs. The pictures were evenly spaced except near the end of the row, where three of the frames hung several inches farther apart.

I glanced behind me. The pensive pianist was focused on the keys, the slow music continuing.

I moved nearer the wall and quietly lifted several frames in turn. There were nicks from previous nails a few inches from the current hooks. The photographs at the end of the line had been moved to hide a missing frame. At one time, another picture had hung there.

I gently straightened the last frame and gazed at the woman. Her lovely face appeared troubled. She half turned toward the wall of pictures, perhaps sensing my movement, perhaps seeking solace. For an instant, sheer misery made her face forlorn. Her hands came down, crashing into a discordant chord.

Now was the time to confront Gwen Dunham.

On the front porch, I glanced around. No one was about. I swirled into place. I took no pleasure in what I was about to do, but someone had pushed Jack Hume to his death and I might be near to knowing why. I pushed the bell.

In a moment, the door opened. The smooth social veneer that keeps misery hidden molded her face into polite inquiry. "Yes?"

"Mrs. Dunham, I'm assisting Kay Clark with her book about Jack Hume. I would like to speak with you—"

"I can't help you." Her voice was thin. "I hardly knew him." The door began to close.

"Jack Hume took your son's hairbrush."

"Oh God." She clung to the doorjamb as if all her strength were gone.

"Hey, Gwen?" The robust call came from down the hall. A burly man with thinning sandy hair and a sun-reddened face strode up the hallway. "Ready to go?"

Violet eyes huge in a blanched face, she held out a beseeching hand to me. "It's my husband. I can't talk to you now. I can't."

"Three o'clock in the gazebo at The Castle."

She nodded jerkily and the door swung shut.

I disappeared. Inside the house, I watched her turn to meet him. The smile slid from his face. "Gwen, what's wrong?" He darted an angry look at the door. "Who was that woman? What's happened?"

She reached out and spread her fingers on the tiled top of the side table in the foyer. She tried to smile, but her face was paper white, her eyes staring. "The woman?" Her voice was uneven, breathless. "I don't know." There was a ring of truth to her voice, truth and puzzlement. "I shouldn't have opened the door. I have a terrible headache. I'm going upstairs. I'll lie down for a while. Go on to lunch without me. Tell Ted and Tracy I have a headache." She turned and moved blindly toward the stairs.

He came after her, reached out to take her arm. "I'll help—"

She pulled away. "No. I need to rest. Everything will be all right. I'll take some medicine. Please, go on without me."

He watched as she climbed, using the banister to pull herself from one step to another. His face held uncertainty. He moved toward the stairs, stopped, shook his head in frustration. He walked down the hall, a man deep in thought. Clearly the thought was not pleasant.

The terrace room at The Castle reflected a taste for Moorish architecture. A long wooden table near the French windows apparently served the family for lunch. Evelyn looked remote and unapproachable. Diane's sundress was too youthful, exposing bony, freckled arms. Jimmy's square face looked set and hard. Kay's dark head was bent toward Diane and Kay seemed to hang on every word. Laverne and Ronald Phillips weren't in evidence.

Diane's face glowed with eagerness. " . . . Laverne gives so much of herself. She is absolutely *drained* after a séance. I worry about her . . ." Her praise continued.

Jimmy ate stolidly, his face drawn in a frown.

Evelyn ignored the conversation except for an occasional disdainful glance.

Obviously Kay hadn't shared her information about Laverne and Ronald with Diane. I wondered if Kay had spoken yet with Laverne. But that could wait until later. At the moment, I was impatient to talk to Kay.

I dropped down beside her, bent to whisper in her ear. "Remain calm."

Kay stiffened. Her expression became glazed.

"Meet me downtown at Lulu's in twenty minutes."

I sat at the counter and smiled at my reflection in the mirror. I no longer felt the need to appear businesslike, at least not for lunch. A jade green cotton top with a square neck and cap sleeves made my eyes look even greener. Green is good for redheads. A short white skirt with green-stemmed daisies and white sandals completed my ensemble.

I took a last bite of hamburger as Kay slid onto the next stool.

Providentially, the space was open, even though Lulu's was at the height of the lunch crunch.

The waitress filled up my tea glass, cast a professional eye. "Dessert today?"

"Lulu's special." After my successful morning, I deserved fresh apple pie with melted Cheddar and a scoop of homemade vanilla.

"Coming up." She glanced at Kay. "What'll you have?"

"Key lime pie and coffee."

When our desserts arrived, I forked flaky crust first.

Kay slid here eyes toward me. "Where have you been?"

She gave the distinct impression she would have been happier had I never reappeared. Fortunately, I wasn't sensitive. "I had an instructive chat with Alison Gregory."

Kay looked bored. "So Alison's sinking her piranha teeth deeper into the Hume fortune. What else is new?"

"Not so fast. Evelyn wasn't interested in a partnership, nor was Alison. Jack wanted Alison's help. He made a special effort to be charming to her at The Castle one evening, asking her to describe some of the paintings to him."

Kay looked puzzled. "Describe the paintings to him? Why? He was as much a connoisseur as Evelyn. Jack's wife was an artist and they often spent time at galleries in Europe."

I shrugged. "I suppose it was a way to be friendly with Alison. In any event, it wasn't art that brought him to her gallery. He wanted to talk to Alison about Evelyn."

As Kay listened to my report, her eyes widened and her fork with a mound of key lime pie remained on her plate. When I finished, she sat silent for a moment, then shook her head. "Paul was Jack's best friend. Why did Jack lie to Paul about Evelyn planning to go into a partnership with Alison?"

"Maybe he didn't. Maybe Alison Gregory lied."

Kay looked efficient. "There's a quick way to answer that."

She pulled out her cell, dialed. "Evelyn, this is Kay. I may have misunderstood Jack in a phone conversation before he died. We were talking about Gregory Gallery. Are you considering becoming a partner with Alison?" She listened, then said smoothly, "Actually, I was on my cell and there was static. He must have said something about you and Alison working so closely together in your art acquisitions, a real partnership." She ate a bite of pie. "I understand. It's a minor point, but I wanted to clear it up. Thank you." She clicked off the cell. "Jack lied to Paul. Why?"

I hadn't known Jack. I didn't know how closely—or not—he hewed to truth, but there could be an explanation. "Paul and Jack were old friends, but would Jack necessarily want to discuss Evelyn with him? Instead, he made up a story to give Paul a reason for his curiosity."

"I suppose." Kay didn't sound convinced. "The whole conversation seems off-kilter to me. Jack might dissemble with Paul if there was an important enough reason, but I don't see Jack asking a woman he barely knew for advice about his family."

"He'd been gone a long time. From all accounts, Evelyn and Alison are very close. There was real affection in her voice when she spoke of Evelyn." I finished the last delicious scrap of apple pie. "We can be sure it's never occurred to Alison that Jack was pushed or she wouldn't have told me what Jack said about Evelyn." I quoted, " 'My sister hates me. If she had the chance, I think she'd shoot me.' "

Kay shivered. "He must have sensed enormous anger on Evelyn's part. She has a very strong personality. I think if she were angry, she'd be frightening." Kay pushed away the rest of her pie. "No matter what we discover, I never feel that we are getting any closer to the reason Jack was killed. I don't see how I'm going to find out who's guilty. Even if I do, what do I do then?" Her voice was forlorn.

It was a surprise to see Kay discouraged. Possibly I should encourage her to give up. I looked into her dark eyes, filled with doubt and sadness. Where was the Kay who never met a challenge she wouldn't take? No doubt she was weary. Her sleep must have been disjointed, what little she had achieved after the crash of the vase. But if she quit, she would always look back and feel that she had failed a man who had been a treasured, if troublesome, part of her life.

I weighed my choices: encourage Kay to leave Adelaide, thus keeping her safe, my prime responsibility, or urge her to fight the good fight, for herself and for the memory of a man she'd loved.

My lips parted.

Kay sat up straight, her eyes blazing. "I have to keep going. No matter what it takes, I'll find out who's guilty."

Here was the Kay I'd come to respect. I didn't even consider suggesting she leave the task to me. For her own peace of mind, she had to finish the course. "I'll do everything I can to help." I meant every word of my offer.

"Thank you."

Was there a hint of appreciation in her eyes?

She gave me a thumbs-up. "I'll catch Jack's murderer." She hesitated, then spoke in a rush. "You're a big help. Thanks for the update."

Since she didn't ask if I had learned anything else, I felt under no compulsion to describe my visit to the Dunham home. If my talk with Gwen Dunham at the gazebo proved to be relevant, I would report what I learned as if I'd discovered all my facts from Gwen. I would leave Paul Fisher out of the equation altogether. I not only believe in young love, I believe in late love.

Kay gestured to the waitress, who nodded, and in a moment placed Kay's check and mine on the counter. As Kay started to rise, I spoke fast. "Did you get anywhere with Laverne and Ronald?"

She settled back on the stool. "Not far. I cornered Laverne alone on the lower terrace and here came Ronald." She looked thoughtful. "It's hard to square your version of him and the one he presents when he's with Laverne. He played the diffident, adoring husband to the hilt, but, thanks to your tip, I watched her. She slid her eyes toward him, time and again. I'd hoped to talk to her alone, but I got the real clear feeling that wasn't going to happen, not if he could help it. I was as pleasant as could be and said I'd heard some interesting facts from Helen Cramer's daughter. Laverne looked like one of Poe's apparitions had her by the neck." Kay paused and gave me an uncertain glance.

Heavens, I would hope I'm never guilty of being overly sensitive. I waved a negligent hand. "'No offense meant, none taken.'" I smiled as I remembered Sergeant Buck, who faithfully served Colonel Primrose in the Grace Latham mysteries by Leslie Ford. I'd recently read her latest, evocatively southern and drenched with the scent of magnolias. Oh. Perhaps I shouldn't share that little fact about Heaven. Dismiss the possibility from your mind that your favorite authors write merrily away in their Heavenly abode. But you might remember the first stanza of Rudyard Kipling's "When Earth's Last Picture Is Painted" and draw your own conclusions.

Kay cleared her throat. "Ronald wasn't fazed. He gave Laverne a glance that meant 'get that terrified look off your face,' then he went on the offensive. He claimed that Laverne had been set up by Carol Cramer, Helen's daughter. He said one afternoon when Helen was resting, Carol encouraged her to look at some old albums and that's why Laverne's fingerprints were on the albums. The fact that Carol surreptitiously obtained her fingerprints from a teacup and had them compared to the prints on the album certainly indicated that Carol was not trustworthy. Laverne had only looked at the albums to be polite and was appalled when Carol poisoned her mother's mind against her, convincing Helen that the intimate details recounted during séances had been taken from the albums. As for the money, it had been freely given as a gift in appreciation for Laverne's great service in affording comfort to Helen. However, when there was a lawsuit, Laverne felt so dishonored she decided not to keep any of the money even though it had been freely given to her by Helen. By the time Ronald finished, Laverne didn't look quite so spooked. Oh. No offense meant."

"None taken." I laughed aloud.

Kay's lips quivered for an instant in amusement, then her amusement fled. She sighed and turned her hands up in a gesture of defeat. "As for the historical society, Ronald was as smooth as silk. He said he was greatly interested in Adelaide's history and was working on a monograph about the founding families, the Humes and the Pritchards."

"What an eel." I pictured an eel with carefully coiffed silver hair and cold blue eyes.

"He has an answer for everything and Diane will always take their part." Kay looked disgusted.

"I imagine she will. However, exposing Laverne and Ronald isn't our main concern. The point is to catch Jack's murderer." I looked into the distance as if seeking enlightenment. I do believe I might have excelled at acting. Possibly that's why I felt such an affinity with auburn-haired, velvet-voiced, witty Myrna Loy. Those who loved her films will be delighted to know she is as urbane and delightful . . . Oh. There I go again. Never mind. One day you will know. Perhaps my inner soliloquy made my expression even more arresting. I widened my eyes. My lips parted. I turned to Kay with a happy look of triumph. "Kay, you are so insightful, so clever, with such an unerring sense of character. There is an avenue open to us that only you are suited to follow."

She looked at me warily.

Was her inner hogwash detector vibrating? I glanced at the mirror. I have never seen anyone look more sincere than I and the light was very flattering to my hair. "Thanks to your good efforts, we know everyone who was present at The Castle the night Jack was killed. However, we must discover which one was angry enough or desperate enough to murder him. You can use your investigative skills to put together their psychological profiles." This project would be a nice, safe diversion for Kay while I followed more fruitful lines of inquiry. "I'll—" I broke off. The mirror gave a good view of everyone entering Lulu's.

Chief Cobb stood in the doorway. Despite the heat, he wore a brown suit, white shirt, and tie. The temperature outside probably hovered around ninety-seven. He looked hot, wiping a hand across his sweaty face. He started toward a booth.

I bent near Kay and whispered, "Pay my check," as I disappeared.

Kay flinched. "I wish you wouldn't do that." Her voice was sharp.

The waitress turned. She was a big woman with a broad, freckled face. "Ma'am?"

"I wasn't talking to you."

The waitress looked at the pudgy man on the stool to Kay's left. He was turned away, deep in conversation with a little boy in thick glasses and a backward ball cap. Her gaze moved past Kay to my empty seat. She stared. "Where'd that redhead go? She hasn't paid."

Her raised voice caught the chief's attention. He glanced toward the counter.

"I'm paying for her." Kay added my check to her own.

The waitress looked to the front door and back to my empty space. Her face creased in a frown. "She was there when I turned around to get the coffeepot." She held a metal pot with a red rim. "All I did was get the pot and turn back around."

The chief stood behind my seat. "Hey, Imogene."

"Hey, Chief." Imogene jerked a thumb toward the door. "Did you see a redhead go out just now?"

Sam Cobb's heavy face was suddenly alert. "A redhead? No." He looked at Kay. "Good to see you, Mrs. Clark. Is your assistant here?"

Kay maintained her poise. "Not at the moment."

"Where did she go? That's what I want to know?" Imogene had met the inexplicable and she gripped it tighter than a dog with a bone as she automatically cleared the counter.

Kay smiled. "She moves quickly. But it doesn't matter. I'm paying." She started to rise.

Chief Cobb blocked her way. "I'd like a moment of your time, Mrs. Clark." He was polite, but commanding.

Kay sank back onto the stool and the chief slid into my place. "The usual, Imogene." He turned toward Kay.

Her dark eyes looked apprehensive, but her face was molded in pleasant inquiry. "What can I do for you, Chief Cobb?"

He studied her. "I've looked into your background. You are exactly who you claim to be, a successful nonfiction author and a longtime friend of Jack Hume's." There the slightest emphasis on *friend*.

Her expression didn't change. She said nothing.

His bulldog face was intent. His dark eyes were not so much combative as stern. "You claim to be writing a book about him. I did a little checking. Your publisher never heard of that book. Apparently, the usual procedure would be for you to submit a proposal. You haven't. According to your editor, you're writing a book about Meg Whitman."

The waitress brought iced tea and shot another puzzled look toward the door.

Kay folded her arms. "Jack's death prompted me to honor his

request that I write a book about him. I have every intention of completing the other manuscript. However, I didn't believe I'd have another opportunity to interview those who spent time with Jack here in Adelaide."

Imogene slid a plate in front of the chief.

He cut a cheeseburger in half, then gave Kay a level, searching look. "You may be interested to know I wasn't the first person to ask about the book. Apparently a reporter for the *Adelaide Gazette* called your publisher yesterday afternoon. I contacted the *Gazette*. You might be interested to know that no *Gazette* reporter made that inquiry."

"A man or a woman?" She stared at him, tense and eager.

"Summer colds are nasty, aren't they? The caller apologized for hoarseness. Could have been either a man or woman." He ate part of his hamburger, dipped a french fry in ketchup. "Now, you're a lot better at asking than answering. I won't waste your time and mine with questions. Instead, I'll tell you the way I see it." His deep voice was matter-of-fact, but he exuded the tough competence of a cop who looked hard and missed little. "You are contacting the people who were at The Castle the night Jack Hume died. Last night you arranged to meet someone in the garden. That cul-de-sac is a nice secluded spot for a quiet chat. I imagine someone left you a note." His eyes never left her face.

Kay's gaze dropped to the counter.

"You were a sitting duck when somebody pushed that vase. We got a 911 call, but not from you. If you hadn't insisted that the vase toppled in an accident, we could have investigated last night. Now we're blocked. Evelyn Hume won't file a complaint. More-over, I'd bet my season tickets to the Sooners that somebody's been busy on that pedestal, smoothing away any evidence a chisel was used to loosen the vase." His brown eyes were hard. "My take is that you believe Jack Hume was murdered and you're stirring up people you suspect. You've started down a path and there's nothing I can do to stop you. However, you can do me a favor. Fill me in on what you've learned."

"Why?" Her question was short and crisp.

"When somebody finds your body, I'll know what you know." His dispassionate tone made the words even more chilling.

Kay drew in a quick breath. Slowly, she faced him. "Am I correct that you won't actively investigate right now?"

He nodded. "I'm blocked. But if something happens to you . . ."

The unspoken proposition was grim: if someone killed Kay, he would have a head start if he knew what she now knew.

"All right. I get your point." Her voice was steady, though thin. "I found a note in my room after dinner. She quoted, 'Be on the terrace at midnight in the cul-de-sac. I know what happened to Jack.'"

He gave a short, hard shake of his head. "What did you think the murderer wanted to do? Confess?"

"I intended to be careful." She didn't mention the gun.

"You are"—he bit off the words—"a damn fool, Mrs. Clark. Murder is my job, not yours."

"Chief Cobb, if I could prove Jack was murdered, I would have come to you first. I don't have proof. I came to Adelaide because he was angry and upset with several people. If you started an investigation, I would never have a chance to get information from any of those people."

"I've been talking to suspects for a long time. I'll share a little fact with you." His tone was sardonic. "People lie."

She lifted her chin. "They are more likely to tell the truth if they don't know they are suspects."

"Maybe." He didn't sound convinced. "Sometimes they squeal like pigs on their way to slaughter to show they are innocent and fall all over themselves to pitch dirt about other people. But one of them may make sure you don't find out too much."

Kay slid from the stool.

He looked after her. "Of course, you may be lucky. You said your assistant was with you last night. Your redheaded assistant, Francie de Sales." Cobb took a bite of cheeseburger, wiped his lips with a paper napkin. "According to your editor, you've never had an assistant, always worked alone. We ran some checks in the Dallas area. No luck with Francie de Sales."

Kay managed a smile. "I don't know too much about Francie. She seems capable enough."

It wasn't what I would call a sterling endorsement.

"Anyway, she was with you last night. I'm betting she pushed you out of the way of the vase. Am I right?"

Now it was Kay who stared with wide eyes. "Yes."

"You could even say"—his tone was ruminative—"that your being saved was miraculous."

His gaze held hers and between them passed an understanding.

Kay swallowed. "You've seen—"

I pinched Kay, once, hard.

She jumped.

A kind of smile tugged at Chief Cobb's broad lips. He looked speculatively about. Certainly he couldn't see me, hovering above and slightly behind Kay. I had no doubt he knew I was near.

"Yeah. Sometimes we can't explain everything." He stirred sugar into his coffee, gave her a sober look. "You can't always count on miracles, Mrs. Clark."

CHAPTER TEN

I waited until the convertible was well out of sight from downtown before I swirled into the passenger seat. "I've been thinking."

"What an accomplishment." Kay's tone didn't invite me to share. She shot a searching glance at me. "I gather you and Chief Cobb have a history."

I tried to look modest. "I've been honored to assist the department on previous visits."

Slowly, her lips curved into a smile. "I'll bet there are some stories behind that sweet modicum of words. Maybe someday the chief and I can let our hair down and trade ghost stories."

I cleared my throat. "Just in case Wiggins is about, perhaps you might refrain from comments guaranteed to distress him."

"Oh, boy. Wow. I sure wouldn't want to distress the head spook—"

The rumble from the backseat sounded like a cross between a water buffalo's bellow and the strangled gurgle of a suddenly unplugged drain.

Kay hunched over the wheel. "Just kidding. One sp— One helper is all I need."

"Spook!" Wiggins's deep voice quivered. "Bailey Ruth, this is the fruit of your transgressions. Constant appearances and open interaction with your recalcitrant subject have now"—and his anguish was obvious—"caused me to breach Precept Three."

Kay glanced in the rearview mirror at the empty backseat. "Precept Three?"

"'Work behind the scenes without making your presence known.'" Wiggins was chagrined. "My lapse clearly reflects that I have succumbed to the temptation against which I warn all emissaries. I have become too much *of* the world instead of pursuing my duties unseen, unnoticed, and unsung *in* the world. I succumbed to the worldly sin of anger." His voice fell lower than I had ever heard him speak, a man in despair.

"Wiggins, your instinct trumped the rules." My voice was fervent in admiration. "You have come to the rescue. Who would have thought you would be this clever! Of course, you are always on top of your job. But your appearance now, at this moment"—I gave Kay a sub rosa pinch—"has made all the difference. Look at Kay." Was I adroit enough to pluck Wiggins from his abyss of contrition?

I pointed at Kay.

Kay appeared startled and a shade (sometimes I succumb to pun fun) apprehensive. Kay also looked youthful and very attractive as the wind whipped her dark hair. Her gaze continued to flicker toward the backseat.

"I'm looking." Wiggins sounded resigned, but I thought I sensed the faintest hint of hope that I could restore his equilibrium.

Kay's peek in the rearview mirror reconfirmed the emptiness of the backseat. Her shoulders tightened.

"Kay regrets her failure to fully cooperate." I was counting on Kay's obvious desire to see—uh—hear the last of Wiggins. "Since I appeared solely to prevent the reckless firing of her gun in the garden last night and thereby was glimpsed by a resident of the house, remaining invisible at all times was no longer possible for me and I put aside my personal wish to honor each and every Precept."

The silence in the backseat seemed somewhat receptive.

So far, so good. "Your well-timed arrival emphasizes the importance the department places upon Kay's safety. I'm sure before you depart, Kay will pledge her willingness to follow my directives so that I may remain unseen, unnoticed, and unsung, except, of course"—my tone suggested this to be a trifling matter—"for those household moments now required by my initial appearance." This not only gave me latitude, but reemphasized the point that my actual presence on the scene had become essential. "Before you leave—is there anywhere you are needed at the moment, Wiggins?"

"Well . . ."

I pictured Wiggins tugging at his walrus mustache.

"There is one small matter, a too-diffident emissary at Ulaa Lodge in Patagonia. From one extreme to another." He sounded exasperated.

I chose not to respond to the latter comment. "Please, don't let us delay you. Quickly, now, Kay, so that Wiggins may depart in good conscience, repeat after me: I, Kay Clark—"

She shot me a look of unadulterated fury.

My left hand wasn't visible to Wiggins. I poked Kay's arm and jerked a thumb toward the backseat.

Kay took a deep breath. "I, Kay Clark—"

"—do hereby solemnly promise on my word of honor—"

"—do hereby solemnly promise on my word of honor—"

"—to cooperate fully with Department of Good Intentions Emissary Raeburn."

"—to cooperate"—she sounded morose—"with Department of Good Intentions Emissary Raeburn."

I firmly believe formality encourages decorum. Ask any former high school English teacher. Ah, *Department of Good Intentions Emissary Raeburn*! If that didn't have a ring! Possibly I might design a card. *DGIE Bailey Ruth Raeburn* would look impressive in bright red script. I have a fondness for red.

I gave Kay a magnanimous smile, then looked over the seat. "Thanks to you, Wiggins, our ship is now on course. Have a great trip to Ulaa Lodge."

"You are very kind. Bailey Ruth, I know you do your best." If he took comfort in that conclusion, it wasn't evident from voice. "But, please, try harder."

"You can count on me."

Possibly I heard a sigh that faded away on the wind.

As the convertible started up the hill to The Castle, Kay still clutched the wheel in a tight grip.

Halfway up, I reassured her. "He's gone."

Her sideways glance was cold. "Is blackmail included in your Precepts?"

"Now, now."

"What exactly do you want me to do?"

"The psychological profiles—"

"Spare me." Her words were clipped. "If you want to send me off to twiddle my thumbs, say so."

"That is an unworthy accusation." I didn't dispute its accuracy. "Actually, you can accomplish a great deal by finding out what makes these people tick. Paul Fisher can tell you everything about them."

"Paul Fisher?" She spoke his name with a mixture of hesitancy and eagerness.

"He's the obvious choice. He knows these people intimately and he was Jack's best friend." Moreover, I felt confident Kay would be absolutely safe in his company. On the day of the murder, the lawyer had dined in Oklahoma City with golf friends and not returned to Adelaide until late. He could not have slipped through shadows to push his old friend down steep steps. Nor had we discovered any hint of a rift between the two men. It was true that Paul hadn't told Kay about Jack's interest in Gwen and Clint Dunham, but the lawyer didn't know that Kay's questions had to do with murder, not a biography. "See what you can find out from him this afternoon. Then we'll have a better idea on where to concentrate our efforts."

"'Our' efforts? What will you be doing while I round up insights?"

"Popping here and there."

"Mine but to do, mine not to question why?" The Corvette turned into The Castle drive. "Okay. I'll play your game after I talk to Diane, Jimmy, and Margo."

I held up my hand. "Leave them to me. They know you were close to Jack. How forthcoming do you think they will be? But me, I'm the help. I didn't know Jack Hume. They are much more likely to drop their guard with me."

She looked thoughtful as she braked. "Much as it galls me to admit it, you've got a point."

I glanced at my watch. I had a little over an hour before my meeting at the gazebo with Gwen Dunham. There was much to do. "I appreciate your cooperation. Let's go inside and I can meet my hostess." And possibly others. "Then you can be on your way to Paul Fisher's office."

I glanced around to be certain no one was observing the car, then transformed my appearance. Gone was the jade green cotton top with a square neck and cap sleeves, short white skirt with green-stemmed daisies, and white sandals. Instead, I wore a drab, too-large taupe smock, black slacks, green tennis shoes, and Ben Franklin granny glasses. Most painful was the lack of makeup. Even red hair and appearing twenty-seven didn't save me from looking like a street waif.

Kay's eyes widened. "Have you had a nervous breakdown?"

I pushed the granny glasses higher on my nose. "Would you worry about talking to me?"

Diane Hume had changed from her gardening clothes to an Irish linen blouse in a robin's-egg blue, perfect for her faded blond prettiness, and navy slacks. I was glad the light was fairly dim in the main hallway, though she apparently hadn't noticed my transformation from stylish assistant in the gazebo to Francie Frump in the hallway.

Diane's smile was shy and welcoming. "Just leave your suitcase here." She gestured at the base of the broad stone stairway. "Margo will bring it to your room. Margo's our wonderful housekeeper. If you need anything, Margo will see that you get it." Diane looked at Kay. "Francie will be in the white room, just down the hall from you."

I felt warmly toward Diane. Perhaps she'd noticed my hair, which flamed while the rest of me drooped, and decided the white room offered the proper background.

"That's excellent." Kay's enthusiasm seemed to be well contained.

Diane said diffidently, "If you'd like, I'll show Francie the main rooms on the lower floor before we go up, and then she'll know her way around."

Kay looked like someone marooned on an island who sights a cruise ship. "That would be such a help. I'll slip away. I have an appointment at the historical society." Her glance flicked toward a shadowy alcove.

Diane looked impressed. "I know you have so much you need to learn. I'll take good care of Francie."

My gaze swung to the alcove. Ronald Phillips stood very still, his figure almost invisible, except for the telltale gleam of white buck shoes.

White buck shoes might be passé, but I suspected they added a buoyancy to Ronald's steps. He no doubt saw himself as quite the dandy fellow, and he continued to be a man who never hesitated to eavesdrop. Was he observing Diane? Or did he have suspicions about Kay?

I didn't envy his shoes, but I loathed my current pair. Appearance does matter. A beautifully patterned, swinging silk makes a woman feel butterfly free and just as lovely. I wasn't enjoying being Francie the Frump. Perhaps better shoes would lift my spirits. The green tennis shoes gave way to adorable ruffled orange leather flip-flops.

Kay drew in a sharp breath and shook her head warningly.

I gave her a reassuring pat on her elbow.

If Ronald hadn't been watching, I suspect she would have chastised me. My smile was blithe as she walked away.

Diane had turned toward an archway. "The living area is this way." I followed Diane through the main living and dining rooms. The heavy Victorian furniture was massive, lightened by occasional Chinese chairs and couches, many of them either red or gold, an odd but intriguing combination of styles. She flicked on lights to illuminate paintings and statuary. She paused in the dining room to look up at an enormous painting of an angel garbed in denim blue holding a small drum. Two lines of blue feathers accented huge golden wings. "This is one of my favorites. James says the drumbeat is so soft it seems as though you are listening to God's heart. He knows." She turned limpid, trusting blue eyes on me. "You see, my friend Laverne—you haven't met her yet, but you will—is able to reach out to James. That's my husband. He died five years ago." Tears made her eyes brilliant.

"Hearing from him must bring you great comfort." Hopefully Wiggins was deeply engaged at Ulaa Lodge. I well knew the stricture in Leviticus 19:31. I intended to unmask Laverne as a fraud before Kay and I left Adelaide. You might well ask how it was that I, admittedly a spirit, abhorred spiritualism. Ah, the difference is that I had been dispatched from Heaven to help. Mediums claiming to contact those who have passed over were initiating contact from earth. Legitimate contact came solely from Heaven.

Diane clasped her hands beneath her chin. "I don't know what I'd do without Laverne." Her voice quivered.

"I suppose when you face a big problem, or a fear, she is able to seek James's counsel." And gouge more money from you.

Diane's eyes looked huge and her face was wan. "Usually."

"I hesitate to speak." Have I ever uttered a less accurate statement? "And, of course, we are strangers." How much easier it is to confide in someone who is not a part of your world. "But I sense that you are in great distress and you aren't sure how to proceed. Maybe I can help."

Diane's fingers hooked around the big beads of her costume pearl necklace. "I can't tell anyone. I hope James will tell me what to do. Truly, Jimmy didn't mean—" She broke off, clapped a hand to her mouth.

"That's all right." I made a reassuring sound. "Kay's told me about Jimmy. She understands how upset he was."

Her eyes grew enormous. "How did Kay know?"

"Kay's a marvel." My tone was admiring, though, of course, I deserved the kudos. However, I am selfless in carrying out my duties.

Diane's delicate features suddenly set in a mask of anger. "I thought Margo heard Jimmy. Well, she can't pretend she wasn't mad at Jack, too. I know what happened years ago. She never got over Jack dropping her, and Shannon running after Jack made Margo furious. But she shouldn't have told Kay what Jimmy said."

"I'm sure he can explain everything when I talk to him. Is he here this afternoon?"

"Somewhere." Her voice was faint. "He's researching a paper for one of his professors. He's worked hard this summer." There was a trace of defensiveness in her voice. I wondered if her background had been less privileged than that of her husband. Perhaps she thought even rich kids should have summer jobs.

"That's wonderful. Certainly it will be important to have his views of his uncle in the book."

"The book." She looked as wilted as a chrysanthemum corsage left out in the sun. "Please, don't put in what Jimmy said. He didn't mean a word of it."

"Let me see what I have." I delved into a shabby straw purse and pulled out a notebook. I flipped past a few pages, peering intently. "Of course, comments often get garbled when they are repeated. Jimmy said something to the effect that he intended to push Jack?" I ended on a questioning note.

"He didn't threaten to push him." Diane's denial was vehement. "If Margo said that, she should be ashamed. It was Saturday afternoon and Jimmy was upset about Shannon and how she was chasing Jack. Jimmy said the next time he saw Jack, he was going to knock him flat. But Jimmy came to dinner and he and Jack didn't say a word to each other, so that shows Jimmy was only blowing off steam. He would never hurt Jack. That's how boys talk. Boys make a lot of noise and don't mean anything serious. Everybody knows Jack fell. His death was a terrible accident." There was terror in her eyes.

Kay was sure Jack had been murdered.

So was Diane.

I would have enjoyed exploring the subtleties of the white bedroom. Wherever I looked, I saw unusual decorations: a photograph of a polar bear on an ice floe with brilliant blue sky the only note of color, an ivory miniature of the Taj Mahal at sunset, a framed Alençon lace bridal handkerchief with the intertwined initials *CKH,* an all-white spiral seashell in an alabaster box lined with red velvet, a lustrous white costume pearl necklace dangling from a red coral branch. Instead, as soon as the door closed after Diane, I became invisible and followed her.

In the hallway, I hovered near the frescoed ceiling, white clouds shot through with gold against a blue sky. Diane stood at the landing, her head turned to look up toward the third floor. She shuddered and whirled away. She hurried downstairs, her shoes thudding on the steps as if she could not go fast enough.

I dropped by the Phillipses' suite. Laverne lay back on a chaise longue, a magazine loose in her lap. Alone, all pretense of imperiousness was gone. Her heavily made-up face sagged, lines of uncertainty and foreboding pulling at her lips. She lifted a shaking hand to massage one temple.

I bypassed Diane's suite and the unoccupied guest rooms. Jimmy Hume wasn't in his room. At the other end of the hall, I entered Evelyn's suite. The impress of her personality was everywhere, from Stickley furniture to art-glass windows to Mission-style lighting to a vibrantly warm still life by Helen Clark Oldfield. The oil painting in an understated white frame hung by itself in the center of a cream stucco wall. On a teak table rested a silver-handled magnifying glass. How much did Evelyn see when she held the oversize glass close to the canvas? Perhaps a dim mélange of Oldfield's rich colors. Was possession of beauty enough in itself to give her pleasure?

Downstairs, Margo worked in the kitchen. Her face was pinched in thought. She looked dour. Evelyn Hume sat at a piano in an alcove off the living room, her expression remote, her hands forceful as she played a polonaise. Ronald of the white shoes was not in any of the ground-floor areas, nor did I find Jimmy Hume or Shannon Taylor.

I stood in the central hallway. I almost materialized to go to the kitchen when I decided to look over the grounds. The sound of a steel guitar led me over a row of poplars. Below was a sparkling swimming pool in the shape of a *T* and a cabana.

Green-and-cream-striped awnings provided shade. Jimmy Hume lounged on a cushioned deck chair. He wore swim trunks, but they appeared dry, and a laptop was propped on his knees. The music thrummed from speakers mounted on the cabana. I floated behind him, read over his shoulder.

. . . and the oil-bearing layers are reminiscent of a sponge, in that . . .

I moved to the other side of a hedge and swirled present as Francie the Frump. My soft-soled flip-flops made no sound as I strolled around the greenery and crossed the deck. "Hello."

He looked up in surprise, but put aside the laptop and came to his feet.

I appreciate good manners. He was also a hunk, dark hair thick on his tanned chest, flat stomach, powerful legs, and the good looks of the Hume men.

"May I help you?" His voice was youthful, but confident. Millions in the bank have a way of instilling confidence.

"I'm Francie de Sales, Kay Clark's assistant. I wondered if I might visit with you for a moment." I pushed up the granny glasses and endeavored to appear innocuous. Of course, that is always a challenge with red hair, despite a lack of makeup.

He closed the laptop and gestured toward a white wrought-iron table and chairs. When we were seated, he looked at me inquiringly, but said nothing. He reminded me of a long-ago movie actor, Montgomery Clift.

I explained in a diffused and rambling fashion that I was gathering material for the book about Jack's life. I leaned forward, pen poised above an open notebook, my expression earnest and slightly dim-witted. "I hope you will describe your uncle's last few days. I understand you had a difficult exchange with him the day he died." I made my tone confidential and sympathetic.

His face twisted in a frown. "So who's mouthing off about me?"

"My sources are confidential." I sounded regretful. "Of course, that's why I am asking you. Everyone deserves to defend themselves."

"There's nothing to defend." He was clearly angry. "I tried to talk to Jack and he blew me off." There was depth of pain in Jimmy's anguished eyes. "He treated me like I was a stranger."

I felt an instant of connection with Jack Hume. That final day a powerful force had driven him. Something mattered terribly to him, mattered so much he couldn't take the time to understand his nephew's distress.

I was also touched by Jimmy's misery. There was grief in his eyes as well as anger. "Did you want to talk to him about Shannon?"

"Jack blew her off, too. I'd never seen her so upset." Jimmy was gruff. "I didn't want her hurt, not like that. She had a big-time crush on him and he made her feel like a silly fool. I knew all along that Jack wasn't serious about her, but he shouldn't have dumped her like that. I was going to tell him he was a jerk."

"Is that why you threatened to knock him flat the next time you saw him?"

Jimmy's jaw jutted. "Yeah. I would have. After dinner, I was going to make him pay. I went up to the balcony."

I looked at him in a confused fashion, but there was no confusion in my mind. "Let me see. I thought he fell down the balcony steps. If you went that way—"

Jimmy shook his head. "I was inside. I came up the interior stairs."

I observed his handsome face. I liked him. I wasn't sure I believed him.

"I went through the ballroom and out to the balcony. He wasn't there." Jimmy looked half sick. "If I'd gone down the steps, I guess I would have found him. Instead, I went back into the house."

Shannon Taylor wasn't in the house nor was she attending Evelyn. Outside, I floated above The Castle. In addition to the workshop, I saw a long building with five bays that obviously served as the garage. I caught a glimpse of white beyond a row of willows. In an instant, I stood in front of a modest frame house with a screened-in porch.

Inside, Shannon sat on a cheerful yellow chintz sofa. She looked young and lovely in a rosebud-embroidered mauve tank top and blue chambray shorts. She held a book in her lap. The immaculate, simply furnished room was cool and quiet.

I came nearer. The page was opened to "Nocturnal Reverie" by Anne Finch. Shannon pressed a finger against a line.

I bent to see.

But silent musings urge the mind to seek Something, too high for syllables to seek. Tears glistened in her eyes.

I reappeared on the front porch and knocked.

She was unsmiling when she opened the door. She glanced at my dowdy clothes. "No soliciting permitted."

Before the door closed, I said quickly, "I'm not soliciting. I'm Francie de Sales, Kay Clark's assistant."

"Kay Clark." A scowl marred her young face.

"You can be very important in a book about Jack Hume. I understand he felt a real rapport with you."

Her eyes widened.

"I hope you will share what you know about his last days."

"His last days . . ." Her voice was shaky.

"In his e-mails, he said you were very kind to him and he admired you." I didn't feel that was too much of a stretch. Certainly he'd told Kay how flattering he had found Shannon's attention.

"He did?" Her eyes lighted. "He said that?"

How little it takes when someone hungers for even a crumb from a beloved figure.

"He said you were gorgeous and sweet."

I could not have given her a greater gift. Her face bloomed. She opened the screen and I followed her into the living room.

When we sat on the sofa, I leaned forward and spoke in a confidential tone. "The hope"—I carefully avoided saying this was Kay's hope—"is to know what he was thinking and feeling those last few days."

Shannon talked fast. "He was so much fun. We first spent time together at the pool. If Evelyn doesn't need me, I can do whatever I want. I help Mom a lot, but I have a bunch of free time. We swam together and twice we went canoeing. One night I ran into him at Mama Pat's." She glanced at me and added, "That's a club near the campus. I love old jazz. I go there a lot. He was there by himself, listening to the piano, having a drink. We danced to 'A Nightingale Sang in Berkeley Square.'" Her eyes shone with the memory of a night and the touch of his arms and a smiling face looking down at her. Slowly, the softness faded, replaced by a dumb misery compounded of hurt feelings and puzzlement. "We had fun. I know we did. He liked me. I don't know what went wrong. I thought maybe I'd said something, done something. It was that last weekend and I found him in the study. Maybe I shouldn't have bothered him. He looked upset, and when I asked him if we weren't friends, it was like he didn't even know me. He kind of shook his head and told me to go away, he was busy. I couldn't believe he'd act like that after the way he'd held me. It wasn't right." There was aching humiliation in her eyes and passionate denial in her voice. "I found out he was seeing that woman next door. She's old. I don't know what he saw in her. But they had something going on. I heard the last thing she said to him. 'I wish you were dead.' I hope she feels bad now."

Margo Taylor cracked another egg into the blue mixing bowl. A splash of sunlight through the kitchen window emphasized lines of discontent that flared from her eyes and her mouth. "I don't want to talk about Jack Hume."

"I understand you were in love with him at one time." She pressed her lips together and clipped another egg on the side of the bowl. "He dropped you for another woman."

A flash of satisfaction gleamed in her green eyes.

Her unexpected response caught my attention. I doubted that she harbored kind feelings toward the woman who had supplanted her. She could only feel pleased if in some way she had caused difficulty for her long-ago rival. I remembered Kay's description of the photograph which she had assumed pictured Jack

Hume on his graduation. Photographs of a darkly handsome boy covered a wall in the Dunham home. A photograph was missing from the Dunham wall.

"You slipped the photograph of Ryan Dunham under Jack's door." I had no doubt in my mind.

For an instant, Margo stood rigid, one hand gripping an egg. She didn't drop her eyes to the bowl quite quickly enough to hide a quiver of shock. Then she cracked the egg with a snap.

"Why did you want Jack Hume to see that picture?"

She picked up a whisk, gently whipped the eggs. Her face was set and hard and utterly determined.

My tone was sharp. "Did you guess that Ryan was his son and want to cause trouble for him and Gwen Dunham?"

She placed the beater beside the bowl, turned to one side to pour flour into a sifter.

I moved to stay within her vision whether she acknowledged me or not. "Apparently your daughter made a spectacle of herself, chasing after Jack."

Margo combined dry ingredients with the flour in a smaller bowl.

"Were you angry because he charmed your daughter, then dropped her? Did it remind you of what happened to you?"

She added the dry ingredients to the larger mixing bowl.

"If you decline to offer information, the book may contain material from others that you won't find pleasing."

She paused and looked at me, her gaze level and challenging. "Have you ever heard of invasion of privacy? Now, if you don't mind, I have work to do."

CHAPTER ELEVEN

Hidden from view behind crape myrtles with lavender blooms, I swirled into the elegant blouse and slacks I'd worn when I spoke with Gwen Dunham. Although I expected she'd be too upset to notice, the contrast between Francie the Frump and Bailey Ruth, aka Francie with a shopper's paradise at her disposal, might be disconcerting. I decided Francie's future wardrobe would be subdued, not dowdy. Subdued can be stylish. Besides, nice clothes made me feel like doing a cartwheel. The lush green grass around the gazebo looked thick and inviting.

Cartwheels could wait. As I climbed the gazebo steps, I remembered long-ago summers and a skinny redheaded girl in the twilight, listening to the cicadas and crickets, whirling from one end of a dusty brown lawn to the other with no thought beyond that moment. It was as if those magical days would last forever.

The air pulsed with heat, and I welcomed the shade of the gazebo. I sat in a comfortable wicker chair and watched the opening in a tall green hedge of Nellie Stevens holly trees that marked the boundary between The Castle and the Dunham property.

Gwen Dunham came slowly along the flagstone path, walking as if she carried a heavy burden. At the gazebo steps, she stopped for a deep breath, then slowly climbed. Her face was shaded by a wide-brimmed crocheted raffia hat with a blue camo-ribbon trim that matched her blouse. Dark glasses masked her eyes. Her patrician features might have been chipped from granite.

She walked across the plank flooring and stood a few feet away from me, her arms folded. "How did you find out about Ryan?" Her tone was anguished. "What do you want?"

I came to my feet and said gently, "I don't intend to cause trouble." Unless, and this was the qualification in my mind and heart, she had ended a man's life to protect herself and her family.

"I don't believe you." Her voice shook. "Why else did you call and say you knew about Ryan and you'd be back in touch and hang up?"

I looked at her gravely. "I didn't call you. Nor did Kay. Was the caller a woman?"

"The voice was just a whisper. It could have been a man. The call came from The Castle. Just a few minutes ago." If she'd looked desperate before, now she was frantic. "Who else knows?"

"The person who took Ryan's photograph knows." But Margo wasn't the only possibility.

Gwen's hands gripped each other, twisting and turning. "Where's the picture now? Where's Ryan's brush?"

"I don't know who has the picture. The hairbrush is in a safe place, where it will stay until it is discarded."

"Why are you doing this? Do you want money? I'll buy the hairbrush from you." She talked fast, the words running over each other. "How much do you want? I'll pay you. I'll get the money today."

"I don't want money. Moreover, I don't have the hairbrush. Unless circumstances change"—if I didn't have to tell Kay and Kay didn't give the information to the police—"we won't reveal anything to anyone." Paul Fisher had apparently decided against pursuing the truth about the young man who was a mirror image of Jack Hume when he was Paul's quarterback. Perhaps Paul felt that Jack's quest was understandable when he was alive, but revelations after his death would cause heartbreak for no good purpose.

"If you don't want money, what do you want?" Gwen's voice was harsh.

"Kay and I want to understand what happened in the last few days of Jack Hume's life. Kay has no intention of including everything she learns about Jack's last days in her book, but she is a careful investigator. If she felt there was good reason to exclude some information, I'm certain she will."

"Good reason?" Her voice shook. "Is my son's trust in me and his dad a good reason? Is leaving a happy family alone a good reason?" She flung out a hand. "Don't you see, it was so long ago and only one night and it shouldn't matter now. Jack came home for James's wedding. I was Diane's maid of honor. There were parties and dances and one wonderful night on the balcony of The Castle." She lifted a hand to clutch at a rose-quartz necklace. "He was handsome and we talked and he held me in his arms. I've never felt that way about anyone else. It was a kind of madness. That night we went to the Hume cabin on the lake. My parents thought I'd stayed at The Castle. The next morning he asked me to come to Africa with him. Just fly away and leave Adelaide behind. I wanted to go with him." Her voice wobbled. "I couldn't do that to Clint. He had a summer job in Houston. He was coming home in three weeks for our wedding. I couldn't treat Clint that way. I love Clint. He's good and kind and he adores me. He came home and we married. I didn't know I was pregnant. When I found out, I thought everything would be all right. I thought the baby was Clint's." Her tone was defiant. "When Ryan was little, I suppose I knew then, but I pushed away the thought. That night didn't matter. Clint is Ryan's dad. Don't you see? Clint is his dad."

"Weren't you afraid someone would notice Ryan's resemblance to Jack?"

She threw out shaking hands. "Why would anyone think of Jack when they saw Ryan? There was no reason to make that connection. When Jack came back from Africa with an eye patch and a scar on his cheek and white hair, he didn't look anything like he did when he was young."

Someone had remembered the youthful Jack with painful clarity. I was sure that Margo Taylor, bitter over his long-ago dismissal of her, fearful of her daughter's pursuit of him, had entered the Dunham house and taken Ryan's graduation picture. She had pushed the photograph beneath Jack's door. Whatever her motive—revenge, jealousy of Gwen, or a wish to distract him from Shannon—she had unleashed violent emotions, Jack's fury at the son denied to him, Gwen's fear at a revelation she believed might destroy her family, and Shannon's youthful heartbreak at Jack's abrupt lack of interest.

Gwen began to pace. "I wasn't concerned when he came back. There was no reason to do more than say hello to him. Ryan is a counselor at a camp in Missouri this summer. I made it a point to have Diane to my house, rather than dropping in to see her at The Castle. That last week, Diane came over several times. She was terribly upset because Jack accused Laverne and Ronald of fraud. Poor little Diane." Gwen's face softened. "She's kind and good and generous, but she's credulous. She's sure she is actually hearing from James and that makes her happy. Jack should have left her alone. It may be a fool's paradise, but what harm was there?"

"Possibly he didn't want Laverne and Ronald to fleece Diane. Possibly he felt delving into the occult was irreligious."

"The Humes have more money than they can ever use. As for the occult"—she made a dismissive gesture—"actually it wasn't, because it was all fake."

Gwen's reasoning was faulty, but this wasn't a moment to pursue theology.

"Anyway"—she was sympathetic—"hearing from James makes Diane happy. Destroying her connection to James would be cruel. Of course, Jack knew they were taking advantage of her. He'd made up his mind to get rid of them. When he told Diane, she cried until she was sick. I don't know what would have happened if he'd lived. He was"—her voice was ragged—"frightening when he was angry. He came to my house Friday morning. He forced his way inside. He had Ryan's picture. He said someone pushed it under his door. He showed me a note with Ryan's name and birth date. Thank God Clint was at his office. Jack found the wall of our pictures. He looked at them and saw the empty place and then he turned on me. He asked me how I could I have done this to him, how I could have cheated him of his son. But when I knew, what was I supposed to do? I'd heard Jack was getting married. Clint was my husband. Jack yelled at me. He stormed up the stairs and found Ryan's room—"

She was suffering, but Jack had suffered, too. Long ago his little daughter died, and at that moment in the Dunham house, he saw a room filled with mementos of a child's life he hadn't shared.

"—and took Ryan's hairbrush. I tried to get the brush away from him and he pushed me away, said he'd have the brush, no matter what." She slumped against a pillar, her fingers once again clasping the hard stones of her necklace. "I begged him. He said he had to know Ryan. He said he would give me a week to tell Clint and Ryan. If I didn't, he would find Ryan himself and by that time he would have proof that he was his father."

The DNA from Ryan's hairbrush would have provided all the proof Jack would ever have needed.

"What did you tell Clint?"

She pushed away from the pillar, stood stiff and still. "I didn't tell him. He doesn't know anything." But her eyes glittered with fear.

"You met Jack at the gazebo Friday night."

If possible, she looked even more terrified. She scarcely managed to speak. "How did you know?"

"You were seen."

She hunched her shoulders.

"Does your husband know you quarreled with Jack at the gazebo?" I watched her carefully.

"Of course not. I waited until Clint was asleep. I slipped downstairs and called Jack, told him I had to talk to him. I hoped he might remember how we'd felt and be kind. He came to the gazebo, but he started in again about telling Ryan. I begged him to leave us alone. He wouldn't listen. Then Diane's dog barked. I was afraid—" She broke off.

"Afraid?"

"I thought I'd heard someone near, a rustle in the bushes. I didn't want anyone to see me there."

Had she feared her husband had awakened and followed her?

"Anyway, there was no use. Jack had made up his mind. I ran home. I wish I could run away now." She looked despairing. "But it's no use, is it? You know about Ryan. Someone saw Jack and me in the gazebo. How many people know?"

She felt surrounded by nameless, faceless enemies. I wished I could reassure her. There was perhaps one positive note I could add. "I don't believe the person who saw you in the gazebo knows about Ryan."

Some of the tension eased from her body. Her face was taut in thought. Then she gave a short, knowing murmur. "Shannon must have followed him." Her smile was mirthless. "Dazed by his magic. I suppose she thought . . . well, it doesn't matter what she thought. You think she doesn't know about Ryan?"

"I'm sure."

"So there's you and Kay and the person who called and whoever has Ryan's brush. Oh, I suppose Kay has the brush. It was probably in Jack's things. That's how you found out." She held out her hands in a plea. "If it's you and Kay, then I beg you. Please don't be cruel. There's no reason to bring up all of this. It was long ago, one crazy night in all of Jack's nights. Don't let that one moment ruin my life and Ryan's and Clint's. Please."

"Jack said he'd give you a week. What were you going to do?"

Her face once again was a hard, resentful mask. "What difference does it make now? Jack is dead. Ryan will never know. Don't destroy my life. You can write your book about Jack, but don't rake up something from the past that will do nothing but break our hearts."

"I can promise that your family won't be included in the book." Since the book would never be written, I felt comfortable reassuring Gwen.

For the first time since she'd reached the gazebo, there was a hint of hope in her strained face. "Ryan won't find out?"

I wondered if it had ever occurred to her that her son had a right to know the identity of his birth father. From the happiness and warmth obvious in the family photographs in their den, it seemed unlikely that Ryan would ever consider anyone other than Clint to be his dad.

"He won't be told anything by Kay or by me."

Her voice was thin. "I hope you mean what you say."

"Let us know if you get another call about Ryan. Don't pay blackmail. Let us help."

"Ryan mustn't know. I'll do anything to keep Clint from finding out." She could not have made her decision clearer. If she had to pay blackmail, she would. "If only Jack hadn't come home." She whirled and ran down the steps and walked swiftly toward home.

I opened the door and stepped into Kay's room.

She sat at the desk with a pen and pad. She put down the pen and looked up. "If I could swoop through the air unseen, it would be my choice of transport."

I waved a dismissive hand. "That's old hat. I enjoy being." I glimpsed my silk georgette blouse in the mirror. It was truly lovely. "And I'm parched."

"Mine but to serve," Kay murmured, but she popped up and moved to the wet bar.

"Club soda, please." I settled in a comfortable easy chair by the coffee table.

The club soda fizzed as Kay poured it into a tall tumbler filled with ice. She selected a Coke from the refrigerator for herself. She turned from the wet bar and carried the glasses to a clear glass coffee table, then brought a bowl of cashews.

"Thank you." I reached for the glass. Plain club soda was always my drink of choice, bright, fresh, and not a trace of sweet. I selected five cashews, ate them slowly, felt a pop of energy. I pushed a cushion behind my back and stretched to admire my sandals. Perhaps they'd be even prettier with a green trim. Oh, yes. I nodded approval.

Kay retrieved her notebook and pen and sat in a webbed leather chair on the other side of the table. A shaft of late-afternoon sunlight through the west windows of Jack's sitting room revealed the fine lines that feathered from her eyes and lips, reflecting a life filled with humor and thought and adventure and empathy.

I spoke rapidly. "I talked to Diane, Jimmy, Shannon, Margo, and Gwen. Diane thinks Jack was murdered . . ." And I concluded, " . . . Someone is trying to blackmail Gwen."

Kay looked up from her notebook as I finished. "How's this for a summary? Diane's terrified that Jimmy pushed Jack. Jimmy admitted he intended to confront Jack, but claimed he found the balcony empty. Shannon heard Gwen Dunham say she wished Jack was dead. Margo refused to answer any questions and you believe she pushed Ryan's picture beneath Jack's door." Kay's expression softened. "And there's Gwen Dunham. Poor woman."

Kay's gaze swung toward the windows to look at the hedge between The Castle and the Dunham house. "I have two sons." The sentence was filled with understanding and compassion. "I wouldn't trade my years watching Kyle and Connor grow up for anything in the world." She tapped her pen on the notebook. "Gwen Dunham had the most to lose."

"The dog barked."

Kay looked bewildered.

I was following my own line of thought. "Gwen Dunham was not the only person who was threatened by revelations about Ryan. Friday night, Shannon followed Jack to the gazebo, where he met Gwen. Shannon tried to get near enough to hear, but Diane's cocker started barking. Gwen said she slipped from the house, leaving her husband asleep. Was he asleep? Did he follow her? Did the cocker bark at him or at Shannon? How upset would Clint Dunham be if he thought the son he loved would learn Clint wasn't his father? Clint had a motive for murder. Or was someone else out there? Ronald Phillips has a talent for slipping around unseen. He may be planning to blackmail Gwen."

"There are too many possibilities." Kay sounded discouraged. "How can we figure out who is guilty?"

"Which one was capable of murder? Was Paul helpful?"

Kay looked at me unhappily. "I feel like I took advantage of him. These people are his friends. He thinks I wanted his perspective so that I could more effectively interview them."

"Jack was Paul's quarterback."

Some of the tension eased from her face. "Thank you." Her glance said more than her words. Paul's admiration and respect mattered hugely to her. Someday, if Kay revealed the truth about Jack's death, Paul would understand.

"I believe Paul's view of them is as honest a picture as we will find. So"—she was brisk—"Gwen seems an unlikely suspect. He describes her as gentle, self-effacing, unwilling to cause controversy. She loves Adelaide. Clint had a chance some years ago to go with Travelers Insurance in Dallas. Gwen didn't want to leave Adelaide."

I looked back over years, considering how Gwen had dealt with a once-in-a-lifetime chance for love. "Jack wanted her to come to Africa. She wouldn't—or couldn't—break out of the mold of her life. Keeping the status quo mattered more to her than passion. If she clung to a kind of life that had barely begun, what would she do if something occurred which threatened to destroy her long-established, secure world?"

"Gwen hated him that night in the gazebo." Kay's eyes narrowed. "Shannon heard her: 'I wish you were dead.'"

I cautioned, "We have no proof of what Gwen said. Shannon may have lied."

"Why?" Kay sipped the soft drink.

"You are forgetting one small matter."

Kay raised a questioning eyebrow.

"The vase."

"Oh. Of course. The murderer is quite sure questions from you or me have nothing to do with a book and will take every opportunity to direct suspicion elsewhere. That means the response of one of them has to be filtered through the possibility of guilt. Clever of you." She gave me an admiring glance. "You aren't as ditzy as you look."

Every time Kay and I seemed to be forging a bond, she said something tactless. I suppose pique was evident in my expression. I stiffened. Had I heard a faint chuckle? I looked around the room. If Wiggins was here, he remained, of course, unseen.

He whirled into being behind Kay, visible only to me, chestnut hair burnished in a stream of sunlight from the window, broad genial face equable, mustache quivering in amusement. He gave me a thumbs-up, pointed into the distance, and disappeared.

I was swept by elation. Despite my continued appearances, Wiggins had clearly awarded me the Department of Good Intentions Seal of Approval. If Wiggins didn't have a seal, I'd be happy to help design one. Perhaps a dear sea lion perched astride bright red (of course) letters trumpeting: YES! For an instant, tears of joy filmed my eyes.

"Don't cry." Kay was obviously distressed. "I didn't intend to be disparaging, but, frankly, you are so young and pretty, it's hard to take you seriously." She clapped a hand over her lips, looked appalled. "Did I say that? How many times was I treated like that when I was your age!" She shook her head in bewilderment. "Of course you aren't that age, even if you look it. How confusing is that?"

My, a seal of approval from Wiggins and a compliment and an apology from Kay. I felt like giving another Rebel yell, but settled for a pleased smile. "'No offense meant, none taken.'"

Her laughter was genuine and appreciative. "Anyway, you've done excellent work." She bit her lip, flashed me an impish glance.

"For a pretty young woman. Okay." Her smile fled. "If Shannon pushed Jack, she'd try to steer suspicion to someone else. Do you suppose she knew about Ryan?"

I drank the fizzy club soda, slowly shook my head. "She'd have told me, especially if she was trying to implicate Gwen."

Kay stirred the ice in her Coke. "Paul was circumspect when I asked about Shannon. She'd been a client. I asked the circumstances. He said the matter had been settled and he wasn't at liberty to discuss it. When I got back, I checked with Evelyn. She was more forthcoming. When Shannon was fourteen she rammed her bicycle into a teenage boy who was throwing rocks at a cat. She knocked him down and he ended up with a broken nose and five stitches in his chin. His parents sued. Jimmy got his dad involved. The suit was settled. Evelyn didn't know whether James had provided money, but she thought so."

It was my turn to murmur "oh." "Hotheaded. Impulsive. Lacks control."

Kay glanced at the notebook. "Shannon's not the only one with a temper. Paul said Evelyn is quick to anger, slow to forgive. The Castle matters more to her than people. She takes enormous pride in the art collection. Although she dutifully responds to charitable requests, her gifts are respectable, but not overly generous. She never hesitates to spend several hundred thousand for a painting or sculpture that she wants."

I was puzzled. "How can art matter that much to her when she has such poor vision?"

Kay shrugged. "Pride of possession? Perhaps having Alison describe a work and knowing that the painting hangs at The Castle is enough. Maybe the art collection gives meaning to her life. Paul said Evelyn was resentful, angry that she'd never met anyone to love, that she'd spent her time caring for her father without any support from her brothers."

Kay glanced again at her notes. "As for Diane, Paul said she's timid, easily flustered, affectionate, and vulnerable. Paul thought it was a shame Jack hadn't dislodged Laverne and Ronald. He said"—Kay's eyes met mine—"that Diane would fight to the death to keep them at The Castle."

I remembered Diane's pitiful "I'd rather die" when she spoke of losing Laverne. "When a weak person is backed into a corner, the response can be vicious."

Kay said briskly, "'Dangerous if threatened' sums up Diane. Jack had no intention of easing up on the Phillipses."

"Wouldn't Diane wait until she was certain he could prevail?" I had no doubt Diane was desperate to keep Laverne near, but I thought the threat would have to be certain before she would act. "Is she decisive enough for preemptive action?"

Kay was thoughtful. "For all we know, Jack may have spoken to Diane Saturday evening. I think she would have to be absolutely desperate to commit murder."

"Paul's take on Jimmy?"

Kay's face softened. "Jimmy reminds me of Jack when he was young. Paul feels the same way. Although"—her tone was suddenly dry—"unlike Jack, Jimmy's been a one-woman man since he and Shannon went on a Halloween hayride in middle school. Shannon is volatile and known to flirt. In fact, she dated another guy last summer." She paused. "Jimmy slouched around looking morose. That's when he took up hang gliding."

I quoted Coleridge: "'And constancy lives in realms above; And life is thorny; and youth is vain; And to be wroth with one we love, Doth work like madness in the brain.'"

"The old boy had that one right." Kay's words were flippant, but her eyes were somber with understanding. "Yet, when you talked to Jimmy, nothing he said suggested an effort to implicate anyone else."

"Unless"—I felt sad making the suggestion—"he was artfully making clear the extent of Shannon's unhappiness with Jack. In fact, he may be a wily murderer and still very angry with Shannon. What did Paul say about Margo?"

"Beaten down. She grew up in Adelaide in modest circumstances. She was nineteen when Jack came back for James's wedding. Jack gave her a big rush and then he met Gwen. He dropped Margo. Later, she married a rodeo cowboy, Rollie Taylor. Shannon was born the next year. Margo followed Rollie on the circuit for a half-dozen years, but he ran around on her. They had a bitter divorce and she got a pretty good settlement. He was a big prizewinner. A few years ago, he was paralyzed when he was thrown from a bull. He needed money. She told him nothing doing. After the divorce, she worked part-time, went back to school, and got her degree. She was a flight attendant for American for a half-dozen years till all the layoffs. She came back to Adelaide because her mother, Phyllis, had Alzheimer's. Phyllis had been the housekeeper at The Castle for fifteen years. Evelyn and James were happy to have Margo take over her mother's job and that made it possible for Phyllis to stay here until she died last year."

Kay drew a string of question marks across the top of her pad. "Margo must have been furious when Jack came home and spent time with Shannon."

I nodded. "She was angry enough to slip Ryan Dunham's photograph under Jack's door. My guess is that after you came, she took the photograph from his box."

Kay was puzzled. "Why not leave the picture there?"

I had an idea. I hoped I wasn't right. "Did Paul appraise Margo's character?"

Kay shot me an irritated look. "Do you take special pleasure in non sequiturs?"

Possibly my swiftness of thought wasn't appreciated. I resisted the temptation to quote Damon Runyon: "The race is not always to the swift, nor the battle to the strong, but that's the way to bet." However, I felt Kay's patience had reached its limit. "Someone called Gwen, clearly to set her up for blackmail. The caller may have been Margo."

"Would Margo commit blackmail?" Kay shrugged. "I don't think she'd try to get money. That might not be the point. Maybe she wants to turn the screw a little tighter on Gwen." She wrote on her notepad. "Paul was fair, but he has a negative view of Margo. He's mostly positive about Alison Gregory. He's grateful for Alison's kindness to his wife and he admires Alison's success, but he said she blocked the establishment of a competing gallery by a friend of his. Alison persuaded the financial backers to pull out. Paul shook his head, said she might have been smarter to welcome a new gallery, the-more-the-merrier philosophy of the big chains when they build across the street from each other. Paul said he understood Alison's dependence upon Evelyn Hume as a primary customer, but her cultivation of Evelyn sometimes seemed excessive."

I didn't find Alison's focus on Evelyn surprising. Possibly not completely admirable, but definitely not surprising. "If we checked the provenance of artworks purchased by Evelyn, I imagine many of them were provided by Alison."

Kay looked indifferent. "Jack had a list. We can probably check and see, but I don't think it would tell us anything. Anyway, Alison is smart, aggressive, and plenty tough beneath the charm. Although I don't find her all that charming."

I laughed. "Of course you don't. You've never fawned over anyone in your life."

"Thanks."

I was glad that she cared what I thought of her. That was definitely a step forward.

"However, speaking of fawning—"

Two minds that worked as one. I nodded. "Laverne and Ronald Phillips."

"Scum. That's how Paul sees them." Her face furrowed. "Diane's their golden goose."

"There's a séance tonight?" I spoke with distaste.

"Every Wednesday at eight in the library. Diane told me all about it. Breathlessly. I've heard what James says and how happy he is to be with her." Kay shook her head. "Poor Diane. She's easy pickings for the Phillipses."

"Who attends?"

"Diane and Laverne. As you would imagine, Jimmy thinks it's all nuts and Evelyn has no patience with the supernatural." Kay abruptly looked gleeful. "It would be a hoot to introduce you to Evelyn as my ghost-in-chief. She's so arrogantly in command. I'd like to see her in a situation she couldn't control. Come on, Bailey Ruth, how about it?"

I was appalled. "Precepts One, Three, Four, Five, Six, and Seven. I would be drummed out of the department."

"Okay, okay. No need to get hot and bothered." Her eyes crinkled as she smiled. "Why do you ask? Do you want to attend? No problem. Disappear and go." Once again, her eyes held a wicked gleam. "Hey, you could add a spot if excitement. You—" She broke off. "Have I said something unacceptable? You don't look amused."

"Remember"—I knew I sounded uncommonly serious— "those who are alive must not seek to contact those who are dead. That way lies evil. If Heaven, as in your case, sends a spirit to you, that is for good."

Kay reached out, patted my arm. "I got it. Not a two-way street. I'm sorry. Your fur is definitely ruffled. I apologize. We'll ignore any and all séances."

That was my definite intent. "Diane is too transparent to be discreet. We can easily find out what happens tonight. I'm sure Ronald Phillips has some mischief in mind. He said, 'The Great Spirit's going to put on a good show.' He told Laverne he had a few more things to find out, then he asked if this was Diane's afternoon with James. What did he mean?"

"James died at four o'clock on a Wednesday. Every week at that time, Diane takes fresh flowers to the cemetery."

"Ronald told Laverne to meet Diane there."

Kay's gaze narrowed. "You make that sound sinister."

"I think it is." I glanced at the clock. It was five minutes to four. I started to disappear, stopped.

Kay's eyes widened. "Don't be half here. That's too spooky for words."

I swirled back. "I'm off to the cemetery. I may be able to find out what Ronald is planning. While I'm gone, lock your door"—I pointed toward the hall door—"and stay put until I return."

"You may be ghost-in-chief." Her voice had its familiar acerbic tone. "You are not nanny-in-chief."

I looked at her sternly. "It may seem far in the past, but less than twenty-four hours ago you escaped death because I pushed you to safety."

"So I'm appreciative." Kay was impatient. "Take my thanks as a given. I'm also not stupid. I'll be careful. I've been thinking about Alison Gregory. It still doesn't ring true to me that Jack talked to her about Evelyn. So, if that wasn't the subject, what was? I'll drop by the gallery, tell her I found some enigmatic notes about her and that guy out at the college." She looked at me inquiringly.

I shook my head. "Your plan is good. Your timing is not. Tomorrow I'll go with you."

"What do I do in the meantime?"

I gave her an encouraging smile. "Cultivate patience. As Charlie Chan advised, 'Anxious man hurries too fast—often stubs big toe.'"

"He also said"—Kay's eyes glinted—"'Hours are happiest when hands are busiest.'"

"Very true."

Her eyes lighted.

I shook my head. There would be no wanderer's blessing from me. "You're extremely smart, Kay." Praise worked wonders when I taught English and generous comments smoothed my path in the mayor's office. "You've found out everything possible about Jack's last few days. Going back to the well won't accomplish anything. Instead, put that fertile brain of yours to work. We have a logjam of facts. Figure out where to poke in a stick of dynamite and change the landscape."

"In other words"—her drawl was dangerously pleasant—"I'm confined to quarters?"

"Here in a locked room you are one hundred percent safe."

"Maybe I should ask that grizzled police chief to lock me up." Her eyes widened. "Get that considering look off your freckled face."

I folded my arms across my chest. "If you don't stay, I don't go."

"Oh, for Pete's sake. You are a pain."

"You are recalcitrant." I had a happy memory. I lifted my right hand. "I, Kay Clark, do hereby solemnly promise . . ."

She made a rude gesture, then raised her arms in surrender.

CHAPTER TWELVE

I loved the cemetery that adjoins St. Mildred's. Rustling leaves of cottonwoods, elms, and oaks shaded old granite tombstones and newer bronze markers from the blistering summer sun. A light breeze stirred the fronds of a willow near our family plot. I smiled at the memorial column that Rob and Dil, our children, had placed there in our memory.

I took a moment, as had been my custom in years past, to visit the marble mausoleum of the Pritchards, one of Adelaide's leading families. My Christmas visit as an emissary had been to aid Susan Pritchard Flynn's young grandson. Inside, I stroked the marble greyhound at the head of Maurice Pritchard's tomb and slid my hand over the head of the elegant Abyssinian on his wife Hannah's tomb. That homage, according to Adelaide legend, always led to good luck. With the spirits of a stalwart dog and a wise cat on one's side, good fortune seemed assured.

I felt in need of a hearty dose of luck as I skimmed below the trees, seeking Diane. I understood Kay's impatience to be out and about. She and I had discovered a great deal about Jack Hume's final days, but we were leagues away from knowing whose hand had pushed Jack to his death.

I curved around crape myrtle. Inside a wrought-iron fenced area lay the Hume graves. Diane knelt next to a grassy mound. The granite stone read: JAMES JEFFREY HUME, BELOVED HUSBAND AND FATHER, APRIL 22, 1953–JANUARY 9, 2004, WHITHER THOU GOEST, I WILL GO.

In a metal vase, Diane arranged a mass of rainbow-colored plumeria and lavender daylilies. " . . . counting on you, James. I'm frightened for Jimmy. Everyone knows he was angry with Jack. So was I." Tears trickled down her face. She lifted a hand and brushed the soft, worn gardening glove against her cheek. "I couldn't go on if I didn't feel you were near. Every time Laverne brings you home again, it's as if you are in the next room and I can walk in there and find you. And you've shared so many wonderful memories. Last time, you remembered my gardenia wrist corsage at the wedding and even described your grandmother's beautiful lily-of-the-valley handkerchief that I carried. Oh, James, our wonderful, glorious, beautiful night. I miss you so much." Her delicate face, despite age and wrinkles and sorrow, reflected abiding love.

I felt a swift surge of anger. Ronald Phillips had done his research well. How easy to find the newspaper account of Diane and James's wedding and pick out the details of the bride's ensemble. Had his lips curled in a cold, satisfied smile?

A shoe scraped on the bricked path that curved around a cottonwood.

Diane looked over her shoulder. "Laverne!" Her voice echoed surprise.

Laverne Phillips approached in jerky, reluctant steps. Tight coronet braids emphasized her sharp features. Her all-black at-tire, fringed blouse, billowy slacks, low-heeled patent pumps, gave her an aura of doom. "Diane." Laverne hesitated, then blurted, "I need to talk to you about tonight."

Diane pushed up from the ground, her eyes flaring in concern. "Is something wrong? You aren't leaving, are you? I must talk to James. I must."

Laverne stopped at the foot of James's grave. Her gaze was glassy. "I'm not leaving. But"—a long, thin hand reached up to press against one temple—"I've been struggling all day. My head hurts so bad." She squeezed shut her eyes. "I can't get away." There was an underlying thread of hysteria in her voice, and a haunting note of truth.

Laverne was in the cemetery unwillingly, but she was there. Ronald had insisted. I didn't doubt she had her lines prepared, but the pain in her eyes and the slackness of her face indicated misery.

"What is it?" Diane's voice was faint.

"James." Laverne shifted her stance. She looked away and down, telltale signs that she was now lying. "I keep having im-ages." She lifted both hands, pressed her fingers against her tem-ples. "James is upset."

Diane gave a low cry, one hand spread against her chest.

Diane was desperately afraid. Was she afraid for Jimmy? Or for herself?

"I get flashes, pictures. They aren't clear to me." Laverne's gaze fixed on the broken stump of cedar, split by age. "It's night. I see a figure on the balcony. The scene shifts. I didn't see Jack's body at the base of the steps, but now I see him. He's lying there, dead."

"Jack?" Diane's voice quivered.

"James's voice is in my head, over and over again." Laverne wrapped her arms across her chest. "Every time the message is the same: 'Bring them back. Bring them back. Bring them back.'"

Diane stepped toward her, imploring, "Bring who back?"

Laverne shuddered. "I have to get him out of my mind. I see James and then the faces come, over and over again, you and Jimmy, Evelyn, me, Ronald, Margo, Shannon, Gwen and Clint Dunham, Alison Gregory. James's words hit at me like the flick of a whip: 'Bring them back, bring them back, bring them back.'" Laverne's voice rose higher and higher as she repeated the phrases. "They must all be at the séance tonight, everyone who was in the house the night Jack died."

"James wants all of us tonight?" Diane looked upset. "I don't think they will come."

"They must." Laverne swung to look fully at Diane. Her sharp features were set and hard, her gaze demanding. "They must." Laverne's desperation was clear. Failure to arrange a gathering of those who had been in The Castle the night Jack died would be unacceptable to Ronald. Laverne reached out a bony hand. "Tonight they must be in the library at eight o'clock or I can't answer for the consequences." Head down, she turned to walk away.

Diane ran after her, gripped her arm. "What will happen if they won't come?"

Laverne hunched her shoulders, dipped her head. "James has spoken. If his cry isn't answered, we may never hear his voice again."

Evelyn looked up from the rosewood desk in her bedroom, her imperious face registering irritation. She gave Diane a short nod. "I trust you have good reason to interrupt me?"

Diane bolted across the room. Wind-ruffled hair framed her face. Her small mouth worked, the lips trembling. "Evelyn, please."

Evelyn laid down her pen, aligning it precisely near a magnifying glass next to a large-print art catalog. "Are you ill?"

"You laugh at me." Diane's voice shook. "You don't believe James comes. But he does." She clasped her hands and they twisted and turned. "Tonight he wants everyone to be in the library, everyone who was in the house the night Jack died. Please. Come to the library at eight. I beg you."

"Try for a modicum of control, Diane." Behind the thick lenses, Evelyn's milky eyes stared fuzzily at the convulsed face of her sister-in-law. "What brings about this hysterical plea?"

Tears trickled down Diane's cheeks. "Laverne doesn't know what's wrong, but James is very upset. James has sent her messages. He's very clear." Her voice was earnest. "Everyone who was at The Castle that night must come."

Evelyn's gaunt face was impassive. "Laverne has heard from James? That's very interesting." Those milky eyes narrowed in thought.

Evelyn was unlikely to be persuaded that James's spirit desired this gathering. I watched her with growing interest. If she were not concerned about revelations that might be forthcoming from so-called spirits, she would dismiss Diane's passionate request. I recalled her cool comment about her sister-in-law welcoming charlatans, as Evelyn described them: . . . *fools deserve to reap what they sow.*

Diane's face flushed. "You don't believe me. But James told Laverne someone was on the balcony with Jack when he fell."

Evelyn sat utterly still. "Who?"

Diane shivered. "I don't know. I'm afraid that's why James is upset."

"Indeed. However, one might expect that Jack would be the proper spirit to consult."

"Don't make fun of me." Diane's voice shook. "We may find out tonight."

"Laverne's claims are interesting." Evelyn's tone was thoughtful. "Very well, Diane. I am not a believer in the occult. However"—there was the slightest dryness in her voice—"I would hate to disappoint James."

I remained a moment after Diane's departure to study the self-possessed woman seated at the elegant desk. She appeared to be deep in thought, the art catalog no longer of interest. Was her willingness to attend the séance dictated by fear or curiosity?

Her features were somber. "Laverne. What a second-rate, cheap, lying fake." She spoke with distaste. "Diane is a fool. I wonder what kind of trouble Laverne plans to cause?"

I assumed talking aloud to herself was a habit of long standing. Perhaps Evelyn believed herself to be the only intelligent conversationalist in The Castle.

"Someone else on the balcony . . ." Her dark brows drew down into a frown. "I'd better go."

Jimmy turned and looked up from a paperback of *The Amber Room* by Steve Berry. I admired the striking bright red (nice color) cover.

Diane began without preamble. "Jimmy, I never ask you to do things for me. But I want you to promise you will do as I ask."

He looked up at his mother with a mixture of affection and wariness. "What's up, Mom?"

She bent forward, stretched out a shaking hand. "Please. Promise me."

He frowned, his good-humored face puzzled. "Promise you what?"

"I need—your father needs—"

His face tightened.

"—for you to come to the library tonight."

He pushed to his feet. "Mom, I can't stand that stuff. If it makes you feel better to hear that woman mutter in the dark, I guess it's okay. But I don't want to listen to her act like Dad's speaking. It makes me sick."

"Jimmy, please, just this once. Your daddy's upset about Jack." Diane's words tumbled out; her eyes were bright and glittering. "It's all about Jack. Not your dad. Maybe we'll hear Jack tonight. Somebody was on the balcony with him."

Jimmy stared at his mother, his face taut. "Who said so?"

"Your daddy told Laverne. Everybody who was in the house the night Jack died has to come. Please, Jimmy."

"Laverne." Jimmy looked tough, pugnacious, and worried. "Yeah. I get it. Mom—" He broke off, shook his head. "I'll be there." His voice was grim.

The long, flagstoned dining room befitted a castle: arched ceiling, gleaming oak walls, slotted stained-glass windows, heraldic flags and shields, and a massive mahogany table. Shannon set crystal wineglasses at each place. She had changed from a tank top and shorts to a pale blue blouse and navy slacks.

Diane's shoes clipped on the stone floor as she burst through the archway. "Shannon, is your mother in the kitchen?"

Shannon looked surprised. "Yes. May I get her for you?"

Diane, fluttery and frantic, interrupted. "I need to talk to you both. Now. Please come with me. I have to hurry." She whirled and moved swiftly to the serving door and held it open, her body tense, her posture shouting her impatience.

In the kitchen, Margo stood at a counter, studying a recipe in a cookbook resting on a stand. An acrylic cover protected the pages from spatters. She looked absorbed, her at times discontented face relaxed and happy. Measuring spoons and cups and a mixing bowl sat to one side.

Diane rushed across the kitchen to the counter. "Margo, I need for you and Shannon to come to the library at eight."

Shannon slowly followed, her face puzzled. "What's going on?"

Margo frowned. "This is Wednesday. Are you talking about those séances Laverne puts on?"

"Laverne hears things from James." Diane's eyes were huge. "James wants everyone who was in the house the night Jack died to come to the séance."

Shannon's face lost its bloom. She looked both sad and angry. "That's hideous. Jack's gone. Don't make him part of a stupid—"

Margo interrupted her daughter. "Everyone deals with loss in a different way." Her tone, however, was cool and remote, rather than encouraging. "Neither Shannon nor I is interested in trying to contact the dead."

"No one's asking you to do anything but come." Diane's voice shook. "James told Laverne that someone was on the balcony with Jack. I don't know what that means, but we have to be there tonight."

Margo gripped the cookbook stand. The cherrywood base squeaked under the sudden pressure. The sound was loud in a suddenly stiff silence.

Shannon took quick steps and faced Diane. "Someone was on the balcony with Jack?"

"That's nonsense." Margo's voice was harsh. "Laverne doesn't know anything."

Shannon's young voice wobbled. "Maybe she does. Maybe she knows everything. I'll be there."

Diane gave a glad little cry. "You'll come. It's important. Everyone has to be there." Diane looked at Margo.

Margo's face was hard. "Talking to the dead is nonsense. But I don't suppose it will do any harm. We'll come. Now, I've got to see to dinner." She kept her voice even, but her quick glance at her daughter was uncertain and fearful.

Diane shut the library door behind her. Eighteenth-century un-bleached wood bookcases sat against three walls. The pilasters and moldings of the French antique featured rosettes, sprays, and tiny pineapples. Louis XV chairs, their blue and gold paint muted by time, sat at either end of each bookcase, ready for a reader to select a book and sink onto a cushion and thumb through the pages. An unabridged dictionary lay open on a mahogany reading stand near one of four arched windows framed by gold velvet drapes. Natural light speared into the room, illuminating the parquet flooring. The reading stand was adjacent to a Victorian chaise longue upholstered in red velvet. Louis XV chairs were arranged on either side of a long English oak writing table in the center of the room.

The chair nearest the dictionary stand was turned a little, as if the occupant had just arisen and left the room. Horn-rimmed glasses rested next to a legal pad and an ornate silver-and-black Montblanc fountain pen.

Diane pattered to the table, pulled out the next chair, and perched on the edge of the cushion. "James, I'm doing what you asked, but I don't know what will happen tonight. I'm afraid the others are skeptics." She looked unhappy and fearful. "Laverne says you're unhappy. You aren't unhappy with me, are you?"

Old walls and thick windows made the room a cocoon of quiet.

Diane clutched at the Venetian glass beads of a blue-and-white necklace. "Are you sure you want Alison Gregory and the Dun-hams to be here?" Her fingers opened and closed on the beads.

"That's what Laverne said. They were here the night Jack died." Her hopeful face was slightly tilted to one side, as if straining to hear. "Bring them back. That's what you told Laverne. I'll call them, but I don't know if they will come."

Diane plunged her hand into her pocket and pulled out a sleek black cell phone. "I don't like Alison. I don't think she's kind. James, you'll come even if she says no, won't you? Please." She closed her eyes.

The stillness of the room was cavelike, but a cave might hold a spatter from trickling water or the rustle of a bat's wing. The library held only the faint, uneven breathing of a burdened woman.

Diane opened her eyes, nodded twice. "I'll call. I must, mustn't I, James?" She punched numbers.

"Alison, this is Diane Hume. I don't want to bother you, but I'd like to ask a favor since you are such an old friend of the family."

I arrived in Gregory Gallery.

Alison sat behind a burled walnut desk in an office that was absolutely free of clutter. She leaned back comfortably in a green cushioned chair that made her white-blond hair even more striking. The office contained only one painting, a brilliant mélange of colors, arresting, evocative, and faintly disturbing. The expensive surroundings provided a background that emphasized success and power. Alison's smooth face held a trace of impatience, but her voice was friendly. "What can I do for you, Diane?"

As Alison listened, her finely drawn brows drew down. "I don't understand." Her blue eyes narrowed. "Someone was on the balcony with Jack?" Her face was abruptly intent, her expression considering. Jack Hume had fallen from the balcony. Last night a vase had been dislodged from the balcony to crash into the garden. This morning Alison had insisted the vase had been vandalized until she realized Evelyn Hume was determined that its fall be deemed an accident. Alison surely saw a link between the two events.

"What does that have to do with me?" Her tone was puzzled. "My presence at The Castle the night of Jack Hume's death is completely coincidental." She listened. "Eight o'clock? Diane, I fail to see how my presence is necessary." Her face folded into a tight frown. "Oh. Very well. I'll come."

Alison clicked off her cell. She pushed back her chair and rose. Her expression suggested she was thinking and thinking fast.

I wondered if she was remembering chisel marks on the pedestal that held the vase. Or perhaps, she was focused on Jack Hume's visit to her gallery and his grim words about Evelyn: *My sister hates me. If she had the chance, I think she'd shoot me.*

In the Dunham house, Clint was alone in the den. He sat in a brown leather chair, holding an open newspaper. He wasn't reading. He stared at the wall of family photographs. His roundish face sagged in despair.

Quick steps sounded in the hallway.

He lifted the paper.

Gwen stood in the doorway. "Does salmon sound good tonight?"

The paper was lowered. He looked up, his face genial, though his eyes were somber. "Are you sure your headache's gone? I can pick up hamburgers."

Gwen forced a bright smile. "I'm fine now." She didn't meet his gaze.

The phone rang.

Clint picked up the portable phone from the small table next to his chair. He looked at the caller ID. "Diane Hume." He answered. "Hello . . . Hi, Diane." There was no warmth in his voice. "Gwen?" He looked toward his wife.

Gwen walked to him and took the phone. She turned away, walking swiftly toward the hall. "Got a minute, but I'm in the middle of dinner." Gwen hurried down the hallway and pushed through a swinging door into a cheerful kitchen.

I liked the yellow daisies blooming in the wallpaper and a golden cherrywood table in a clean contemporary design.

Gwen stopped short in the middle of the room. If she'd looked pale before, now her face was stark, blank white. "I can't."

Her back was to the swinging door. The panel ever so slowly and carefully eased open a crack.

I flowed through the door. Clint was an odd figure for melodrama in a stylish white-, pink-, and gray-striped poplin shirt, gray cotton twill slacks, wrinkle-free, and highly polished cordovans. He bent forward, every muscle rigid, and listened to his wife's soft, halting voice.

I flowed back into the kitchen.

"Oh, Diane, I simply can't . . . Someone on the balcony with Jack?" Gwen reached out to grip the kitchen counter.

For a moment, I thought she would faint.

The door widened a half inch.

Gwen braced herself against the counter. "I don't understand . . . Laverne Phillips? Oh, that's—" She broke off.

I wondered if Gwen had intended, in a natural, rational response, to insist that Laverne could not possibly have heard from James, that whatever Laverne said was a figment of her own imaginings. Or did Gwen realize in the same, chilling instant that Laverne Phillips might well know something and have learned that fact in a purely worldly way.

Gwen asked sharply, "What exactly did Laverne say?" She closed her eyes briefly, opened them. Her voice was wooden. "I understand, Diane. I don't believe in this kind of thing at all, but if it matters to you that much, I'll come."

The swinging door eased shut.

When Gwen reached the den, Clint was seated, holding the paper.

"Clint."

Once again he lowered the paper. He looked inquiring, but the newspaper rustled until he made his arms rigid.

Gwen tried for a smile. "Darling, the most absurd thing. Diane and that awful woman are having a séance tonight. Poor Diane. They have one every Wednesday night." It was as if she kept talking, her words would fill the emptiness in her husband's face. "Everyone who was at The Castle the night Jack Hume died will be there. It sounds perfectly dreadful. I don't like the idea at all, but I was afraid Diane would be hysterical if I refused. Do you mind terribly"—her hands twisted, belying the studied casualness of her tone—"if we go?"

A muscle worked in his jaw. "Diane's a fool." His voice was gruff. He dropped his eyes, lifted the newspaper to hide his face. His words came from behind the shield. "All right."

Gwen turned away.

When the swinging door to the kitchen soughed shut, Clint crumpled the newspaper in his hands. Fear glittered in his eyes.

Kay sat at the dressing table. She opened a jewel box, selected a necklace of large, diamond-cut blue beads separated by silver oblongs. The blue matched her summery blue chiffon dress with a pattern of silver swirls. She reached back to fasten the necklace. In the mirror, she looked elegant, her feathered-short dark hair flattering to her fine bone structure. "Blackmail." Her voice was crisp. "Ronald thinks he knows something someone will pay him to keep quiet about. I don't get the public venue. Maybe the idea is, here's what we know and more can come out. Maybe he plans to put the touch on several people. The evening will be like a houseware party. Everybody come and look over the goods.

"While confined to quarters this afternoon"—her glance at me in the mirror was chiding—"I had an idea. It's time to add Sturm und Drang. I could call everyone together and announce that Jack was murdered. But Ronald may save me the effort. Now, I need to wangle an invitation to the party." She glanced at her watch. "I'll catch Diane before dinner." At the door, she gave me a brilliant smile. "Fortunately, you don't need an invitation."

I started to speak, but the door closed. I shook my head. Kay might be eager for Sturm und Drang, but I knew what was verboten for me. No séances, thank you. I strolled to a chaise longue and settled comfortably. However, I was uneasy. I wondered if there were a way to warn Ronald Phillips against a risky gamble. Unless, of course, he was the killer and hoping to cast suspicion on others.

I popped to my feet and disappeared.

In the Phillipses' suite, Laverne lay on the bed, a damp washcloth on her face. "I can't do the séance tonight."

Ronald looked up from a leather chair. His blue eyes were cold. "You will do as I say." He looked down at a thick travel brochure with a picture of dark blue water and an elegant cruise ship. "This one visits seven ports. We'll fly to Copenhagen."

I carefully eased open the drawer to a writing desk. I found a pen and cream-colored stationery with the emblem of a castle.

"I'm frightened." Laverne's voice was muffled.

I wrote in block letters:

CANCEL SÉANCE. JACK HUME MURDERED.
DANGER!

He turned a page in the brochure. "You don't have to do anything but be a dandy little parrot tonight. Say your piece and say it right." His tone was threatening. "You won't have to do anything more. I'll take care of everything else."

I scooted the sheet of paper across the floor, going slowly so a flicker of movement wouldn't catch Ronald's eye. I placed the sheet just inside the door, as if it had been slipped beneath the panel.

I flowed into the hall, rapped smartly on the door, returned to their bedroom.

Ronald looked around. His expression was alert with a feral wariness. He flipped the travel brochure to a side table and walked to the door. As he reached for the knob, he saw the sheet of paper. He bent, picked it up. He yanked open the door and looked into the hall.

The hall lay quiet and empty.

Ronald shrugged and closed the door.

Laverne propped up on one elbow. "What was that?"

A swift, exultant smile touched his face. "Oh"—his tone was careless—"just a little confirmation of my theories. Nothing for you to worry about."

I paced back and forth in Kay's room.

The door opened and Kay stalked inside, her expression frustrated. "Diane's always had the backbone of a noodle."

"Not this time?"

Kay dropped onto the small seat at the dressing table. "I was sure I could finesse an invitation. I knocked on her door and smiled prettily and said I hoped we could have a few minutes after dinner, there were some points in my notes that weren't clear. She looked frazzled and said we'd get together tomorrow, but tonight there was the séance. I pretended utter, heartfelt fascination and said in a tremulous voice that I wanted to reach out to Jack. Instead of embracing me as a convert to the Hereafter, she got this stricken look and muttered that the evening was only for those who were here when Jack died. She shut the door in my face. So"—she pointed at me—"you have to do your thing and find out what Ronald knows."

My reply was swift and definite. "Count me out."

She frowned. "Come on, Bailey Ruth. Tonight will be a gold mine of information. We have to find out what happens." She looked exasperated. "Why are you staring at me like I'm Dracula?"

I glanced at my reflection. I admired my black jersey dress with a dramatic white floral print. It was perfect for a summer-evening dinner at The Castle. The vivid black was an excellent choice for a redhead. I smoothed back a shining curl. I wasn't, of course, being prideful. I simply took to heart the charge against hiding a light beneath a bushel. But my normally vivacious (even though I say so myself) expression was gone. In fact, I definitely looked perturbed. "Leviticus 19:31."

Kay blinked in surprise, then shook her head. "I remember. Summoning the occult is a bad, bad idea." She drew out the *a* in the adjective. Her tone was amused. "Chill, dearie. Laverne isn't summoning the occult. She'll be working off hubby's script. And"—she was abruptly serious—"if your spook routine was ever essential, it's tonight. I can't be there, ergo you take the baton."

"I can't attend a séance." I wasn't sure I could make Kay understand. "There will be the trappings of the supernatural. Wiggins wouldn't want me to be part of that." I suddenly felt as though I were bathed in a beatific glow. I looked around.

"Uh-oh." Kay stiffened.

My expression of seeking someone clearly hadn't escaped Kay. She made a little shushing motion with one hand. "Is he back?

Honestly, one of you is enough. Really and truly. But you have to be at the séance tonight." She swung around on the cushion, her eyes darting around the room. "Wiggins." She sounded a little choked at using his name. "Hear me out. We don't believe in sé-ances. Right? None of us here believe in that kind of thing. Al-though—but no, no. I remember. You sent Bailey Ruth. I didn't ask for her to come. Oh, that's for da— That is definitely true. No request came from me. Anyway, I understand the distinction be-tween an authorized emissary and attempts to make a fraudulent connection with the beyond."

I nodded in admiration. Kay put the matter very well indeed.

"However, you know and I know and Bailey Ruth knows that our participation—"

Was there a faintly heard rumble?

Kay continued hurriedly. "Actually, her unwilling presence, very unwilling, would in no way signal approval of the fraud per-petrated by Laverne Phillips upon poor Diane. However, since we are well aware the séance is a fraud, that knowledge surely permits Bailey Ruth to attend. Ronald Phillips intends to blackmail Jack Hume's murderer. Bailey Ruth may gain evidence to avenge Jack. Possibly if we follow those leads, we can prevent Ronald from put-ting himself in grave danger."

I shook my head. "A moment ago, I warned him." I described the note and my knock on the door. "He took the note as a signal that he was right. The séance will proceed."

"Danger." Wiggins's voice was as deep as the lowest timbre of a pipe organ.

Kay's eyes flared wide.

Wiggins boomed. "Danger indeed for the immortal souls of all who traffic in such nonsense."

Kay shot me a panicked glance.

Truly, it mystified me that she had come to terms with me, but still found Wiggins's unseen presence unnerving. "Wiggins." As always I was respectful. "Possibly we should realize that Precept Six—don't scare anybody—outweighs Precept Three—stay out of sight. Of course, it is always your intent, nobly so, to work behind the scenes. However, in this instance I believe we can have more civilized discourse if Kay can see you." He was such a wonderful, reassuring man. In person. A booming voice alone didn't give the proper impression.

"Hmm."

Kay stared toward the sound of his voice, hunched her shoulders.

"Oh, very well." A swirl of colors and Wiggins stood a few feet from us, shining chestnut curls bright above his ruddy face. "Kay Clark, please understand this is not the usual protocol."

Kay lifted a shaky hand to touch her upper lip.

Wiggins's walrus mustache was a thing of beauty. His stiffly starched, high-collared white shirt gleamed. He was true to his period in gray wool trousers—thankfully, the air-conditioning in The Castle made the room quite cool—and suspenders as well as a thick black belt with a silver buckle.

He looked at Kay. "Now, now, my dear." His voice was suddenly gentle. His rubicund face creased in that warm, welcoming smile I had come to love.

The tension eased from Kay's body.

His dark brown eyes glowed with kindness. "The mission of the Department of Good Intentions"—he spoke with quiet pride—"is to combat evil."

Kay's look was imploring. "That's why Bailey Ruth must be at the séance tonight."

Wiggins tugged on one end of his mustache. He stood in thought for a long moment. Finally, he spoke in a considering tone. "The intent behind tonight's gathering is reprehensible in several ways: the spurious offering of contact with the beyond, the deliberate effort to create fear on the part of those present, the nefarious purpose of profiting from evil. However"—his eyes brightened—"I can see that Bailey Ruth's attendance would in no way offer sanction, but may lead to a successful completion of her mission." He folded one large hand into a fist, smacked it into his palm. "Very well. I approve."

Colors swirled and he was gone.

From long-ago charity functions, I remembered the glories of The Castle's drawing room, gold damask curtains, pale-rose-and-blue brocaded furniture, eighteenth-century English mirrors, and above the Adam mantel a portrait of old J. J. Hume, whose broad, pugnacious face beamed down in eternal triumph.

Kay went directly to Evelyn Hume, who was seated in a Louis XV armchair. She appeared regal in a summery blue silk dress and a lustrous pearl necklace. "Evelyn, this is my assistant, Francie de Sales."

Evelyn looked up, but her gaze didn't center squarely on me. "We are pleased that you can stay with us, Francie." Her tone was gracious. "Jack's life was exciting and I'm confident Kay will create a fascinating book. Have you met everyone?"

I smiled. "I've met all of the family."

Kay looked around the room. "Francie hasn't met Laverne and Ronald."

Diane fluttered toward us. "Laverne and Ronald won't be dining with us. Just a light repast in their suite. Laverne said she is under great stress. Because of this evening." She took a deep breath. "Tonight holds special significance. We will be gathering together, everyone who was here the night Jack died."

Evelyn was gruff. "I doubt our guests are overly concerned

with the presence or absence of Laverne and Ronald. Francie can meet them in the morning. Francie, I hope you are enjoying your visit here in Adelaide." She looked past Kay and me. "I believe our dinner is ready. Francie, I'd be pleased to have you sit by me." She rose and gestured for me to accompany her. "Are you aware that the Chickasaw Nation . . . "

CHAPTER THIRTEEN

D rawn velvet curtains blocked any vestige of late-summer sunlight from the library. Golden light from ecru-shaded bronze wall sconces offered soft pools of illumination around the periphery of the room. The twin chandeliers remained dark. Near the oak writing table in the center of the room, Laverne Phillips lay propped against the end of the red velvet chaise longue, one hand draped on the carved back, the other dangling limply over the side. Her face was indistinct in the gloom. No details of her all-black clothing could be distinguished.

I floated above the long oak table, studying the family and guests seated in the Louis XV chairs.

Diane plucked nervously at silver charms on a bracelet and darted worried glances around the table, perhaps fearful that those she'd persuaded to attend would leave, perhaps fearful that James would not appear.

Jimmy's shoulders hunched. He looked young and uncomfortable, as if he held anger barely in check. His occasional glances toward Laverne were filled with loathing.

Evelyn's strong face was untroubled, her hands quietly folded on the table. She had a magisterial dignity. Disdain was evident in the faint downward curl of her mouth.

Shannon sat stiffly, her face somber. Her eyes flickered uneasily toward the somnolent woman on the couch. When Laverne's breathing became labored, Shannon's hands bunched into fists.

No one was seated in the slightly turned chair at the place with horn-rimmed glasses, legal pad, and fountain pen.

Ronald stood by the door, clearly visible in the golden light from a nearby wall sconce. In a cobalt blue shirt with white collar and cuffs and cream slacks, he was at ease, assuming the role of host. With his silver hair and Vandyke beard carefully groomed, he was magazine-model perfect. He glanced at his watch. "It is almost time to begin, even though several of those expected tonight have not yet arrived. Laverne is slipping deeper and deeper into the reverie demanded by the spirits. She shall soon be connected to the beyond." He spoke in the hushed tone affected by television golf commentators.

Diane began to push back her chair. "I'll call them." She was desperate to make certain nothing impeded a connection to James.

He held up a hand. "There must be no sudden movement, no noise. If necessary, we shall start without them."

Diane sank back onto the seat. She looked close to tears. "They said they'd come." It was as if she spoke to someone unseen.

"Quiet." Ronald spoke in an urgent whisper. "Laverne must not be disturbed."

A muffled rap.

Ronald opened the door, held a cautionary finger to his lips.

Alison Gregory's confident entry was in stark contrast to the stiff reluctance of the Dunhams. Margo Taylor followed and Ronald shut the door. Ronald pointed peremptorily toward the empty seats opposite the family. "Take your seats. No talking." He had the air of a funeral-home employee directing mourners.

A low moan issued from Laverne. She rolled from side to side, as if in pain.

Shannon gave a gasp. "What's wrong with her?"

Ronald looked toward the chaise longue. "The spirits are near. Laverne is in their possession. Please remain silent. She loses contact if there is distraction."

Alison gave Ronald a contemptuous glance as she slid into a seat as far from Laverne as possible. She murmured softly, "That would be a shame." Her elegant face looked as if she saw something repugnant.

Gwen and Clint Dunham took the chairs across from Diane and Jimmy. Gwen's lovely face was rigid. She stared straight ahead, her hands tightly clasped. She looked like a woman awaiting doom. Clint's big face had the hurt, bewildered appearance of a wounded animal, suffering and without the power to alleviate the pain.

Margo was the last to be seated. She brushed back a strand of hair, covertly watching her daughter.

Ronald slowly closed the door. He waited a moment, then walked toward the recumbent figure of his wife. His steps were measured, the *thump-thump-thump* loud on the parquet flooring. He stood slightly behind the chaise longue.

Laverne's stertorous breathing sounded loud in the strained silence.

I wondered if Ronald had any sense of the forces he might unleash. Not figures from beyond. They were not at the beck and call of Ronald or Laverne. This dim room seethed with here-and-now emotions of suspicion, fear, anger, hope, despair, and malevolence.

Malevolence.

One of those who watched and waited was as dangerous as a marauding tiger and as ready to destroy. A hard shove and Jack Hume had crashed to his death. Steady pressure on a crowbar and a vase had plummeted down toward Kay.

I had warned Ronald. He refused to see what he was doing. He had made his choices, consciously, greedily, manipulatively. I could not change them.

Laverne rocked back and forth. Words came in spurts, her voice deep and leaden. " . . . the Great Spirit is here . . . Great Spirit, we beseech you . . . James, where is James? . . ." Laverne breathed spasmodically, then slowly the gulping eased. " . . . torn from happiness . . ."

The last phrase was in a different voice, a lighter, tenor voice with an unmistakable Adelaide drawl.

" . . . no longer can we delight in our happy days . . . the night of the wedding . . . you were beautiful . . ."

Diane drew a handkerchief from her pocket, stifled a sob.

Jimmy turned toward his mother, shook his head angrily. "That's not Dad."

Laverne wailed, a high eerie cry that faded into loud, irregular breathing.

Ronald took five quick steps to the table. He loomed over Jimmy. "Outbursts such as that may end the session. Her spirit is not her own. If she is pulled back, there can be damage."

Diane gripped her son's arm. "Hush, Jimmy." Her whisper was anguished. "Daddy's here. I know he is. I can feel him in the room. Oh, please, Jimmy, please."

A furious scowl twisted Jimmy's face. He glared at Ronald, awkwardly patted his mother's shoulder.

Ronald waited a moment more, then returned to his station behind Laverne. She twisted and turned, her dress rustling with the jerky movements. He murmured, his voice low and soothing, "All is well. Be at peace. Welcome James, bring him back."

I would have liked to yank his dandy little beard, an inexplicable, unnerving, jolting out-of-the-ordinary tug, a little one-on-one with a spirit who despised sappy. *All is well. Be at peace.* What appalling nonsense. I folded my hands together, the better to resist temptation.

Ronald continued to murmur.

I wondered how long he would hold the stage. But he revealed a showman's sense of timing. His words came ever more softly, then he fell silent.

Gradually, Laverne quieted. She gave a low moan. " . . . Jimmy's ninth birthday . . . the calliope and the merry-go-round . . ."

Adelaide was a small town. I was willing to bet the *Gazette* ran a sweet little story on the society page about Jimmy Hume's ninth birthday party.

" . . . the good times . . . darkness now at The Castle . . . trouble draws me back . . . hear me and do as I wish . . . jealousy and resentment growing over the years . . . family secrets . . . the father . . . handsome boy . . . desperate mother . . ."

Gwen Dunham was utterly still, her pale face stone hard as she watched Laverne.

Her husband remained rigid next to her. There might have been a gulf as wide as a canyon between them.

" . . . stolen photograph . . ."

Margo's eyes flared in alarm. She had made no answer when Francie de Sales accused her of slipping the photograph of Ryan Dunham beneath Jack's door. Now she stared in shock toward that mumbling figure dimly seen on the chaise longue.

" . . . Jack upset . . . young love spurned . . ."

Shannon drew in a sharp breath. She began to shake her head. Her mouth opened.

Before Shannon could speak, Margo reached over and gripped her arm.

" . . . oh, Jimmy . . . desperate measures . . ."

Jimmy's head jerked up.

Diane made a desperate sound deep in her throat. "James, what are you doing?"

Laverne sagged against the chaise longue. " . . . bright red poppies in a field . . . sharp light and a magnifying glass . . ." Laverne pushed to a sitting position, clapped shaking hands to her temples. " . . . someone on the balcony with Jack . . . a quick blow to his back . . . down the steps, down the steps, down the steps . . . murder . . ."

"Murder." Margo breathed the word in a shaky whisper.

"Nonsense." Evelyn's deep voice was harsh. "I demand to know what's behind this highly contrived exhibition." She turned a reproachful face toward Diane. "What are you trying to do? Destroy the family?"

"Murder?" Shannon's cry was high and piercing.

Alison pushed back a thick strand of white-gold hair, gleaming in the dim light of a sconce. "Hey, wait a minute. Don't the spirits have anything for me?" She feigned disappointment, clutching her throat. "Oh, woe, when will I know what the spirits foretell?"

"This is stupid." Clint's voice was gruff. He shoved back his chair. "Come on, Gwen. That's enough of this woman's idiocy." He stood and reached for his wife's arm, pulled her to her feet. "This has nothing to do with us." But his voice was hollow.

Laverne buried her head in her hands. " . . . pain, so much pain . . ."

The overhead lights came on. Ronald stood by the light switch. "I'm sorry. Vocal outbreaks destroy the link to the other world." He didn't sound disturbed. In fact, his tone was bland. "The séance is over."

I felt sure Laverne had completed her assignment.

Alison's cool blond elegance was unruffled, her expression amused. "Hey, how about an encore? Let's have an out-out-damned-spot moment."

Shannon stood and pushed back her chair. "Who was on the balcony with Jack?" Her cry was shrill. "Laverne, you have to tell us. What do you know about Jack? Are you saying someone pushed him down the stairs?"

Laverne looked up with a glazed, blank expression. She shuddered. "I don't know anything. I never remember what has been said. I don't know what happens. The spirits come through me, but I am not aware."

Jimmy strode toward Laverne. "Don't give us that I-don't-know-a-thing claim." His voice was rough. "It's all smoke and mirrors, totally phony. You make stuff up to get money out of my mom."

Diane rushed unsteadily to Jimmy, clutched his arm. "Oh, no, Jimmy. Laverne doesn't control the spirits. Everything at the séances is true." Her face shone with a believer's intensity. "There are so many things your daddy has talked about at séances that only he and I knew. Some notes he wrote to me . . . I still have them, but no one else has ever seen them . . ."

Apparently Ronald not only did excellent research at the historical society, he or Laverne had snooped among Diane's most private and personal mementos, much as they'd filched information from the family albums of Laverne's victim in Gainesville. Yet Diane hadn't made that connection when Kay told her what she'd discovered. Diane would not, perhaps emotionally she could not, believe any fact that destroyed Laverne's credibility.

Diane was nearing hysteria. "Everything in the séances comes from the beyond. You mustn't drive Laverne away. I need your daddy. Oh, Jimmy, I have to have your daddy."

"Mom . . ." His voice was anguished.

Shannon darted toward Laverne. "Who was on the balcony with Jack?"

Ronald moved swiftly to stand between Laverne and Shannon. He gently helped Laverne rise, smoothly placed her on the opposite side from Shannon, and began to walk toward the door, speaking softly. "You can rest now, Laverne. Your task is done. The spirits came. They have spoken through you."

"That's absurd." Evelyn held tight to the back of a chair. "I insist you explain this charade."

Clint Dunham banged the door against the wall. His hand on his wife's elbow, he pushed her a little ahead of him and they were in the hallway.

Alison picked up her purse from the floor. "It looks like the party's over. I never knew séances could be so much fun." She moved purposefully toward the door.

Near the door, Laverne leaned against Ronald, her face pale and drawn. He looked calm, but there was a gleam of malicious satisfaction in his cold blue eyes as he cockily stared at Evelyn. "Laverne is nothing more than a conduit. If there are questions, perhaps you can answer them among yourselves. As James said, there appears to be trouble in the family." He slid an arm around Laverne and guided her into the hall.

Shannon flung out her hands. "Did you hear what she said? That was supposed to be James's voice saying someone murdered Jack." Shannon stared at Diane. "Do you think that was James?"

Diane's face crumpled. "Oh. If James said so . . ."

Evelyn clapped her hands. "Diane, you are the world's biggest fool. The dead do not communicate."

Hmm. That all depends. Generally speaking, Evelyn was

right. Certainly in this instance she understood a scam when she saw it.

Evelyn folded her arms, her gaunt face grim. "James is not speaking through that absurd woman. In between those fake heavy breaths, she spewed disconnected, senseless phrases. James was never imprecise in his life. Or, I imagine, in death. Your dear friend Laverne and her smooth-tongued husband used the cover of a séance to allege that Jack was murdered. If they had proof, the responsible action would be to notify the police. However, they obviously have no proof. I fail to understand their objective. Possibly they simply wish to create unpleasantness. My advice to everyone present is to dismiss this evening's performance and remember that Jack died in an accidental fall." She moved majestically toward the door.

There was an instant of silence, then Alison nodded approvingly. "I'm with Evelyn. And now good night all. I won't claim this was the most enjoyable evening I've ever spent here, but it certainly has been one of the most interesting."

Shannon swung toward Alison. "How can you act like this is all funny? Jack's dead. Jack's dead!" She burst into tears.

Jimmy took a step toward her. "Don't cry, honey."

She stared at him, her eyes wide, her face stiff. "I heard you say you were going to hurt him. Did you?" She plunged past him.

Margo hurried after her running daughter.

Jimmy looked shocked. He called after her. "Shannon, come back."

Running steps were his answer.

His mouth twisted in despair. He walked heavily toward the hallway.

His mother reached out a hand. "Jimmy . . ."

He didn't look back.

Diane was alone in the library. She stumbled to the chair that had belonged to James Hume, sank into it. She picked up his glasses, cradled them in one hand. Tears streamed down her face. "James, I'm frightened."

Upstairs, Ronald stood at the wet bar in their suite. He poured Scotch into a tumbler, added soda.

Laverne slumped back in an easy chair. She looked ill, her eyes staring and glazed, her face raddled. "That was terrible."

He lifted the glass in a toast, took a deep drink. "To the contrary, you were never better. That's the best James you've ever done."

She lifted a shaking hand. "Didn't you feel it?"

He was impatient. "You know it's bogus."

Her lips worked, and the words were almost indistinct. "I used to feel things. I could help people. I knew things no one else knew, but you pushed me and made me tell people things for money. Now there's nothing there. I said what you told me to say, but there was something terrible in that room. Didn't you feel the hatred?"

He smiled. "Hatred? Who cares? They're scared." His voice was soft. "I watched them. If you think we got money before, wait and see what I do now."

A sudden flush stained her cheeks. "I hate you."

"Poor Laverne." There was cold dislike in his eyes. "Don't pretend you don't like money. I know better. If you want money for Jenny, you'd better keep your mouth on straight."

She stared at him and spoke as if she hadn't heard his words. "Tonight you had me say that Jack Hume was murdered. Is that true?"

He looked amused. "Of course. Why do you think someone tried to kill Kay Clark last night?"

Laverne moved uneasily in her chair. "Someone pushed that vase?"

"Someone pushed that vase and I know who." He sipped at his drink.

"What are you going to do?"

He gave a little shrug. "Nothing for now. I'll let the pot simmer tonight. Tomorrow I'll make some calls, offer some constructive advice, and pick up some consulting fees."

"Ronald, I feel danger. Something dark and terrible—"

"'I feel danger.'" He mocked her. "Save your performance for the fools, Laverne."

"You don't understand." Her voice rose. "I know—"

"I like that vibrato. It gives Diane chills. It doesn't do a thing for me. Look"—and he was suddenly good-humored—"you've had a long day. You'll feel better tomorrow. You may have to do some hand-holding with Diane." He walked to wet bar, splashed water in a glass, carried it to Laverne. "I'll get you a pill. All you need is a good night's sleep."

She sank back against the chair, waited until he returned, handing her two capsules. She swallowed them submissively. "Yes. I'll go to bed." Tears trickled down her cheeks. She rose and moved heavily into the bath. When she returned in a pale ivory nightgown, she was already drowsy.

I wondered if she often took powerful, quick-acting narcotics.

He placed his drink on a coffee table and strolled to a closet. He returned in a moment in a T-shirt and boxers and settled on the sofa. He picked up the glass and smiled, a man enjoying a nightcap, obviously pleased with a productive day.

I popped to Kay's room.

No Kay.

I took a deep, steadying breath. She'd promised to stay put. Of course, she very likely had expected me to make a prompt report on the séance. With her door open, she'd have been sure to hear people walking to their rooms.

I wasn't as fearful now for her safety. I expected the murderer was totally occupied assessing what danger might emerge from the séance. Evelyn Hume's cold conclusion that nothing could be proved might reassure the murderer. Everything depended upon how much Ronald knew and what he intended to do with the knowledge.

But I didn't like the idea of Kay roaming around The Castle.

I pressed my fingertips to my temples. Hadn't I seen Myrna Loy do that in a film? Lo and behold, an answer came. When I didn't return, Kay must have gone to the library seeking me. I dropped through the ceiling into the library. Such a fun way to maneuver.

Kay sat next to Diane.

Diane was a wreck, her makeup streaked by tears, her nose red from rubbing with a handkerchief, her untidy hair more frazzled than usual. She looked earnestly at Kay. " . . . you're very kind to offer to help me make sense of everything."

Kay spoke soothingly. "Start at the beginning, from the moment you reached the library . . ."

I hovered next to Kay, whispered in her ear: "I'll be in your room in half an hour."

She froze for only an instant, gave a tiny nod.

"After everybody finally came . . ."

. . . .

In a marble-walled bathroom, Gwen Dunham sat at a vanity counter. She poured facial cleanser onto a washcloth. Her movements were automatic. Not even the harsh light from theater-dressing-room-style lights diminished the perfection of her features. Whether young or old, she would always be beautiful. She wiped away makeup. Her deep-set violet eyes stared unseeingly into the mirror. Whatever she saw, it was not her image.

A step sounded. Clint stood in the doorway. He was still dressed. He looked toward his wife, his face anguished. "We have to talk."

She stiffened. "Not tonight, Clint. Tomorrow." She rose and turned on a spigot, held the cloth beneath the rushing water. Squeezing out the excess, she lifted the wet cloth to her face, covering her eyes and nose and mouth.

Her husband waited a moment, but she made no move, said nothing. Slowly, he turned away.

Her shoulders quivered. She pressed the cloth harder, muffling sobs.

In the bedroom, he gathered up a pillow and a light blanket. He turned and moved out of the bedroom. The sound of the closing door brought Gwen into the room. She saw the pulled-down spread and missing pillow. She turned and leaned against the frame of the door, defeat and misery in every line of her body.

In the den, Clint tossed the pillow onto a leather sofa. He made no move to undress. Instead, he slumped into a chair, massaged knuckles against one temple. His face was hard with anger.

Kay worked at Jack's desk. She wrote quickly, her face absorbed and intent.

I had much to report, but I was desperately thirsty. I opened the small freezer compartment, scooped ice into a tumbler.

Kay's head jerked up. She stared toward the wet bar. "Will you please announce when you're here? An ice scoop dangling in the air bothers me. There's something awfully weird about it."

"Certainly," I murmured agreeably. "Here I am. Almost." I enjoyed my reflection in the mirror behind the wet bar, the colors wheeling and whirling and solidifying, and there I was. I gave a satisfied nod. The carnelian necklace was very attractive. "I aim to please." I filled the tumbler to the brim with water and drank it half down.

She raised an inquiring dark eyebrow. "Thirsty work?"

"Very." I took another drink and described the séance. "Diane was anxious for the séance to begin but obviously afraid of what she might learn. Jimmy . . ."

Kay wrote furiously to keep up. When I concluded, she flipped back a few pages of her legal pad. "Your account is a good deal more coherent than Diane's." She paused. "Thank you."

I smiled. "You're welcome. As it played out, no one there, except for Diane, was under any illusion about trafficking with the beyond."

Kay tapped the desktop with her pen. "Why didn't he simply put the squeeze on someone? Why the drama?"

I drifted to the sofa and dropped gratefully onto the soft cushions. "I think he took pleasure in publicly gigging people. Plus, the séance was a clever way to make everyone present exceptionally uncomfortable and nervous about what she might say next. The obvious threat is that the séance was only a prelude. As he told Laverne, he's going to let everyone worry and then he'll make his move."

Kay looked eager. "Bailey Ruth, we're getting close. You can monitor everything he does for the next few days. As soon as he sets up a meeting with the killer, we can alert the police chief. You can be there in your cop uniform and video the whole thing."

In the white bedroom, I admired again the effect of the pearl necklace hanging from red coral. It was a subtle, but commanding use of color. Although it would have been lovely if the circumstances had been happier, I had enjoyed my stay at The Castle. I agreed with Kay that we were nearing the end of her quest. I would follow Ronald to a fateful meeting. If all went well, Jack Hume's murderer would be revealed and arrested. Soon I would hear the whistle of the Rescue Express and once again leave my beloved Adelaide.

I glanced at the clock. It was a quarter to ten. I felt everything was under control. Until morning, I was free. It would take only a moment for me to see those I loved. Emissaries were under strict orders never to contact family or friends, but a quick peek did no harm. As Wiggins stressed, the living must not be preoccupied with the dead. Moreover, I always felt close to Dil and Rob because whenever they thought of me, I was there for an instant.

My daughter, Dil, her red hair frosted with silver, dished up ice cream at her kitchen counter. Ice cream had always been the bedtime snack at the Raeburn house. Bobby Mac liked chocolate with slivers of almond and chocolate syrup. I poured chocolate over a generous serving of vanilla and crumbles of a Reese's Peanut Butter Cup. Dil was a purist, plain vanilla. Our son, Rob, added slices of banana and peanuts to a dip of strawberry. Each to his own taste.

Dil hummed as she added spoons and carried two bowls to the den.

Her husband looked up with a smile. He had a nice, crooked smile that indicated good humor and a wry insight.

Dil settled across from him on a comfortable chintz sofa.

"Hugh, the funniest thing. In the kitchen I started thinking about Reese's Peanut Butter Cups. My mom . . ."

I blew her a kiss.

I found Rob and Lelia in their den. Rob groaned, clapped his hands to his head. "He threw the ball away. He threw it away."

On the television screen, a first baseman scrambled after a ball that had zoomed over his head. A base runner in visitors' gray rounded second and flew toward third.

Rob groaned again. "If they lose this game, they'll be four behind in the wild card."

His wife, Lelia, made soothing noises, but didn't look up from her book.

I craned to see. Oh, a novel by Dorothea Benton Frank. Lelia had excellent taste. I would add the author to my reading list.

Rob looked despondent. "They were ahead at the end of May. I should have known they couldn't hold it. Oh, well. That's baseball. When I was a kid, my mom loved that Yogi Berra quote: 'This is like déjà vu all over again.'"

Lelia looked up. "Funny you should mention your mom. Today I saw someone who looked so much like a picture of your mom when she was young. A redhead in a yellow convertible."

If I'd ever felt like the stereotype of a ghost with hair standing on end, this was the moment. I held my breath.

"This redhead was really young and pretty. It made me smile to see her." Lelia's tone made clear that she had no inkling the woman she'd seen was me. I relaxed. After all, I certainly hadn't been twenty-seven when the *Serendipity* went down in the Gulf.

Rob grinned. "A redhead in a yellow convertible is Mom's kind of woman." He glanced toward a studio portrait of Bobby Mac and me. The affection in his eyes brought tears to mine.

Cars were picking up kids from the rectory of St. Mildred's. Dear redheaded Bayroo, my grandniece, stood on the back steps, waving good night to friends. Her dad, Father Bill, dropped paper plates into a trash sack. Her mom, Kathleen, swiped the top of the picnic table. "Mom, that was the best watermelon yet this summer."

At the Pritchard house, a little boy slept with one arm around the neck of a plush bear. Downstairs a young couple on a rose-colored sofa held hands. Peg looked at Johnny. "Saturday."

"You'll be the most beautiful bride in the world."

She moved nearer, lifted her face to his.

I felt joyful as I returned to The Castle. My children were fine and those whose lives I'd touched in previous visits were well and happy.

The front hallway light was on but the house was utterly silent. The Castle walls were old and thick.

In the white bedroom, I appeared and chose a pale blue nightie. I glanced approvingly in the mirror. The bedroom was an excellent background for coppery red hair and the nightgown. I propped two puffy pillows behind me, sank into softness. The pillows were almost as comfortable as floating on a cloud. You object to the concept of support from a cloud? Clouds, you point out, are simply particles of mist. But in Heaven . . . Oh, of course. Yours to wonder about, mine not to tell.

I turned off the bedside lamp. Hopefully, tomorrow Ronald would lead me to a killer.

CHAPTER FOURTEEN

Evelyn and Jimmy were in the dining room when Kay and I arrived. She looked up as we entered, her strong face pleasant. "Good morning." Her deep voice sounded good-humored. Jimmy pushed back his chair. "Good morning." He was polite, but formal.

Kay was quick. "Please don't get up. We'll take care of ourselves."

He returned to his breakfast, and we moved toward the sideboard. I chose bacon, scrambled eggs with sausage and jalapeño, a waffle, fruit, and orange juice. I glanced in the mirror and admired my outfit. I had still opted for restraint in fashion, but my pale lime blouse had adorable embroidered parasols on it. A matching trim adorned my beige linen slacks. This morning I opted for beige woven leather moccasins. I felt ready for a busy and productive day. After breakfast, it would be time to disappear and take up sentinel duty with Ronald Phillips.

We carried our plates to the table and sat near Evelyn. Jimmy was reading what appeared to be a geology text.

Evelyn held up several sections of newspaper. "Would you care for the newspaper?"

Kay and I declined.

Evelyn lifted a section and became immersed.

Mindful of our ostensible roles, I murmured to Kay, "Do you want me to visit the historical society this morning?"

Clattering steps sounded in the stone hallway.

Diane hurried into the dining room. Her hair poked up in sprigs. She wore no makeup. Her housecoat was open to reveal pink-striped pajamas. "Did someone let Walter out last night? I thought he was inside, but maybe he went out. I whistled and called and he's not in the house. I went to the back porch and called for him and he didn't come. Has anyone seen him?"

I glanced at Kay.

She murmured, "The dog."

Jimmy looked up. "He's probably chasing a rabbit, Mom."

She looked doubtful. "Jimmy, please go out and look. Walter's always on the back steps in the morning if he's been out at night." Her voice wobbled.

Jimmy put down his coffee cup. "I'll find him. He's too cantankerous for anything to have happened to him."

Diane nodded jerkily. "I'll get dressed and come help."

Kay gave me a quick nod. "Francie and I will help, too."

I disappeared when out of sight from the terrace. I floated above The Castle grounds. The heat was already building. Though it was early, I judged the temperature to be in the high eighties, which augured one-hundred-plus degrees by midafternoon. Heavenly residents find whatever climate they enjoy, from deserts to polar ice caps. Bobby Mac and I lazed away cheerful days in sparkling bays reminiscent of the Caribbean, but, at this moment, I took delight in the Oklahoma summer. I skimmed above the trees and kept a sharp eye for the old dog.

In the distance, I heard Jimmy whistling and calling: "Hey, Walter. Where are you, you decrepit old reprobate. Found a lady somewhere? Come home, buddy."

Suddenly I heard a faint yipping.

I swooped down as Jimmy came around the corner of The Castle. He was grinning as he walked to the workshop. He opened the door and Walter burst out, barking in a frenzy. The cocker wobbled around Jimmy, nipped toward his hand, then turned and pelted unevenly toward the house.

The old dog strove mightily but he was slow, hampered by an arthritic back leg. Laughing, Jimmy caught up with him. Jimmy reached down, grabbed him up. "How'd you get in the workshop? Dumb old dog. Mom's frantic. Come on, stop wriggling, I'm taking you in."

Before Jimmy came around the corner of the house, I dropped down by the back door and appeared.

Kay jogged up, her eyes darting nervously around. "What if somebody saw you do that?"

I wasn't worried. "So they didn't see me for a minute. Now I'm here."

Kay held the door for Jimmy.

Walter squirmed, trying to get down. He snuffled and quivered, his rheumy eyes bleary.

Jimmy carried him through the kitchen and into the main hallway. "Hey, Mom. Walter got trapped in the workshop."

Diane hurried to the top of the stairs. "I was just going to come down and help. I'm so glad you found him."

Jimmy carried the dog upstairs and placed him on the floor. "Here he is. No worse for the wear."

Walter trotted toward Diane.

Beaming, she picked him up and buried her face in golden fur, murmuring.

Suddenly the dog stiffened. He yipped, his tone high and shrill. "Walter . . ."

The cocker wriggled free and dropped to the floor.

Diane called him, "Come here, you bad dog." But she wasn't scolding him. Her tone was loving and indulgent. "Come back here, Walter. Tell Mother where you've been." Her voice faded as they moved away from the top of the stairs.

Jimmy grinned at us. "She'd be a lot more upset if something happened to Walter than to me." But there was affection and good humor in his voice. "As dog rescuers, we deserve fresh coffee." He turned to go back to the dining room.

"Walter!" Diane's cry was sharp. "Come back. Their door's ajar. Don't push! Walter, stop that." There was a strangled sound and then a high scream.

Jimmy swerved around Kay and me. He reached the stairs, took the steps two at a time.

Kay and I raced after him.

Diane stood at the far end of the hall near a partially open door. She was trembling. "There's blood . . . there's blood everywhere."

The door to Laverne and Ronald Phillips's room was partially open. Blood had pooled in a dark splotch just over the threshold into the hallway.

I glanced back. Only Kay was behind me. I disappeared.

Inside the bedroom, I felt as if I'd slammed into a wall. I wouldn't follow Ronald Phillips today. His body kept the door from fully opening. He lay on his back, skin flaccid and grayish.

Dark splotches stained his once-white T-shirt. His temple was disfigured as well. I suspected a gun had been held only inches away and the trigger pulled.

I hovered above the bed.

Laverne lay on her back. Blood had seeped into the pillows and the bedclothes. She appeared to have been shot in her sleep. Had she awakened, groggy from pills, at the rapid staccato of gunfire? I suspected the attack had been sudden, Ronald shot down, then swift movement to the bed and the gun trained on her.

"They're dead." Diane's cry rose from the hallway. "They're dead!" She clung to her son's arm.

Jimmy stared into the bedroom, his young face pale with shock. "Walter." His voice was shaky. He reached out, snagged the cocker's collar, pulled him into the hall. Smears of blood stained the floor. He lifted the struggling cocker, held him against his chest, then slid an arm around his mother's shoulders as she began to sob.

I returned to the hall. I glanced toward the stairs and saw no one. I was behind Diane and Jimmy and Kay. I appeared.

Kay took two swift steps, gazed into the room. She drew in a sharp breath. "They've been killed." Her voice was grim. She pulled a cell phone from the pocket of her slacks and punched 911.

Jimmy turned his mother away from the room. He still held the struggling Walter. "We'll wait for the police downstairs. Come on, Mom." He gave Kay a commanding glance. "Close the door."

Kay moved quickly, pulled the door shut.

Evelyn waited at the foot of the stairs, worry and fear clear in the drawn lines of her face. Margo and Shannon stood a few feet behind her.

Diane sobbed. "Someone's killed Laverne and Ronald. There's blood all over their room."

Jimmy nodded at his aunt. "Laverne and Ronald are dead. It has to be murder. The police are coming."

Check Out Receipt

Central Point Library Branch
541-664-3228

Thursday, June 13, 2019 10:18:04 AM

Item: 0024253155
Title: Dead in the water
Due: 07/05/2019

Item: 0024244923
Title: Silent night
Due: 07/05/2019

Item: 001593133
Title: Dearly depotted : a flower shop mystery
Due: 07/05/2019

Item: 001914786
Title: Ghost in trouble
Due: 07/05/2019

Total items: 4

You just saved $119.97 by using your library. You have saved $12,781.11 this past year!

Starting March 4: holds on all items will be 7 days

On the main floor, with an apologetic glance, I slipped into the guest lavatory. I regretted that I'd succumbed to the lure of fashion this morning. I couldn't at this point change to a frumpier costume, but I added oversize harlequin-frame sunglasses and a green kerchief to cover my hair, then returned.

"The police are coming." Kay spoke quietly. "Possibly we should wait in the drawing room."

Evelyn led the way. She walked to a Queen Anne chair, sank onto it. Diane huddled on a sofa, shaking, words tumbling. Jimmy paced by the fireplace. Margo and Shannon sat side by side on a bench, their expressions shocked and frightened.

Margo asked abruptly, "Are you sure—"

Jimmy interrupted. "They're dead and covered with blood."

Shannon gave a cry.

He started to walk toward her, then shook his head, resumed his quick steps up and down, up and down in front of the fireplace.

The police arrived within five minutes, sirens blaring. Chief Cobb paused in the archway. "Is everyone in the household here?" His gray suit already looked rumpled.

Evelyn wasn't as majestic as usual. She took a deep breath and nodded, big-boned face bleak.

"Remain here." It was an order, not a request. "Officer Cain will be in charge. Officer, take everyone's name." The chief swung away, moving fast for a big man.

I well remembered young and handsome Johnny Cain. His coal black hair was newly cut, his deep blue eyes alert and intelligent. I hoped he wouldn't recall the redhead he'd glimpsed at Lulu's when I was in Adelaide for the Christmas holiday. Of course, on that particular day, I'd worn a particularly flattering jade green blouse and slacks, which emphasized the sheen of my hair. Possibly today was the first time in either my earthly or Heavenly existence that I perceived a negative aspect of red hair.

Truly, once glimpsed, the coppery gleam of my hair is difficult to forget.

Morning sunlight slanted across the Aubusson carpet, its colors faded a dusty rose and pale gold from years of exposure. Each person sat in an island of silence. Johnny Cain moved from one to another. When he reached me, his expression was curious. I could have told him it was déjà vu all over again. Instead, I gave my name in a sibilant mutter and hunched my head to one side as if I had a stiff neck.

When his task was done, he waited near the archway.

Everyone sequestered in the drawing room appeared shocked and subdued. Evelyn clasped the silver head of an ebony cane, her expression somber. Diane slumped against the side of the sofa, occasionally pressing a sodden handkerchief to her reddened eyes. Jimmy paced, frowning as he flexed his hands, opening and closing his fingers into fists. Shannon held tight to one of her mother's hands. Margo kept her gaze trained on the archway, watching as officers and technicians came and went in the hallway. Shannon's face creased in thought. Occasionally, she stared at Jimmy with haunted eyes.

More quick steps in the hallway. A wiry, trim figure in a sport shirt and Levi's trotted past the archway. I recognized the medical examiner. His official pronouncement of death was necessary before the bodies could be moved and the business of collecting evidence begun.

I moved restively in a not very comfortable early Victorian chair. Perhaps Wiggins had been right to discourage appearances. If I weren't a guest at The Castle, I could be upstairs right this moment. Instead, I was trapped in the drawing room.

Occasionally Johnny Cain slid a puzzled glance toward me.

I sat in a shadowy corner with one hand to my face, as if propping up a cheekbone. Upstairs so much was happening . . . I gave a little mental shrug. Nothing ventured, nothing gained. I stood, still with a hand to my face. I veered fairly near Johnny and muttered, "Going to the lavatory. Back in a minute."

He said, "Miss de Sales . . ."

"Got to hurry." Dignity was a small sacrifice for duty.

He followed me through the archway.

I flapped a hand as I opened the lavatory door only a few feet away and stepped inside.

I punched the lock, gave myself a thumbs-up in the ornate ormolu mirror, and disappeared.

In the hallway, Johnny stood where he could keep an eye on the lavatory door as well as the drawing room. In two quick strides, he checked the doors on either side. One opened to a closet, a second to a storage room. Now he could feel comfortable that the restroom had no other exit and I was inside until I came out. I was glad to see he'd lost his tense expression.

In an instant I was upstairs. I hovered above the chief, Detective Sergeant Hal Price, and the quick-talking medical examiner. I spared one admiring glance for Hal Price, the cotton-top detective with craggy good looks, slate blue eyes, and a muscular build. I was always true to Bobby Mac, but I would be disingenuous to pretend my pulse didn't quicken when I saw Hal Price. I knew the attraction was mutual. Perhaps someday I could find the right redhead for him.

" . . . looks like contact wounds, both to the chest and temple." The M.E. pointed at Ronald's body. The doctor stepped to the bedside and looked down, his thin face intent. "Same MO here. That's kind of a puzzle. The guy at the door had to be shot first. There's no suggestion of trauma or struggle by him to prevent the attack. Why did she remain still? Natural thing would be to fling back the covers and fight or run. Instead, she's lying here, and bang, she's dead. Probably a narcotic. I'll run the tests, let you know."

The last words came as he stepped casually over Ronald's feet and edged out of the partially open door.

Several uniformed officers were working around the perimeter of the room, measuring and photographing. One officer on his knees near Ronald's pooled blood looked up. "Hey, Chief. The blood's pretty much dry except in the center. Paw prints go right through it. But there's a smear here"—one finger pointed at a brownish curl—"that looks like the edge of a shoe."

Chief Cobb stepped nearer. "That's critical. Get a good photo, then try for an impression. Whether we get it or not, the murderer may have stepped in blood. If we get a suspect, we can get a warrant to check shoes. There may be microscopic traces that will send somebody to jail."

Cobb was thoughtful. "Here's how I figure it. Late last night there was a knock at the door. Phillips gets up. Probably he's foggy with sleep. He opens the door, the gun's jammed against his chest, and bingo. As he falls, the murderer steps inside, gun in one hand, flashlight in the other, and kicks the door shut. A couple of strides to the bed." The chief matched action to his words. "Gun to her throat, pull the trigger. Back to the guy on the floor, maybe he's moaning. Maybe he's still alive. Gun to the temple and that's the end of the story."

Hal looked at him quizzically. "Three, maybe four shots, and nobody heard?"

Cobb raised a sardonic eyebrow. "If anybody noticed the shots, they haven't shared that information with us. I don't think there was that much noise. A gun fired against his body muffled the first shot and very likely that was the only shot fired from the doorway. Once Phillips was down, the murderer stepped inside and shut the door. The Castle walls are old, thick, and well insulated. If anyone in bed heard a pop, it didn't register as gunfire. I doubt the entire attack required more than three or four minutes. When they were dead, the gun was tossed down beside him"—the chief pointed at the gun lying on the floor—"and the door opened. The murderer likely waited long enough to be sure no one was stirring, then returned to his or her room. Or left The Castle."

The chief looked at Hal. "Process the weapon, then see if anyone in the drawing room can identify it. I'll find a place downstairs and interview those who are in the house."

I reappeared in the lavatory, unlocked the door, and was back in my chair when Price appeared in the archway.

"I am Detective Sergeant Hal Price. We appreciate your patience. Chief Cobb will speak with each of you individually in the library." He glanced at a card in his hand. "Ms. Francie de Sales?" He looked inquiringly around the room.

As we walked down the hall, I held a hand to the side of my face. In my peripheral vision, through the spread of my fingers, I saw Hal Price give me a long, searching look.

He held the door to the library. "Ms. de Sales, Chief."

I sat down with my hand apparently stuck to my jaw.

Price started to pull up a chair to one side of the oak table.

The chief tapped a legal pad. "I'll take care of this interview." His bulldog face was bland. "Check upstairs on the evidence collection."

"Yes, sir." Hal moved out of my view. I heard the door open, then shut.

Chief Cobb and I sat on opposite sides of the oak table in the library. His heavy face looked purposeful and determined. His tie was loosened at the throat of a pale blue shirt. "You can take your hand down. He's gone."

I yanked off the kerchief and sunglasses as well, tucked them in a pocket.

He laughed, then quickly sobered. "What do you know?"

He didn't ask how I knew, which I considered tactful. He wanted information. I gave him everything.

He wrote fast, then looked up with a grim face. "You'd think a man who'd threatened to expose a murderer might have been more cautious. Probably Phillips answered the door because he was foggy with sleep. From what you've said, he was a cocky little guy. He had planned to let his victim stew, get more and more nervous and worried, then make a move. The murderer didn't give him that chance."

I wasn't surprised. Jack Hume posed a threat and he'd been pushed to his death. Kay Clark arrived, asked too many questions, and a vase crashed down where she waited.

I finished with the story of Walter, the cocker, shut in the workshop. "If only Walter could talk."

The chief looked at me in surprise.

"If Walter was outside last night, wouldn't that indicate the murderer came from outside the house?"

The chief shrugged. "Whether the dog was in or out, he had to be put where he couldn't raise an alarm."

I understood. Walter loved a frolic. Someone in the house walking in a hallway would attract the dog if he were inside. The answer: scoop him up, carry him outside, stroll to the workshop, shut the dog inside. Then the murderer would be free to slip back to the house and approach Laverne and Ronald's suite.

If the murderer came from outside The Castle, either Alison Gregory or one of the Dunhams, it was also essential to prevent Walter from barking.

Chief Cobb was suddenly formal. "Thank you for your assistance, Ms. de Sales."

When I was at the door, he called after me: "Should any other information come to your attention, please let us know." He sounded bland, as if I were simply Kay's assistant, but his eyes held mine for a moment.

He knew who I was.

I knew that he knew.

Neither of us intended to say more.

I smiled. "I will certainly keep you informed." As I stepped into the hall, Detective Sergeant Price came around the corner.

Quickly, I yanked the sunglasses from my pocket, put them on.

He walked more swiftly. When he stopped and looked down at me, I was grateful for the dark lenses that hid my eyes.

"Ms. de Sales."

I waited.

He cleared his throat. "Ask Kay Clark to come to the library." He lingered only an instant too long, then stepped past me.

I walked swiftly to the drawing room. "Kay, they want you in the library."

Evelyn Hume's face folded in a disagreeable frown. "I fail to see why we are being held here and why you and Kay have been summoned before me." Her sense of entitlement was powerful. After all, she was Evelyn Hume.

I was conciliatory. "Obviously, Kay and I aren't important witnesses. I never met Mr. and Mrs. Phillips and Kay had only a brief acquaintance with them. I'm sure the chief wished to speak to us first so that he can concentrate on the people who matter, the ones who knew them quite well."

I wasn't surprised that my pleasant statement was not reassuring to the occupants of the drawing room. Evelyn's lips folded into a tight, hard line. Diane broke into fresh sobs. Jimmy stopped pacing and jammed his hands into the pockets of his chinos, his expression grim. Margo looked wary. Shannon moved uneasily.

Kay and I turned away and walked down the hall. As we rounded the corner, the corridor to the library lay empty. I disappeared.

I hovered near the ceiling. I didn't expect to learn anything from Kay's visit with the chief, but I didn't want to miss his other interviews.

In a few quick questions, Chief Cobb made certain Kay could add nothing to the information I'd provided. "Mrs. Clark, please keep our conversation confidential as well as the murders. Nothing has been released to the news media. There are witnesses I wish to interview before the crime is publicly known."

"I understand." She rose, then looked at him somberly. "Did Ronald and Laverne Phillips die because of me?"

His rumbly voice was patient. "Did you advise Ronald to try blackmail?"

She shook her head, understanding his query was rhetorical. "If I hadn't come back to Adelaide, he might not have realized Jack was murdered." Her dark eyes mirrored her distress.

The chief lifted his bulky shoulders in a shrug. "Phillips could have contacted us. He chose another path. You came to The Castle because you suspected a crime. When we spoke at Lulu's you admitted as much. If there had been a basis for me to investigate, I would have done so. There is an important distinction between your suspicions and Ronald Phillips's knowledge. He knew something. It may have been nothing more than a glimpse of someone climbing the stairs to the third floor. If he had informed us, I could have taken that fact and investigated that person."

Kay pushed back a strand of silky dark hair. "Person." Her tone was puzzled. "You talk about a person. Last night at the séance, Laverne's ramblings obviously referred to more than one person."

Chief Cobb sketched a noose on his legal pad. "Phillips was an equal-opportunity blackmailer. People will pay to hide secrets, even though innocent of murder. But one of his listeners was a murderer. Phillips made a fatal error."

As Kay left, Detective Sergeant Price stepped inside. He carried a gallon-size plastic bag zipped shut. Clearly visible was a dark metal handgun. He shut the door behind him, lofted the container in triumph. "Homegrown, Chief. There's a chip on the lower right edge of the grip. Evelyn Hume said her father brought the gun back from the Pacific in World War Two. Army-issue Colt .45. One bullet left. What are the odds the other five will be retrieved during the autopsies?"

"I'm willing to take that bet. In the affirmative." Cobb's eyes gleamed. "Where was the gun kept, when was it last seen, who is responsible for it?"

Price answered in order. "Her father's upstairs office hasn't been changed since he died. Kind of a shrine, I guess. I checked out the desk. Huge. Mahogany. Drilling plats unrolled and open. Some drilling logs. Evelyn Hume said the gun was kept in the lower right-hand drawer. When I opened the drawer, no gun. Apparently the desk wasn't kept locked. The old dame simply gave me a cool stare when I asked if the gun was secured. Nothing, she told me frostily, is kept under lock and key at The Castle. I suppose the implication is that only hoi polloi live in houses where they have to lock up the silver. In fact, they hardly lock up anything here. No alarm system. As for keys, they sprinkle them around like confetti. The plumber has one, ditto repair companies like air-conditioning, heating, handyman. You name it, someone has a key."

Evelyn kept her left hand slightly extended, touching the side of a bookcase as she entered the library. She made ever so slight an adjustment and walked directly to the chair opposite the chief. She sat, lifted her head, and looked every inch an imperious grande dame. Instead of waiting for his question, she spoke, her words swift and clipped. "Last night was reprehensible, from start to finish. Laverne Phillips . . ."

The chief made occasional notes as she described Laverne's exploitation of Diane's grief, Jack's determination to discredit her and Ronald, Shannon's pursuit of Jack, Jack's apparent lack of interest, Margo's hostility to him, Jimmy's anger with his uncle.

"I mention these facts because the murders of Ronald and Laverne indicate her claim last night that Jack was murdered may be true. I suppose it was a suspicion of murder which drew Kay Clark here. Possibly she had some communication with Jack prior to his death which suggested to her that he might have been in danger."

The chief nodded. "Please describe the séance."

Evelyn accurately reported on the performance in the library.

He glanced down at his notes. He quoted: "' . . . bright red poppies in a field . . . sharp light and a magnifying glass' . . . Were those phrases directed at you?"

She appeared intrigued and not in the least alarmed. "I'm the only person in The Castle dependent upon a magnifying glass. I suppose the reference may be to the Willard Metcalf painting in the grand hallway outside the ballroom. A glorious burst of red poppies. Many of the best paintings in our collection are hung there. However, I see no reason why that should excite Ronald's interest. We've had that painting"—her brow furrowed in thought—"for at least ten years."

"Did you see either of the Phillipses after the gathering in the library ended?"

Her expression was sardonic. "Did I shoot them? No. Nor do I know who did. I went directly to my room and I heard nothing during the night. However, I may know one fact of interest to you. A few days after Jack died, I was coming down the upper hallway. I heard a door open. I turned and saw Ronald coming out of Jack's room. He had no reason—or right—to be there. I asked him what he was doing in my brother's room." A dour smile touched her lips. "He claimed he thought he heard the dog scratching on a door and feared Walter might have been trapped inside. An odd coincidence that Walter apparently was trapped behind a door last night. However, I am sure Ronald was lying."

As soon as Evelyn rose and turned toward the door, I picked up the pen by Chief Cobb's legal pad.

His eyes fastened on the pen, then he moved his gaze toward the doorway.

I was startled when I felt his hand cup over mine.

In the hallway, Detective Sergeant Price faced the table as he held the door for Diane Hume.

I wrote swiftly, despite the weight of Cobb's hand above mine. I released the pen.

Cobb grabbed the pen.

Diane sagged into the chair. Her frizzy blond hair was untidy. She wore no makeup and her face looked sickly. She glanced toward the chaise longue and more tears spilled down her cheeks.

Chief Cobb read my sentence.

As Detective Sergeant Price turned to leave, Cobb called out, "In the murder suite, look for a picture of a young guy in a cap and gown."

The detective sergeant nodded and pulled the door shut behind him.

The interview with Diane, punctuated by her sobs, revealed little. " . . . someone must have crept into the house last night . . . poor Laverne . . . terrible . . ."

Chief Cobb regarded her with an objective, measuring gaze. "We have discovered that Mr. Phillips directed Mrs. Phillips to float the provocative statements in the séance for the purpose of blackmail."

Diane's head jerked up. Her red-rimmed eyes widened in a glare. "That's not true." Her voice was shrill and rising. "Laverne heard from James. It's dreadful"—now she was shaking—"that James had to tell us someone killed Jack." She pushed back her chair, struggled to her feet, trembling. "I can't believe this has happened. No one in the family would hurt Jack. But Margo hated Jack. She and Shannon live in a little house on the grounds. She could have put Walter in the workshop. She'd know about that gun in J. J.'s desk. She knows everything in the house." Diane rushed to the door, yanked it open, and ran into the hall.

Both the chief and I looked after her thoughtfully. Yes, Diane had depended upon Laverne, revered her. Yet if Diane had slipped up behind Jack, a desperate creature driven to violence, and Ronald knew, he might have wanted much more than a nice steady income from Diane. Diane was a very wealthy woman. Or Diane might have feared for her son.

Could indecisive, sweet-natured Diane have shot two people?

In the spear of sunlight through the library window, Margo Taylor's face held little echo of youthful beauty. Lines of dissatisfaction radiated from her eyes and lips. She had an aura of unhappiness. " . . . have no idea what happened last night. Shannon and I have our own house. I'm quite sure Shannon didn't go out after we went to bed. Nor did I."

Chief Cobb looked skeptical. "How can you be certain?"

"I sleep with my bedroom door open. I would have heard her door. I slept very poorly last night." Fear glimmered in her eyes. "I heard Walter barking. I looked at the time. It was almost two o'clock. I was surprised. Usually he doesn't bark unless he wants to play with someone. Then the barking stopped."

"You didn't get up to see?"

"No. You see"—and her voice was barely audible—"I thought someone from the house couldn't sleep either and had gone out for a walk and Walter wanted to play."

The instant of silence between them held a vision of a dog bounding up to someone he knew, someone who moved purposefully through the night to The Castle after placing Walter in the workshop.

The chief once again glanced at his notes. "You've worked here for a good many years."

Margo waited, her face still and wary.

"Were you aware of the forty-five kept in the upstairs office?"

"I knew there was a gun there at one time."

"When did you last see it?"

She turned her hands over. "I don't know exactly. Several years ago Evelyn decided that the floor in the study needed to be replaced. There had been a water leak. Alison advised her on how to obtain flooring from that era. Evelyn instructed me to empty the desk drawers and pack the contents. After the floor was repaired and the desk back in place, I returned the proper items to the drawers. That would have been the last time I saw the gun."

"How many people knew there was a gun in the drawer?"

"I have no idea. Actually, a lot of people may have known. Evelyn was very proud of her father. Several times, in order to raise money for charity, small groups have been taken on a tour of the family rooms. That included the study. Evelyn led the tours and she always showed her father's gun. It was a World War Two relic."

I studied Margo with interest. She had managed to imply that all of the outsiders at last night's séance could easily have known about the gun.

The chief's gaze was stern. "Was the gun loaded?"

Something flickered in her eyes. Was she trying to decide which answer best served her? She paused for a fraction too long, then said smoothly, "I don't know."

Cobb straightened his notebook. "Who had reason to murder Jack Hume?"

She looked at him with a blank face. "I have no idea."

"Was there dissension between Mr. Hume and those living in the house?"

"He didn't approve of Laverne and Ronald." Her voice was carefully neutral.

Chief Cobb was sharp. "Clearly Mr. and Mrs. Phillips were not involved in Hume's death. I want to know his relations with his sister, his sister-in-law, his nephew, and your daughter."

She was equally sharp in her response. "Ask them."

He asked brusquely, "You have no opinion?"

"No." She sat quite still, her face carefully expressionless.

The chief leafed through his notepad, paused as if reading notes. He tapped the pad. "Your daughter was furious with Hume because he dropped her."

Margo's eyes glinted with anger. "Possibly he hurt her feelings. She's very young. Her interest in him was a passing thing, an infatuation. That is scarcely a reason for murder."

He looked sardonic. "So you do have an opinion."

She made no response.

Cobb spoke without emphasis. "Years ago, Jack Hume dropped you for another woman."

Margo's smile was cold, her tone disdainful. "Are you suggesting that I waited until he came back to Adelaide twenty years later and revenged myself by pushing him down the balcony steps? That's absurd. If you're quite finished, I have work to do."

Shannon Taylor burst into the library. She hurried to the table, skidded to a stop. She looked very young and very pretty, blue eyes blazing, heart-shaped face cupped by thick brown hair. "You are seeing everybody else first. It's like I don't count, like I'm some kind of kid. But you need to listen to me. Last night I was upset. People have told you about last night, haven't they?" Shannon didn't pause for an answer. "Laverne antagonized everybody. That's why she was killed, and him, too. Laverne knew that somebody pushed Jack. I know who killed him. You have to talk to Gwen Dunham. She lives next door. I heard her quarrel with Jack in the gazebo and she told him she wished he was dead and then he died."

"Sit down, Miss Taylor." The chief's tone was calm. "Your accusations against Mrs. Dunham are interesting. Last night you accused Jimmy Hume of his uncle's murder. To be precise"—he glanced at his notes—"you said to Jimmy, 'I heard you say you were going to hurt him. Did you?' In fact, Miss Taylor, isn't that what you said?"

Shannon looked stricken. "I didn't mean it."

Cobb was stern. "That was your first thought, wasn't it? You accused Jimmy Hume, not Mrs. Dunham." He pointed at the chair. "Sit down."

She slipped into the chair, stared at him with anxious eyes. "Jimmy might have had a fight with Jack, but he would never shoot people. Never in a million years. The minute I heard about Ronald and Laverne, I knew Jimmy didn't have anything to do with it."

"Did you hear the dog bark last night?"

The sudden change of subject caught her by surprise.

Shannon's hands were beneath the top of the table, out of the chief's view, but I could see them open and close, open and close. She was frightened.

"The dog?"

He didn't repeat the question. He waited, his gaze steady and demanding.

"I don't think so." Her hands opened and closed. "I was asleep."

I dropped down, whispered in the chief's ear. "Ask if she heard her mother go outside."

He went rigid for an instant, then cleared his throat to hide the tiny hiss of my words. "What time did your mother go outside?"

Her eyes flared wide. She waited an instant too long to reply, then said quickly, "Mom didn't go outside." There was stark fear in her eyes. "If anybody said so, that's a lie." She pushed up, struggling for breath. "Mrs. Dunham wanted Jack to die. Talk to her."

Jimmy Hume looked tired and somber, his drawn face giving a preview of his appearance at forty if life turned out to be unkind, purplish smudges beneath his eyes, a hard, mournful stare, jaws clenched in worry.

Chief Cobb leaned back in his chair. "You were angry with your uncle. You threatened him."

"For the record"—Jimmy's voice was dull—"I didn't push Jack—"

The door opened. Detective Sergeant Price strode around the table. He carried a gallon-size plastic bag, holding it by the zipped top. He placed the bag on the table.

Chief Cobb looked down at a picture of a handsome young man in a cap and gown. The picture was not framed.

Price pointed. "Found this photograph in the murder suite, slipped into a coffee-table book about Yellowstone. Good work by Officer Woolley. She flipped through the books one by one and noticed that a page seemed too thick. She looked closer and saw tape at the top and bottom, keeping two pages together. When she used a razor to slit the tape, it opened and the photograph fell out. Pretty clever."

I agreed. A clever hiding place devised by Ronald Phillips, a clever officer to find it.

Jimmy craned to see. He frowned.

Chief Cobb glanced from the photograph to Jimmy. "Do you know him?"

"Sure. That's Ryan Dunham." Jimmy appeared puzzled. "I don't see why his picture was in the Phillipses' room. Ryan's a great guy. That's strange."

Cobb made no reply to Jimmy. He looked toward the detective. "Has the photograph been checked for prints?"

Price nodded.

"Then I'll keep it for now. Thanks, Hal."

At the door, Price looked back. "We have everybody's prints here in the house. We'll see if there's a match on the gun. We still need prints from Alison Gregory and the Dunhams."

"I want to talk to them first."

Price nodded.

As the door closed, Cobb turned back to Jimmy. "You were angry with your uncle?"

Jimmy looked bleak. "Yeah. But like I said, I didn't kill Jack. Maybe I would have punched him. I wouldn't kill him. Ditto for Laverne and Ronald." He took a deep breath. "I suppose I have to tell you. I was outside last night. I couldn't sleep." He rubbed the back of his neck. "I took a long walk. There was plenty of moonlight. Maybe I walked a couple of miles, maybe more. I came back by the gazebo. Somebody was walking away from the house, across the grass. I didn't think much about it. Maybe somebody else couldn't sleep. I didn't want to talk to anybody. I was trying to figure out what was going on with the nutty Phillipses. I didn't really think anybody pushed Jack. I mean, that was crazy. I thought that snake—yeah, well, he's dead now—anyway, I thought Ronald was trying it on, thinking he could squeeze more money out of Mom. See, Mom heard me yell at Jack and she's easy to scare. I was trying to decide what to do. But what can you do when somebody says something and you can't prove it's a lie? Anyway, I was mad and tired and I didn't want to talk to anybody. I almost ducked back the way I'd come, but then I saw him stop and look back, almost turn, then head toward me again. I knew it was a man. Maybe that's why I stopped. If it was Ronald, I was going to . . . Well, that doesn't matter now. Anyway, I waited. When he got about halfway to the opening to the Dunhams', I saw it was Mr. Dunham. He stopped again and looked back. I couldn't see his face clearly in the moonlight. He stood there for a minute and then he jerked around and hurried toward the gate." Jimmy's face furrowed in misery. "Clint Dunham was my scoutmaster. Ryan"—he nodded toward the photograph—"is one of my best friends. Maybe Mr. Dunham couldn't sleep, too. Maybe he was outside and heard Walter and wondered about the noise."

The chief's eyes narrowed. "Was the dog following him?"

"No."

"Did you hear the dog?"

"When I was over by the lake, I thought I heard him yipping. But I didn't pay any attention. Sometimes he stays in, sometimes he goes out. If he sees anybody, he barks his head off. Same thing if he finds a rabbit. The thing is"—Jimmy looked burdened—"this morning in the toolshed, Walter had a rawhide bone. It was chewed slick. He loves that stuff. Anytime you want to make Walter happy, give him a rawhide bone."

CHAPTER FIFTEEN

Chief Cobb hooked a finger to loosen his tie. "Hotter than blazes." Beneath one arm, he held the plastic bag containing the photograph of Ryan Dunham.

Hal Price wiped sweat from his face. "Supposed to hit a hundred and one." He carried a black case approximately a foot wide and five inches deep.

No trees shaded the path from the side door of The Castle to the gate in the shrubbery between the Hume and Dunham properties. Both men squinted against the hot, sharp brightness of blistering sunlight.

Much as I enjoyed being in the vicinity of Hal Price, I wished the chief was alone. I had much I wanted to communicate.

As Hal closed the gate behind them, they looked toward an English manor house, not a mansion like The Castle, but a nice, solid home that gleamed with care, the product of years of love. Ferns flourished in blue ceramic vases on the front porch. Red-

and-blue cushions made wicker chairs inviting. Stained-glass insets gleamed in the front door.

At the base of the steps, the chief looked back toward the gate. "Maybe two hundred yards from here to The Castle."

As they climbed to the porch, Price looked around the Dunhams' spacious yard. "If all he wanted was a walk, he had plenty of room here."

"I don't think he was looking for exercise." Chief Cobb pushed the front bell.

When the door opened, Gwen Dunham's patrician face looked pleasant. Spun-gold hair emphasized deep violet eyes. She was lovely in a rose Shaker-stitched silk sweater and cream-colored silk trousers. The elegant, immaculate hallway behind her was a perfect setting for her cool beauty. She looked up at the chief and her face was suddenly strained. Adelaide was a small town. She might not know Chief Cobb socially, but she would recognize him as chief of police.

In the instant before Chief Cobb pulled out his wallet, opening it to provide identification, I gazed at the lawmen as if I were Gwen.

Despite his wrinkled brown suit and slightly askew tie, Chief Cobb looked formidable, tall and powerfully built. Hal Price was a man most women would sharply note, white-blond hair, rugged features, athletic build. Price's slate blue eyes, cool and impersonal, never moved from her face.

The wallet lay open in the chief's large strong hand. "Police. Chief Sam Cobb, Detective Sergeant Hal Price." The plastic bag was still tucked beneath his left arm, the photograph not visible to Gwen.

Price, too, held open his billfold.

Chief Cobb spoke quietly, with no hint of threat. "There has been a crime—"

Gwen's eyes widened. One hand sought support from the doorjamb. The arrival of police with unreadable faces at a front door evoked the terror of bad news, someone dead, someone hurt. "Ryan . . ." Her son's name was a desperate whisper.

"—at The Castle. Detective Sergeant Price and I have some questions about the gathering there last night."

Her relief was followed immediately by dismay. "Last night?"

"May we come inside, Mrs. Dunham?" His voice was polite.

"I suppose so." She sounded uncertain and frightened. She held the door and led the way to a small living room with a white stone fireplace and comfortable chintz-covered chairs and sofas. Densely patterned wallpaper pictured a Chinese vase with stylized flowers. She gestured toward the chairs on one side of a coffee table. She sank onto a small sofa opposite the police officers.

Price placed the polymer case on the floor by his feet. The chief held the plastic bag facedown.

Gwen sat straight and rigid.

Cobb was soft-spoken. "Last night you and your husband attended a séance—"

"Is that the crime? Is it against the law to have something like that, even in a private home?" Her voice was sharp.

"The crime"—his voice was stolid—"is murder. Ronald and Laverne Phillips were shot to death late last night." He watched her, his gaze measuring.

Gwen struggled to breathe, her violet eyes wide with horror. And fear. "Shot?" She appeared to grapple with the enormity of violent crime. "Where?" The word was a faint whisper.

"In their second-floor suite at The Castle. They were not seen again after the séance. Their bodies were found this morning around eight A.M. They had been dead for several hours. We are fully aware of everything that was said at the séance." He placed the bag with Ryan's photograph faceup on a coffee table.

Gwen looked old and stricken, as if every bit of life and hope had drained away.

Sam nodded at the photograph. "Your son."

She reached out a shaking hand. "Please. Don't do this to us. I know what you are thinking. None of it's true."

"Is Ryan the son of Jack Hume?" His tone was quiet.

She trembled. "Oh, he may be." Her face crumpled. "I suppose he is."

"Did you tell your husband about Jack Hume's threat to contact your son unless you informed Ryan?"

"I didn't tell Clint." There was truth in her voice, but terror in her eyes. The cocker had barked the night she met Jack in the gazebo. Did she fear her husband had followed her, overheard her quarrel with Jack?

"Have you discussed Jack Hume and your son with your husband?"

"No." There was heartbreak in her face and in her voice.

I thought of the two of them in their lovely home, marred by strained silence and averted eyes.

She leaned forward, her voice urgent. "What Jack said doesn't matter now. I don't know anything about Jack's death. He fell. That's all I know. Last night, that awful woman"—Gwen's face was hard and angry—"in her silly black dress and beads and thick makeup, pretending to commune with the dead. No wonder someone killed her. But their deaths have nothing to do with me or with Clint. We were here."

"Did you leave the house after returning from The Castle?"

"No." She was vehement.

"Did your husband leave the house?"

"No." Her voice was ragged, her stare hard and bright.

"I see." Nothing in the chief's demeanor revealed the fact that

I'd told him about Clint Dunham making up a bed downstairs in the den or that Jimmy Hume claimed to have seen Clint coming from The Castle toward his house. "Very well. Then I presume you have no objection to Detective Sergeant Price taking your fingerprints to see if there is a match on the murder weapon?"

Price picked up the shiny black case.

"I don't care. Take them." Her voice shook. "I didn't shoot those people. Clint didn't shoot them. Clint doesn't know anything about any of this. Last night at the séance, he didn't have any idea that awful woman was talking about Ryan."

Cobb tilted his head, peered down at her, his expression skeptical.

"Clint doesn't know anything." Her voice was husky with despair. "Don't tell him. Please don't tell him."

Cobb slowly shook his head. "I'm investigating three murders, Mrs. Dunham."

She swallowed, said thickly, "You said they were shot? Well, then, neither of us could have done it. We don't have a gun. We've never had a gun. Ask anybody."

Cobb looked phlegmatic. "I understand you and Mrs. James Hume have been close friends for many years. During that time, you have visited The Castle many times." His gaze was intent. "Were you and your husband familiar with the history of J. J. Hume's office?"

A flash of knowledge moved and shifted in her eyes. "Diane's always talking about The Castle. I never listened closely."

The chief nodded. He glanced toward Hal. "Mrs. Dunham might prefer to have her fingerprints taken in the kitchen. I'll be on my way to my office."

She came to her feet, her face distraught. "I want Ryan's picture. You have no right to keep it."

"The photograph is included in evidence taken from the crime scene. If your son's picture turns out not to be germane to the investigation, you may make a claim for its return."

The chief retraced his steps, walking fast. At The Castle's front drive, he headed for a police cruiser parked in the shade of a cottonwood. He unlocked the door, slid into the driver's seat, placing the bagged photograph in a side pocket. Immediately the air-conditioning hummed.

The passenger seat was not, to put it kindly, tidy. I removed two empty Frito bags, a McDonald's sack, three Styrofoam coffee cups, and a crumpled Baby Ruth wrapper.

As the cruiser pulled out of The Castle drive, he said conversationally, "Nice of you to come along. Make yourself comfortable."

I brushed out the seat and settled back. "I'd be glad to appear." I always enjoyed wearing an Adelaide police uniform. The French blue was a lovely color. I started to swirl into—

"No need to do that." It was as near a yelp as I'd ever heard from Chief Cobb.

Obediently, I retreated. Another time.

As the car curved right at the base of the hill, I observed brightly, "If we're on the way to your office, you could pick up some hamburgers from Lulu's."

"The office was for Gwen Dunham's benefit." As soon as the car was a block away from the Dunham house, he reached forward, punched a button. The siren squealed. The cruiser picked up speed, curved around a corner.

"Ooooh. Fun. You must be as hungry as I am."

"I don't use a siren to go to lunch. Hal will keep Gwen Dunham occupied long enough for me to get to her husband's office before she can call him."

Clint Dunham sat behind an unpretentious, plain gray metal desk in an ebony leather swivel chair. To one side on a shelf was a computer monitor with a keyboard. The room was large enough for two upholstered chairs in a bright floral print, bookcases on one wall, filing cabinets against another. Plain blue drapes framed large casement windows.

He stared at Chief Cobb, his face dogged, determined, and resistant. "I have nothing to say." In a soft blue, short-sleeved polo shirt and khaki slacks, he was an odd figure for high drama. He looked like a man ready for a round of golf, not a man possibly fighting for his life.

The chief sat with his hands spread on his thighs. A fingerprint kit and manila folder were on the floor next to him. "Did you leave your house last night?"

No response.

"Did your wife leave your house?"

No response.

"A witness saw you on the grounds of The Castle."

Clint's eyes flickered, but his face was rigid.

Chief Cobb retrieved the folder, opened it, and placed on the desk the plastic bag with Ryan Dunham's photograph. "Were you aware that Jack Hume is Ryan's father?"

Clint's jaws ridged. For an instant, his hands closed into fists.

The chief looked stern. "Three people have been murdered, Mr. Dunham. If you are innocent, you may hold information which can help solve these crimes. Did you hear the Humes's cocker barking last night?"

No response.

Chief Cobb gestured at the shiny black fingerprint case. "Those who were at The Castle last evening are being asked for fingerprints."

"No."

"I can take you to the police station as a person of interest."

Clint reached toward the telephone. "I'll call my lawyer."

The chief studied him for a moment, then heaved himself to his feet. He picked up the fingerprint kit, slid the plastic bag beneath one arm. "Don't leave town, Mr. Dunham. I'll be back in touch." He paused in the doorway. "You could make this easier. It's important to know whether you heard the cocker bark."

Clint folded his arms.

Chief Cobb's voice was grave. "There's a killer out there, smart, quick-thinking, ruthless. When word gets out that you were on The Castle grounds, you may look into the muzzle of a gun and know in that last instant that you made a mistake."

Chief Cobb turned the a/c on high. He glanced toward the empty passenger seat.

I floated above the seat.

"Might wait a minute before you sit down." He gave a small head shake. "I feel dumb talking to somebody who isn't here. But"—now the words were rushed—"please keep it that way."

I hovered for a moment longer. A car with closed windows in Oklahoma on a hot June day resembles a kiln. The plastic seat was still uncomfortable when I dropped into my place.

The cruiser pulled away from the curb.

"You didn't get much information." I wasn't being critical, simply stating a fact.

"He's scared." The chief was matter-of-fact. "Maybe for himself. Maybe for his wife. Scared and smart. He was on The Castle grounds and he knew better than to lie. But maybe not smart enough to save his life—if he's innocent."

I felt a quick stab of worry. "Is Jimmy in danger?"

Cobb shook his head. "He's told what he knows. If he saw any-one else, he would have spoken up. Or Jimmy may be the killer and he's taking advantage of Dunham being on the grounds. Or Dunham may be the one we're looking for. What I need is proof, a physical piece of evidence linking someone to the crime."

Alison Gregory stared at the chief in wide-eyed shock. "That's horrible." She was as carefully and artfully groomed as always, blond hair gleaming, makeup understated but perfect, well dressed, sophisticated, and self-possessed. But now there was an element of uncertainty in her blue eyes. The hand she lifted to brush back a strand of hair shook slightly. "Shot? That's incred-ible." Sudden worry flared in her eyes. "Is Evelyn all right?"

Cobb sat in a large leather chair, hands planted firmly on his knees. The fingerprint kit rested on a corner of the pine coffee table. "Miss Hume is shocked. She now believes her brother was murdered. I understand he came to see you."

Alison picked up a bronze letter opener inlaid with turquoise and turned it around and around in her hand. "That's correct." She recounted Jack's hope that he could become closer to his sister, but she spoke almost absently, her thoughts clearly elsewhere.

I raised an eyebrow. Alison didn't repeat Jack's words about his sister's anger: *My sister hates me. If she had the chance, I think she'd shoot me.*

As always, the chief's heavy face reflected calmness, with no hint he was aware that Alison had omitted a significant piece of information.

He glanced at his notes. "I understand you recommended Leonard Walker to Jack Hume."

"Leonard?" She repeated the name without interest. "That wasn't important. Except"—she gave a small shrug—"to Jack. He was interested in having a portrait painted of his late wife. Chief Cobb." She sounded embarrassed. "I have a confession to make."

He waited, his brown eyes intent.

Alison tossed back her hair. "I didn't take it seriously about that vase falling the other night. When was it?" She looked as if she were figuring. "I guess it was yesterday that Evelyn called me. So Tuesday night. I'm not too clear on what happened, but I think that woman who knew Jack was in the garden when the vase came down. Evelyn pretty clearly wanted me to look over the pedestal and"—touches of pink flared in her cheeks—"conclude that the vase fell by accident." She looked away from Cobb, as if studying a brilliantly colorful Baranov painting on a sidewall. "Okay." She gripped the letter opener. "There's no graceful way to put it. I went up on the balcony and smudged away traces of a chisel. I figured some vandal had prized the vase loose. It never occurred to me somebody really tried to kill anybody. So"—now she looked at him directly—"I guess I'm guilty of destroying evidence. But with Laverne and Ronald dead, I had to tell you." She looked diminished.

Cobb didn't change expression. "We'll ask you to come to the station and make a formal statement. For now, I want to hear about last night's séance."

Alison spoke quickly. She was accurate and complete.

He read from his notes, his face stolid: "' . . . bright red poppies in a field . . . sharp light and a magnifying glass . . .' Would you have any explanation for this passage?"

Alison's face folded in a puzzled frown. "I didn't take mention of the painting—I'm sure that was the Metcalf painting—to mean much of anything. I thought the séance was a bunch of nonsense until Laverne claimed somebody pushed Jack Hume. That pretty well drove everything out of my mind. Of course, everyone was upset and most of them were angry. I don't blame them. If it was my family, I would have been mad, too. I suppose I was pretty harsh. I said it was all nonsense. I left as soon as I could. None of it had anything to do with me. As for the magnifying glass, I supposed it had something to do with Evelyn, but I can't imagine what."

Chief Cobb's tone was avuncular. "You have been closely connected to the Hume family for many years. I would appreciate your insights as to who might have killed Jack Hume."

Her face drew down in dismay. Slowly, she shook her head. "If I knew anything that I felt would be helpful, I would tell you. But we are talking about people's lives here. I'm not willing to play guess-the-murderer."

Cobb was somber. "We are indeed talking about people's lives, Ms. Gregory."

He waited.

She gave a slight shake of her head. "I'm sorry."

"Very well." He started to rise, then reached for the shiny black case. "We are requesting those who attended last night's séance to provide fingerprints."

Although she looked startled, she managed a smile. "That's the easiest question you've asked. I'll be happy to do that."

I picked up the sack from Lulu's from the car floor. I hoped it hadn't left a grease spot on the plastic floor mat.

Chief Cobb cleared his throat. "I'll carry the sack."

"I could appear." I know I sounded wistful. Wistful usually has a lovely effect upon manly men such as the chief.

"Somebody would see us. Then I'd be asked about the good-looking redhead with me at the lake."

"Oh." Well, if I couldn't appear, a compliment was the next best thing. "How about sitting on the pier?" The forest preserve next to St. Mildred's Church was one of Adelaide's loveliest and coolest places on a summer day.

We found a shady spot a few feet from shore and settled on the wooden flooring, our feet dangling over the edge. The only fishermen were on the other side of the lake in a boat.

Sam—I do think of him as Sam—swiped his face with his handkerchief.

I carefully split the sack, placed it on the dock for a makeshift place mat. I picked up a cheeseburger.

He summarized what he felt were the important points:

"One. Evelyn Hume was ostensibly cooperative, but her only revelation concerned a man who was dead. The photograph of Ryan Dunham was found hidden in a coffee-table book in the Phillipses' suite. Ronald's fingerprints were on the print.

"Two. Diane Hume was quick to accuse Margo, but she revealed that she herself was well aware where the gun was kept.

"Three. Margo insisted neither she nor Shannon left the house last night. I think she was lying.

"Four. Shannon Taylor knows something she isn't telling.

"Five. Jimmy Hume implicated Clint Dunham, but he also implicated himself. He could have been outside to place the cocker in the tool room.

"Six. I think Gwen Dunham lied when she said her husband knew nothing about Jack Hume's claim that Ryan was his son.

"Seven. Clint Dunham stonewalled me. He knows something he isn't telling. But he didn't show shock when I asked him whether he knew Ryan was Jack's son.

"Eight. Alison Gregory did not repeat Jack Hume's comment about his sister's anger toward him. Alison admitted she destroyed evidence about the vase's fall."

I added more salt to the French fries.

The chief chided me: "Salt's not good for high blood pressure."

He stopped, a French fry midway to his lips. "Oh. Yeah. You don't have to worry. You know, it would be kind of interesting if—"

I felt a tap on the back of my hand.

For an instant I was startled. How had Wiggins known where I was? Oh. Of course. He saw the French fry in the air. I waggled my French fry in reply. Surely Wiggins was pleased that I wasn't, so to speak, here. However, I understood his instructions. To head off any discussion of the Hereafter, I broke in quickly, "That's an excellent summing-up. Cogent, clear, concise." Praise is always a good diversion. "Compelling," I concluded with vigor.

Chief Cobb wiped his hand on a paper napkin. "Thanks. But I don't see a direct link to Ronald Phillips and the murderer." He sounded discouraged. "We have plenty of people with motive and opportunity and not a single fact to tie one of them to the crime."

A growly whisper in one ear caught my attention.

"If I had time, I would remonstrate. Conversing with your charge is one thing: discourse with Chief Cobb is definitely another. But, alas, I am needed." As suddenly as he had come, I knew Wiggins had departed.

Hopefully, the diffident emissary in Patagonia required Wiggins's attention posthaste. Certainly no one could accuse me of indecisiveness. Not, of course, that I am being prideful. Heaven forfend.

Chief Cobb made a disgruntled sound in his throat.

Physical evidence . . . I finished a final fry. "How about the rawhide bone?"

He looked toward where I sat. Slowly, his broad mouth curved into a smile. "Probably no prints," he murmured. "Whoever killed the Phillipses was too smart for that. Besides, the bone would have been greasy and chewed up. We can check the dog's collar." His eyes narrowed in thought. "The murderer decided on killing them after the séance broke up around nine P.M. That left very little time for planning. We know the murderer was aware of the gun in the upstairs study. I imagine the murderer carried another weapon, just in case. The murderer also knew the dog might be either outside or inside. Whichever, the dog had to be placed somewhere to keep him quiet. A rawhide bone was a good lure. There's just a chance . . ."

He pulled his cell phone from his pocket, punched a number. "Hey, Hal. Find out if Alison Gregory or the Dunhams have a dog."

I was puzzled for an instant. Oh, of course. If they had dogs, they might have rawhide bones at home.

" . . . check all the convenience stores and late-night groceries. It's a long shot, but maybe someone might remember selling a bag of rawhide bones last night."

Kay ran her hands through her dark curls. She looked even more tousled than usual. Her intelligent features squeezed in a moue of frustration. "So we have to pin our hopes on a cop finding a clerk who remembers a bag of dog bones. All this work and effort and what have we got—a dog bone." She pointed at papers strewn across the desktop. "It could be anybody. The murderer must be giddy with delight."

I pushed a cushion behind my back on the wicker settee. I was comfortable in a white piqué blouse and turquoise shorts. I held up one foot in a white sandal and looked critically at the blue polish on my toenails. Every detail counts.

"Bailey Ruth, if you can focus on something other than your appearance for all of a minute and a half, I want you to take a look at this." She held out a sheet of paper.

I refrained from a searing retort about those who are obviously jealous of redheads and took the sheet.

Kay was crisp. "I've tagged most of Laverne's comments to a particular person."

Diane Hume: . . . hear me and do as I wish . . .

Evelyn Hume: . . . jealousy and resentment growing over the years . . . bright red poppies in a field . . . sharp light and a magnifying glass . . .

The Dunhams: . . . family secrets . . . the father . . . handsome boy . . . desperate mother . . .

Margo Taylor: . . . stolen photograph . . .

Shannon Taylor: . . . Jack upset . . . young love spurned . . .

Jimmy Hume: . . . oh, Jimmy . . .

Kay's eyes narrowed. "Everybody except Alison."

I agreed. "She complained that she'd been left out."

"So why was she there?"

"She was a dinner guest the night Jack died. Laverne insisted Diane bring everyone back for the séance."

Kay leaned back in her chair. "I thought maybe I'd found an anomaly. All the others appear to be linked to a specific comment."

I read the list again, then returned to the entry for Evelyn. "You're right. Laverne's comments seem innocuous unless you know why she made them. Then it's obvious she's hinting at devastating knowledge. Except for these two phrases." I tapped the references to the painting and the magnifying glass. "I don't see anything threatening. Yet there had to be a reason for Laverne to include this as part of the séance."

Kay read aloud: "'. . . bright red poppies in a field . . . sharp light and a magnifying glass . . .'"

CHAPTER SIXTEEN

Evelyn Hume smiled as she pointed toward the painting which I imagined she saw as a diffuse impression of colors. " . . . Metcalf was one of the first American artists to visit Giverny . . . He enjoyed his years in France and even spent two months in North Africa in 1886 . . . his greatest success as an artist came during his years in Connecticut . . ."

Kay stepped nearer the canvas as Evelyn's deep voice recounted facts and descriptions.

I, too, studied the magnificent painting. The colors of the poppies were as red as my hair. Gorgeous. When Evelyn paused for a breath, I asked diffidently, "Have you looked at the painting recently with your magnifying glass?"

She paused in mid-oration, looking surprised. "I haven't done so. I believe I will this afternoon. Often I prefer to enjoy my memories of the paintings before my eyes grew so dim. This painting was a special favorite of my brother James." Suddenly her face softened. "Jack and I looked at it only a few days before he died." She shook her head, was abruptly remote. "Please enjoy looking at the collection. I believe I'll go rest now."

Kay paced back and forth in front of the bedroom's stone fireplace. "If Evelyn has a guilty conscience, I'll jump from the balcony with wax wings." She slapped a fist in the opposite palm. "Why did Laverne stick in the stuff about the Metcalf painting? Ronald must have seen Evelyn looking at the painting with her magnifying glass. Why was that important? The painting belongs to her. She can look at it every day if she wants to."

I wasn't listening. I was seeing Ronald as he slipped quietly around The Castle, watching, looking, noting. Suddenly a different picture filled in my mind. Not Evelyn. Of course, Ronald didn't see Evelyn. He wouldn't have given a thought to Evelyn peering closely at one of the famous paintings. I could scarcely breathe I was so excited. "Kay, listen, what if—" I felt a tap on my shoulder. I looked around inquiringly.

Kay broke off. Her eyes widened. "Is *he* back?"

I felt a wisp of whisker as Wiggins leaned close to whisper in my ear: "I *must* talk to you." I obligingly bent nearer.

Kay pushed to her feet. "Do you have any idea how spooky it is to see you listening to someone who isn't here? Look, I've gotten used to you. I mean, you're here and it's all kind of crazy, but familiarity breeds a certain relaxed feeling. So that's okay. More than one of you makes me feel like I'm a certifiable nut." She darted a haunted look around the room. "For all I know, there are a bunch of you. Maybe that grade school teacher who always made me stand out in the hall. Maybe that married city editor who thought he was God's gift to single girl reporters. Maybe—"

"Kay, we're here to help. There are only the two of us."

She folded her arms, stood as if braced against a high wind. "Let's go back to one of you. One. *Uno. Wahid. Eins.* Please."

It wasn't my place to instruct Wiggins, but Kay was truly distressed. "Wiggins, possibly this is a moment to remember Precept Six."

"I wouldn't have to alarm earthly denizens if I could ever find you by yourself." Wiggins sounded plaintive as he swirled into being. "You're here and there and everywhere and always with someone." He turned toward Kay, his expression earnest. "I beg your forgiveness for my intrusion. Outstanding emissaries"—he shot me a disapproving glance—"neither appear nor"—great emphasis—"converse unseen with earthly creatures. Bailey Ruth means well." There was a singular lack of conviction in his voice. "But she's communicated with you and with the police chief, though at least she hasn't appeared in his presence." His brows beetled as he shot me a demanding glance.

I beamed at Wiggins. "Only as Francie de Sales and, of course, that doesn't count."

Wiggins heaved a despondent sigh and looked morose. "That is a sore point which will require further consideration on my part at the appropriate time."

Uh-oh.

I'd been happy as a bobbing red balloon and now it was as though my energy were seeping away, along with my self-esteem. I couldn't help noticing in the mirror the transformation of my bright, vivid, eager face with glowing green eyes and spatter of freckles and lips poised to smile into a drooping, wan, forlorn visage.

"Oh." Wiggins tugged in dismay at his thick walrus mustache. "Now, Bailey Ruth, that isn't to say you haven't done good work." His reddish face brightened. "Excellent work, in many respects.

In fact, that is what brings me here. You have completed your task. Kay Clark"—he nodded at her respectfully—"is safe from harm. The proper authorities are investigating the murder of Jack Hume. Sadly, Ronald Phillips followed the wrong path, but"— and he gazed at me with approval—"you made every effort to keep him from harm. And you did so"—and here I'm afraid his voice reflected surprise— "without violating most of the Precepts."

I wished he didn't sound as if he found that almost incomprehensible.

"Therefore, I am relieved I am finally able to inform you that the Rescue Express is en route."

In the distance, I heard the throaty, I'm-on-my-way, almost-there cry of an approaching train.

"Oh, no." My cry was heartfelt. "I can't leave now."

Wiggins looked startled. He pulled a watch on a chain from the pocket of a vest. "The train is almost here. When an emissary's task is successfully completed, the pickup time is set. I've been try-ing"—he sounded aggrieved—"to alert you for quite some time now."

Another mournful whistle sounded, louder, nearer. Soon I would hear the clack of iron wheels on silver rails stretching into the sky.

"Wiggins, just as you arrived, everything became clear to me. I know what happened and only I can bring the murderer of Jack Hume and Ronald and Laverne Phillips to justice." I spoke rapidly, laying out my reasons. "There isn't a shred of proof. The only solution is for me to obtain fingerprints and see if there is a match. It is imperative that the fingerprints be secretly retrieved. The police can't do that. But"—and I tried to keep pride from my voice—"I know *I* can succeed." I appealed to his sense of honor. "Surely the Department of Good Intentions won't walk away and leave a calculating murderer free."

Kay watched with her eyes wide, lips parted.

The train whistle shrieked.

Kay clearly heard nothing.

Did I smell coal smoke?

Wiggins tipped his stationmaster cap to the back of his head. "A conundrum, to be sure." He gazed at me in perplexity. "I fail to understand why nothing proceeds in an orderly fashion when you are involved."

I do believe it was the first time I was ever described as a co-nundrum. Possibly the word was intended to be flattering?

He looked almost overcome. "Your methods, Bailey Ruth, your methods! At the very least, you plan upon breaking and entering."

I disappeared, reappeared.

"Oh, I know. You won't need to break inside. But still, I am uneasy."

The thunderous roar of the express rattled the room.

"Wiggins!"

He threw up his hands. " . . . against my better judgment . . . and yet good must be served . . ." He began to swirl away. "The Rescue Express will be here at ten P.M. No sooner. And," he announced, "no later."

I picked up a half-empty Coke can from a side table in the den. I didn't worry about leaving fingerprints. That wasn't a problem when I was invisible.

Footsteps sounded in the hallway.

My heart lurched. The can hung in the air. Swiftly, I flowed behind a sofa. The footsteps continued past the doorway and I heard the distant slam of a door. Still, I was careful. I slithered along the floor to the hall and on to the kitchen. As I poured the soda into the sink, the soft gurgle sounded in my ears as loud as Niagara.

I now faced the difficult challenge of transporting the can safely without blemish to the police station. I would likely have to appear at one point or another since a can of Coke wafting through the air, brilliantly visible against a bright blue sky, might provoke unfortunate attention.

I needed a plastic bag. When I appeared, I wanted to be sure I didn't add my fingerprints or muss those on the can. I opened a cabinet and the hinges squeaked. The kitchen door opened.

Just in time, I placed the Coke behind a trash can.

The footsteps didn't pause, though I scarcely heard them over the thud of my heart. When the room was empty, I opened other cabinets and on the fourth try found a container of gallon-size plastic bags. I unzipped a bag and dropped in the can. I opened the back door and stepped outside. I swooped as fast as possible to take cover within the dangling fronds of a willow.

I appeared and with one hurried glance over my shoulder walked fast. As soon as I was out of sight of the house, I waited until a pickup truck rattled past. I disappeared and joined a large German shepherd intelligently riding on a folded moving pad on the hot aluminum flatbed. I scratched behind his ears and rode until we reached downtown. A block from the police station, I zoomed up thirty feet. I hoped no eagle-eyed passersby would note the traveling can in the plastic bag. I reached the station without any startled cries from below.

I knew from past experience—I had a fleeting memory of a chilly October night and a rope ladder—that Chief Cobb's office windows opened and closed, unlike some in more modern buildings. I pressed against the window shaded by a cottonwood.

Chief Cobb sat at his battered oak desk, his back to the windows. He was in his shirtsleeves, his suit jacket hanging from a coat tree.

Detective Sergeant Price perched on a corner of the desk.

Price's rugged features creased in concentration. He tapped a folder, then thrust it toward the chief.

Cobb flipped the folder open and looked down at the contents. His left hand pulled out a side drawer, fumbled in it, and emerged with a handful of M&M's.

I looked at my watch. It had taken me twenty-four minutes to achieve my first objective and arrive here with my trophy. I placed the plastic bag with its precious contents on the window ledge. The minutes were ticking past.

I flowed into the chief's office.

" . . . no fingerprints on the gun. Nothing on the dog bone." Price grinned. "Didn't make me popular in the lab. Slimier than algae."

"Any luck on dog-bone sales?"

Price shook his head. "I'm supposed to get a buzz if they find anything."

Time, time, time, I had so little time. I moved to the blackboard and picked up a piece of chalk. I came up behind Hal Price and held the chalk above his head.

The chief looked up. He stiffened.

I pointed the chalk at Hal, then at the door.

The chief gobbled a half-dozen M&M's. "Hey, Hal, print out the Phillipses' autopsies. And make some calls and find out who takes care of Evelyn Hume's eyes. I'd like a report on how well she sees."

As the door closed behind Detective Sergeant Price, I was at the window and pulling up the sash. I grabbed the plastic bag.

Chief Cobb watched the plastic bag approach his desk and land squarely in front of him.

"I don't like sodas."

"You'll like this one. Here's what you need to do . . ."

In midstream I paused. "You don't look well."

He pointed at the plastic bag. "How did you get that can?"

"I took it. I needed it. You need it."

"I'll be fired. You can't steal somebody's fingerprints."

I felt impatient. Men are so literal. "Don't worry about it. Once you get these prints, then it will be easy to see if they are also at The Castle. I am absolutely sure they are. Then"—I spoke slowly—"you'll know. Once you know, you can go about getting evidence the way you usually do."

"Good." His voice had a strangled sound. "I'd be all in favor of getting evidence the old-fashioned—" He stopped, his heavy face suddenly excited. "Yeah. If we know, I can either make an arrest or use the knowledge to get big-time cooperation. Threat of arrest on first-degree murder may get me a little canary song."

"Exactly. You'll also need an art expert. That won't be hard." I pulled his legal pad to one side of the desk, began to write. "I have a plan."

Chief Cobb punched his intercom. "I need prints made from a Coke can. ASAP." He frowned in thought, then affixed a piece of tape to the plastic bag, identifying the contents and assigning the case number.

His door opened in less than three minutes. A slender woman in a beige smock and blue slacks took the plastic bag. "Fifteen minutes, Chief."

"Thanks." He reached for his phone.

When Detective Sergeant Price returned, Chief Cobb waved away the autopsy reports. "I got a tip. Here's what we're going to do." He dispatched Price to pick up the expert.

True to her word, the technician returned with a sheet of fingerprints in fifteen minutes.

Chief Cobb smiled. "Thanks, Esther. I want a crime van at The Castle in an hour. Bring these prints. We'll be looking for a match."

As she left, Chief Cobb picked up the phone, punched a number. "Miss Hume? This is Chief Cobb. Our crime technicians will return to The Castle for further testing this afternoon. Some fingerprints may also be checked on the third floor in connection with your brother's death. This is all a matter of routine." His tone was bland. He listened, nodded. "Thank you."

Once again he punched his phone. "Hal, get the expert to The Castle in an hour. I'll meet you there." He clicked off the phone, settled back in his chair, and looked around.

"Good work, Chief." I spoke with warmth and admiration. "Everything's going perfectly."

His expression was wry. "That's assuming there's a match between the Coke prints and the prints you think we will find at The Castle."

"O ye of little faith," I murmured.

"But"—his brown eyes gleamed—"if the prints are there"— he glanced down at my plan—"your idea is swell. I'll request everyone to be at The Castle at eight o'clock tonight, ostensibly to re-create the séance." He tapped the sheet of paper with his forefinger. "None of them will dare refuse."

Kay handed me her cell phone. "Moment of truth," she announced.

I glanced at my watch. It was almost four o'clock. While Kay and I had awaited the chief's call, we'd talked and paced and worried. And now we would know if we had succeeded. "Chief?" I held the phone tightly.

"Everything went just as you planned." He sounded amazed. "The expert confirmed your guess. The prints were exactly where you said they would be. That was my ace in the hole. When I showed up and gave the Miranda warning and started talking about a triple murder charge, there was absolute shock and a pretty credible explanation. Actually"—the chief's voice was thoughtful—"I don't think there was a murder conspiracy. So, the canary sang and is fully on board for tonight. See you at eight." A rumble of laughter. "I guess I won't see you. But I'm sure you'll be there." The connection ended.

Kay looked depressed. "I don't see why I can't come."

I have a fondness for silk sweaters. I tried a seashell pink with pale blue silk crepe trousers. Matching pink leather thongs were lovely. I pirouetted in front of the mirror. The light slanting through the window added a glow to my hair. But . . . I shook my head. Not dressy enough. I changed to a light blue Irish-linen shirt with openwork embroidery and a long A-line skirt with matching embroidery that started six inches above the hem. A different shade for my shoes—sky blue—and I was ready. I added a medallion necklace of ivory. "Perfect." I was admiring the artistry of the clothing, not myself, of course.

Kay stood with her arms folded, glaring. "What is with you? Nobody's going to see you. Why bother?"

Sometimes waspishness disguises disappointment. "I'm sorry you can't be in at the finale."

Kay paced, her narrow face in a tight frown. "Maybe I can slip into the library and hide behind the drapes."

I straightened a curl over one ear. "The library isn't the place to be. That's simply a ruse to get everyone here. After everyone gathers, slip up to the ballroom. Open a door just a sliver." I felt a pang of uncertainty. Our adversary was smart, tough, and strong-willed. "Oh, Kay, if ever you hoped for luck, hope tonight."

In the library, I hovered near a chandelier with a clear view of everyone present.

Chief Cobb stood with folded arms at one end of the oak table, only a few feet from the chaise longue where Laverne Phillips had spun the web that robbed her of life. Although his brown suit was wrinkled and his tie loose at his collar, the chief looked powerful and impressive. The drapes were drawn, but tonight the chandeliers glittered, banishing all the shadows. In the bright, harsh light, wary faces looked toward him.

Evelyn Hume held her glasses in one hand. Her milky eyes made her look vulnerable, but she sat with regal dignity, her soft mauve chiffon dress appropriate for a grande dame. Diane's face was blotched from crying. Every so often, she pressed a tissue to her lips. Jimmy studiously avoided looking toward Clint Dunham. He stared at the tabletop, his face sad and drawn. Clint's shoulders hulked forward, a man in a tense, defensive posture. Gwen Dunham appeared remote and fragile despite her Grace Kelly beauty. Alison Gregory toyed with the emerald ring on her right hand, her gaze shifting from face to face. She was as perfectly turned out as always, blond hair smoothly brushed, makeup understated but effective, yet her cheekbones looked sharp above lips pressed tightly together. Margo Taylor's auburn hair was pulled back in a tight bun, emphasizing deep lines at her eyes and lips. Shannon Taylor darted occasional worried glances toward Jimmy.

Chief Cobb's deep voice was smooth and pleasant. "I am grateful to all of you for your willingness to return this evening to assist us in our investigation. We have made a great deal of progress today. However"—he glanced down at my suggested queries—"in some instances, information has been withheld." He looked at Margo. "Where did you put the tools used to leverage the vase loose from the balcony?"

Margo was by far the likeliest person to have found the tools. I'd left them poking out of the chest in the main entrance hall

Tuesday night. They were gone when I checked early Wednesday morning.

Shannon burst out, "I took them. Not Mom."

Margo turned toward her. "Hush." Her voice was frantic.

Shannon shook her head. "I didn't push that dumb old vase. I was scared. I thought somebody was trying to cause trouble for somebody else." She so obviously kept her gaze from Jimmy that she might as well have marked a huge black *X* in front of him. "I tossed them in the pond." Her gaze was both scared and defiant.

Jimmy looked startled, then touched. "Yeah. My fingerprints would be on the crowbar. I changed a tire on my Jeep last week." His eyes softened as he looked at Shannon.

She looked back and her heart was in her eyes. "You might have socked Jack. You wouldn't sneak up from behind and push him."

"It is helpful to know the whereabouts of the tools. However"—now Cobb's look was dour—"you lied about not leaving your house last night, Miss Taylor."

Shannon drew a deep, shaky breath.

Chief Cobb was brusque. "You went outside. You saw Jimmy Hume. Why didn't you tell us?"

"Jimmy wouldn't hurt anybody." Her voice was shaky, but her tone fierce.

"You might be interested to know that Mr. Hume had already told us he was outside."

It was as if a chill pervaded the room.

The chief glanced at Margo. "You claimed Shannon never left the house. Did you hear her leave? Or return?"

"I was outside, too." Margo talked fast. "I heard the front door. I followed Shannon. She wandered down to the pool and then she came back. That's all she did. She didn't go near The Castle. I saw her go inside our house and in a few minutes I came in."

"Where was Jimmy Hume?" The chief's tone was conversational.

Margo's eyes flickered. "I don't know. I didn't see him."

Shannon reached out, took her mother's arm. "Mom, it's all right. I walked toward the gazebo. That's when I saw Jimmy. But he was walking away from me. I almost called out, but I didn't." She looked toward him and tears spilled down her cheeks. "I was afraid you wouldn't ever want to talk to me again. Jack was amazing, but you're the only one who matters to me. Last night I wanted to talk to you so much, but I was afraid you would be mad at me."

Jimmy's face softened. "It's okay, Shannon. Everything's okay."

I hoped that would be true for them now.

The chief turned toward Clint Dunham. "You were on The Castle grounds as well."

Again, as in the afternoon, Clint Dunham said nothing, his lips pressed tightly together. His heavy face held a look of dumb misery and furious anger.

Cobb massaged his cheek with the knuckles of his right hand. "Mr. Dunham, you saw a woman near The Castle." The chief's voice was flat. It was not a question. It was a statement.

Silence settled in the room, a silence heavy with fear.

Cobb looked grim. "Who did you see?"

Dunham made no response.

A quick peal sounded.

Chief Cobb pulled a cell phone from his pocket. He glanced, tapped, apparently read a text. He lifted his head. Power emanated from him. "We'll go upstairs now. A great deal of new evidence has been uncovered today. In fact, we will be making an arrest shortly. In conjunction with that and before we proceed further here, I will ask you to accompany me to the third floor. We expect the arrival of a witness, who has interesting information." He walked to the hall door, held it wide.

"What kind of nonsense is this?" Clint Dunham slammed a hand on the table.

Gwen reached over and gripped his arm. Her violet eyes were wide and frightened. She didn't speak.

Clint took a breath of aggravation. "None of this has anything to do with us."

"Please, Clint." She clutched his arm, tugged. Perhaps she hoped their cooperation would indicate innocence. Perhaps she was willing to do whatever they were asked to shift attention away from them.

No one else spoke. Chairs squeaked against the floor. Footsteps sounded.

Evelyn Hume led the way, moving with unerring accuracy through the door, walking to the stairs. She rested her hand lightly on the banister and started up.

At the base of the stairs, Diane clung to Jimmy's arm. "I don't like this. Jimmy, why we are going up there? If they ask us to go out on the balcony, I won't go. I can't bear thinking about Jack and those steps."

"It's okay, Mom. Let's get up there and get this over with."

I flowed above them.

Evelyn was the first to reach the third floor. She peered myopically down the hallway at the officers lining the hallway, four on each side. For an instant, her pace slowed, then she lifted her head and moved forward.

Diane clung to Jimmy's arm, whispered, "Why are they here? Jimmy, what's going to happen?"

Jimmy spoke quickly. "I don't know, Mom." His voice was even, but his face was strained.

Shannon drew in a sharp, harsh breath. "Jack came this way." Her face crumpled.

Margo slid an arm around her daughter's shoulders, glared angrily at the chief. "What is this macabre exercise supposed to prove?"

"Guilt." His answer was quick, sharp, and hard.

Gwen Dunham looked at her husband with despair.

Clint blustered, "This has nothing to do with us."

Alison Gregory's eyes glittered, possibly from anger, possibly from excitement.

Chief Cobb led the solemn group midway down the broad, marble-floored hall. He gestured at the paintings hanging on either side. "These are some of the finest paintings in the Hume collection." He stopped in front of the Metcalf painting with its brilliant red poppies. On close inspection, the red of the poppies drew the eye instead of the pale blue water of the river. The intermingling of white poppies added a dramatic accent.

"At the séance"—the chief sounded matter-of-fact—"Laverne Phillips said: ' . . . bright red poppies in a field . . . sharp light and a magnifying glass . . .' We know now that Laverne was following a script created by her husband. There was a reason for each and every comment she made. We wondered at the significance of the description of this specific painting. Of course, we know that Miss Hume"—he nodded toward Evelyn—"requires aid to view paintings."

Evelyn Hume stiffened. Her strong-boned face appeared wary.

"However"—the chief's voice was smooth—"there would be nothing remarkable about Miss Hume observing this work with a magnifying glass. Yet Laverne's comments suggest that Ronald Phillips saw someone with a magnifying glass and light at this painting. What if the person at the painting was not Miss Hume, but her brother Jack? Why would Jack Hume investigate this painting?"

Footsteps sounded on the staircase. "Oh, perhaps the man is here who can answer all of our questions."

Everyone looked toward the stairway.

"Ladies and gentlemen, this is Professor Leonard Walker, who teaches art at Goddard College and is a local artist."

Walker looked uneasily up and down the hallway. "I'm always willing to be helpful to the authorities. I'll be happy to tell you what I know about the painting in question. I understand that you found my fingerprints on the back of the canvas. Let me take a look." He strode confidently to the painting, studied it. "Of course, I recognize it now." His tone was hearty. "This is a copy I made of the Willard Metcalf original. I understood the family wished to raise money with a private sale of the original. Certainly, when I paint copies, it is always with the understanding that the recipients have ordered a copy."

Evelyn Hume bristled. "There are no copies in the Hume collection."

"Ma'am." The artist's tone was shocked. "I assure you this is a copy I produced on the understanding you had ordered it."

Alison Gregory took a step forward. Her face was a hard mask of emptiness with burning eyes.

A police officer moved to stand on either side of her. Johnny Cain rested a hand on his holstered gun. The older officer watched Alison intently, rocking a little on the balls of his feet.

Alison darted swift looks at them.

Walker turned away from Alison. "I'm glad I was able to be of service. If that's all you need—"

Chief Cobb took a step toward him. "Who directed you to paint the copy?"

The artist never looked at Alison. He spoke quickly, the words tumbling. "Alison Gregory ordered the copy for Miss Hume."

Evelyn Hume's face was cold. "I did not order a copy." She slowly turned toward Alison. "Where is the original?"

A pulse flickered in Alison's slender white throat.

Evelyn looked both angry and bereft. "You were my friend. You have betrayed me and stolen from me. How many paintings"—she gestured at the paintings on the walls—"are copies made by him? How much money did you make selling the originals?"

Alison whirled toward Walker. "You fool. You complete fool."

Walker took a step back. "I know nothing about what happened to the original of the Metcalf painting, or"—his eyes flickered—"any of the other paintings. I thought I was creating copies for Miss Hume."

"You knew better than—" Alison broke off. She turned, tried to run.

Officers surrounded her.

Chief Cobb took two quick strides, faced the woman who no longer appeared suave and cool and confident. "Alison Gregory, you are under arrest for the murder of Jack Hume, pushed to his death on the night of June sixth, and Ronald and Laverne Phillips, shot and killed the early morning of June seventeenth, and the attempted murder of Kay Clark, the night of June fifteenth."

CHAPTER SEVENTEEN

Kay folded clothes, stacked them on the bed next to an open suitcase. Her fine dark brows drew down in a frown. "I don't suppose it ever occurred to Jack that Alison was dangerous."

I hadn't known Jack Hume, but I had a memory of the photograph of a man who had stood by Victoria Falls, fully aware of danger in his African home. He had never expected danger in Adelaide. "I imagine he threatened her with prosecution. Unfortunately, she was willing to do anything to protect herself."

Kay's face was hard with anger. "I should have known she was lying when she claimed he came to see her to talk about Evelyn."

I nodded. "That was Alison's effort to put us off on the wrong track. He knew art and he realized some of the paintings were forgeries. She probably promised to make restitution. Instead, she came back after dinner that night and pushed him down the balcony steps."

Kay slipped shoes into plastic bags. "Then I came to The Castle and she knew I was suspicious. She set a trap for me. If you hadn't been there, the vase would have hit me, and my death would have gone down as another unfortunate accident."

I happened to glimpse myself in the mirror above the dresser. I smoothed back a vagrant red curl. "Happily, I was on the job. Although"—I am always ready to admit my mistakes—"I missed a chance to find out what had happened. I'm sure Ronald was somewhere in the vicinity and saw Alison. Later, he put that together with his glimpse of Jack looking at the Metcalf painting. Laverne used Ronald's information at the séance and Alison realized she was facing blackmail. She didn't have time to arrange an accident for Laverne and Ronald. She knew about the gun in the office and was easily able to take it."

I was rather proud of my summing-up. Hopefully, I would be as cogent when I reported to Wiggins. It was essential that I focus his attention on the good outcome of my efforts and not on my, as he would see them, transgressions of the Precepts.

Kay's face folded in a discouraged frown. "We may know what happened, but I don't see how the police will ever prove anything. Maybe they can convict her of fraud and theft. I don't see how they can prove murder."

I admired the scalloping of the cuff on my linen sleeve. It was much nicer to see the delicate blue than simply to know I was wearing the blouse. "Not to worry. People will talk now. Clint Dunham can reveal the figure of a woman he glimpsed leaving The Castle. He was afraid it was Gwen. They've already found Alison's prints on the dog's collar. The crime lab will check her clothes basket and the top of her washing machine for traces of gunshot residue. Certainly she washed what she was wearing, but there may be traces of the residue elsewhere. In the Phillipses' room, the blood was smeared, apparently by the edge of a shoe. They can check her shoes for microscopic traces. Now they can use her photo to find out where she got the leather bone since she doesn't have a dog. They'll get the evidence."

I glanced toward the clock. Five minutes to ten. Did I hear the distant sound of iron wheels? I realized in a rush of emotion that I was going to miss Kay. She'd been stubborn, determined, willful, and acerbic. But . . .

I popped up and gave her a hug.

She looked suddenly forlorn. "Is it time?"

"Almost."

Her expressive face held a mélange of emotions—sadness, affection, admiration. There might have been the tiniest hint of relief. "I never thought I'd say this, but I'm going to miss you, even if you do drive me nuts." Kay grinned. "No offense meant."

"None taken."

The rumble of the wheels clacked nearer.

"Good-bye." I started to disappear. Oh, one thing I'd forgotten. I paused in midswirl. "You'll see Paul Fisher."

Her face was suddenly filled with yearning. "I hope so."

"Be sure and tell him you weren't going to go back to Africa with Jack."

Her smile was wide. "Bailey Ruth, you are one foxy lady. Do you know what that means?"

I laughed aloud. I remembered.

"Thank you, Bailey Ruth. Good-bye."

"Hasta la vista," I called.

Faintly, as I moved through The Castle ceiling into the starlit night, I heard her quick shout: "Yeah. Sure. But, please, not anytime soon."

Here came the caboose. I reached out, clung to the railing.

As the lights receded below, I was torn between earth and Heaven, the diamond-bright glitter of Adelaide receding, the brilliance of the stars bathing me in a silvery glow.

A strong hand clasped my arm, pulled me aboard. Above the rush of the wind, Wiggins shouted, "Well done, Bailey Ruth." A portentous pause. "However, there were a few moments we should discuss." The wind rushed past us. Shooting stars illuminated our arc as we rose higher and higher.

I slipped my arm through his as we turned to enter the last car. As Mama wisely advised, "Talk to men about something dear to their hearts."

"Wiggins, how is the schedule coming with that emissary at Ulaa Lodge?"